WIDE SARGASSO SEA

Jean Rhys was born in Dominica in 1890, the daughter of a Welsh doctor and a white Creole mother. She came to England when she was sixteen and then drifted into a series of jobs – chorus girl, mannequin, artist's model – after her father died.

She began to write when the first of her three marriages broke up. She was in her thirties by then, and living in Paris, where she was encouraged by Ford Madox Ford, who also discovered D. H. Lawrence. Ford wrote an enthusiastic introduction to her first book (1927), a collection of stories called *The Left Bank*. This was followed by *Quartet* (originally *Postures*, 1928), *After Leaving Mr Mackenzie* (1930), *Voyage in the Dark* (1934) and *Good Morning, Midnight* (1939). None of these books was particularly successful, perhaps because they were decades ahead of their time in theme and tone, dealing as they did with women as underdogs, exploited and exploiting their sexuality. With the outbreak of war and subsequent failure of *Good Morning, Midnight*, the books went out of print and Jean Rhys dropped completely from sight. It was generally thought that she was dead. Nearly twenty years later she was rediscovered, largely owing to the enthusiasm of the writer Francis Wyndham. She was living reclusively in Cornwall, and during those years had accumulated the stories collected in *Tigers are Better-Looking*. In 1966 she made a sensational reappearance with *Wide Sargasso Sea*, which won the Royal Society of Literature Award and the W. H. Smith Award in 1966, her only comment on the latter being that 'It has come too late'. Her final collection of stories, *Sleep It Off Lady*, appeared in 1976 and *Smile Please*, her unfinished autobiography, was published posthumously in 1979. She was made a Fellow of the Royal Society of Literature in 1966 and a CBE in 1978.

Jean Rhys, described by A. Alvarez as 'one of the finest British writers of this century', died in 1979.

Angela Smith was born in Selmeston, Sussex, and educated in Eastbourne and at the universities of Birmingham and Cambridge. She taught at Northridge University, California, and for the Open University, and is now a senior lecturer in English Studies and director of the Centre of Commonwealth Studies at the University of Stirling. Her publications include *East African Writing in English* (Macmillan, 1989), and her comparative study of Virginia Woolf and Katherine Mansfield is due to be published in 1998.

JEAN RHYS

Wide Sargasso Sea

Edited by
ANGELA SMITH

PENGUIN BOOKS

PENGUIN BOOKS

Published by the Penguin Group
Penguin Books Ltd, 27 Wrights Lane, London w8 5tz, England
Penguin Putnam Inc., 375 Hudson Street, New York, New York 10014, USA
Penguin Books Australia Ltd, Ringwood, Victoria, Australia
Penguin Books Canada Ltd, 10 Alcorn Avenue, Toronto, Ontario, Canada m4v 3b2
Penguin Books (NZ) Ltd, 182–190 Wairau Road, Auckland 10, New Zealand

Penguin Books Ltd, Registered Offices: Harmondsworth, Middlesex, England

First published by André Deutsch 1966
Published in Penguin Books 1968
This edition published 1997
3 5 7 9 10 8 6 4 2

Set in 11/12.5 pt Monotype Perpetua
Typeset by Rowland Phototypesetting Ltd, Bury St Edmunds, Suffolk
Printed in England by Clays Ltd, St Ives plc

CONTENTS

————

The Editor gratefully acknowledges the help of
Stephanie Newell and Daniel Smith.

INTRODUCTION

Jean Rhys seemed to many of her contemporaries to be a revenant, someone who returns to a familiar place, like Lazarus, from the dead. Francis Wyndham, then literary adviser to the publishing house André Deutsch, was told in 1950 that she had recently died in a sanatorium and in an article referred to her as 'the late Jean Rhys', while at the BBC she was said to have died in tragic circumstances during the war. After the publication of her first five books, between 1927 and 1939, she seemed to have disappeared while she was still living, though in relative poverty and obscurity, and her novels went out of print. She wrote to a friend in 1949 that 'My bitter enemy next door is now telling everybody very loud and clear that I'm an imposter [sic] "impersonating a dead writer called Jean Rhys".'[1] That she seemed a spectral figure, impersonating her dead self, frightened her; her letters show an awareness that the 'dead' writer could be reincarnated in a variety of ways:

I can't resist quoting something Miss Vaz Dias said: 'Dear Miss Rhys – You're so *gentle* and *quiet* – Not at all what I expected!' I gathered afterwards that she expected a raving and not too clean maniac with straws in gruesome unwashed hair. Maybe I should have played it that way.

Never disappoint your audience.[2]

What Vaz Dias was expecting sounds like mad Mrs Rochester in *Jane Eyre*, whose portrayal Rhys regarded as so distorted that she wrote her novel in response to it; what *Wide Sargasso Sea* explores is negotiation of the space between audiences and performers, sanity and madness, expectation and fulfilment, acting and being. The Sargasso Sea lies between Europe and the West Indies and is difficult to navigate, like the human situations in the novel.

It was not only Rhys who was apparently resurrected. The same thing happened to her book. Soon after *Good Morning, Midnight* was published in 1939, Rhys's second husband gave her a copy of *Jane Eyre*. She became very excited about an idea for a new novel and wrote approximately half of it; her husband typed it out from her chaotic handwritten version. Then they had a furious row and she burnt the typescript to punish him; the book, like Brontë's mad Mrs Rochester, perished in the flames, and parts of the handwritten version also got lost. That first response to *Jane Eyre* was called *Le Revenant*, the title suggesting haunting and being haunted. The writer was revisiting familiar places in imagination: she had spent her first sixteen years in Dominica, in the West Indies, and in 1936 returned for her only subsequent visit after nearly thirty years. She was also returning to a classic English novel, and seeing its Creole madwoman in the light of her West Indian childhood and her return to the site of childhood memories. Her ambivalent attitude to the status of Brontë's novel is implied in her tone about it in a letter to a woman friend, as she tries again to write her response to it in 1949, feeling insignificant in comparison with Brontë's canonical position and yet aware that the woman who interests her most in Brontë's novel can only tell her story in snarls and yells:

I think of calling it '*The first Mrs Rochester*' with profound apologies to Charlotte Bronte and a deep curtsey too.

But I suppose that won't do (I'm supposing you've studied Jane Eyre like a good girl).

It really haunts me that I can't finish it though.[3]

The haunting seems to relate to other ghosts; Rhys's letters show that she is obsessed by Brontë's novel: 'It is that particular mad Creole I want to write about, not any of the other mad Creoles.'[4] She describes herself as brooding over 'the all wrong creole scenes, and above all [. . .] the real cruelty of Mr Rochester'[5] to his unwanted wife. Rhys hears voices that Brontë's novel pushes to the margins or out of hearing; in Rhys's version of Rochester's first marriage he is perplexed by the conflicting narratives that lie below the surface of official colonial policy and practice. Christophine tells Antoinette that '"The man not a bad man, even if he love money, but he hear so many stories he don't know what to believe."'[6] Christophine's Creole patois itself suggests a colonial story that is absent from Brontë's text. Rhys's Rochester, who remains ironically unnamed in *Wide Sargasso Sea* although his absent name haunts the text for the reader who knows or knows of *Jane Eyre*, is aware that something always eludes him, that there is a secret. Just at the moment when he has reduced his wife to a zombi, 'her face blank, no expression at all' (p. 107) he hears one of the island's messages; the implication of the way it is represented textually is that Rochester's consciousness is repressing what he knows but does not want, as a Victorian materialist, to acknowledge:

So I shall never understand why, suddenly, bewilderingly, I was certain that everything I had imagined to be truth was false. False. Only the magic and the dream are true – all the rest's a lie. Let it go. Here is the secret. Here.

(*But it is lost, that secret, and those who know it cannot tell it.*) (p. 108)

In 1937 in London Jean Rhys had a West Indian friend for whom she cooked Caribbean suppers; they used to get drunk and then write 'Great is the truth and it shall prevail' on the wall in Latin. This might imply that there is a kernel of truth in *Wide Sargasso Sea* which Rochester must learn, but Rhys's narrative method has much in common with the modernist writers who were her contemporaries; she is like Conrad's Marlow in *Heart of Darkness*: 'to him the meaning of an episode was not inside like a kernel but outside, enveloping the tale which brought it out only as a glow brings out a haze, in the likeness of one of these misty halos that sometimes are made visible by the spectral illumination of moonshine.'[7] The truth that Rochester glimpses, that his perception is skewed, is fleeting and uncertain, quickly suppressed. He is surrounded by people who are acting the parts he has required of them; of Antoinette he says: 'the doll's smile came back – nailed to her face.' (p. 111) Rhys herself confused her acquaintances by the parts she played; she had been an actress and a chorus girl when she first arrived in Britain from Roseau in Dominica, and she used her skills in her literary life to protect herself. When she first met the novelist Rosamond Lehmann, who had asked to meet her, she was a disappointment; Lehmann was hoping for 'someone bohemian and *louche*, someone as daring and unconventional as her books' but she met a woman who was 'impeccably well dressed, like the ladies of Roseau at a tea-party: coat and skirt, hat and gloves.'[8]

When Rhys invited Lehmann to tea with her, the guest arrived to find Rhys lying drunk on the sofa looking unkempt and dishevelled, unable to register her visitor's presence. One way of seeing this would be to say, as Rhys's biographer does, that 'the impossibly proper lady who'd come to tea' concealed 'the cruel, tormented woman beneath'[9], but another perspective suggests that the proper well-dressed lady was partly what Rhys was. She always loved clothes and cared about her appearance; she also loved alcohol and said terrible things when she was drunk, though the fact that they were terrible did not mean that they were necessarily truthful. A related question might be whether the reader feels that the 'true' Antoinette is revealed when she gets drunk and bites and curses her husband, or whether the girl in the white dress who sings in front of her mirror is not equally part of what Antoinette is.

Wide Sargasso Sea was widely and favourably reviewed when it first appeared, and its popularity has grown steadily, perhaps because of the questions of perception and interpretation that are posed to the reader. The novel anticipated late twentieth-century preoccupations in fiction and in critical theory, for instance, the resurgence of interest in the Gothic imagination. *Jane Eyre* is of course itself a Gothic text, with its mad Creole locked away but haunting the lives of her tormented husband and the innocent Jane. In *Jane Eyre*, however, the narrative trajectory is clearly defined, through a series of mysteries that are resolved in turn: the demonic figure is identified and Rochester's attempt at bigamy thwarted as he is about to marry Jane; Jane's suffering and poverty are rewarded when she is revealed to have inherited her uncle's money and to have congenial relations; Jane's obsessive anxiety about Rochester's fate subsides when she discovers him, crippled and blinded but a widower, after his wife has set fire to Thornfield and leapt from the battlements. The Gothic imagination expresses itself quite differently in *Wide Sargasso Sea*; the emphasis is not on the solution of mysteries but on the recognition of them. When Rochester asks Antoinette whether there is another side to Daniel Cosway's story, she replies: ' "There is always the other side, always." ' (p. 82) What haunts the reader of this text is the knowledge of what will happen to Antoinette, and the sense that secrets are hidden because people do not want to see what they see, or know what they know.

Antoinette prays for her mother in the convent as though she were dead, though she knows she is alive; Antoinette describes herself and her family being driven out of Coulibri by a fire, but when Daniel tells Rochester about Annette's second marriage he makes no mention of a fire. When Rochester gives his account of his visit to Daniel he says that Daniel called after him: '"Give my love to your wife – my sister [. . .] You are not the first to kiss her pretty face"' (p. 80) but when he reverts to it, Rochester has rewritten the encounter: '(*Give my sister your wife a kiss from me. Love her as I did – oh yes I did.*)' (p. 102) Antoinette's relationship with her cousin, Sandi, is similarly blurred; Amélie implies that they had a sexual relationship before Antoinette's marriage to Rochester, though she unnerves him by affecting to deny it vigorously. She touches on her most xenophobic fears, using 'marry' as a polite euphemism for a sexual encounter: '"Miss Antoinette a white girl with a lot of money, she won't marry with a coloured man even though he don't look like a coloured man."' (p. 77) The narrative insecurity of the novel teases the reader's imagination; the living dead here, the zombis and revenants, are not the victims of vampires but of colonialism.

Jane Eyre opens with an authoritative statement: 'There was no possibility of taking a walk that day.' *Wide Sargasso Sea*'s opening sentence sets a hesitant tone: 'They say . . .' Caliban's isle was full of noises, but this isle is full of voices, speaking different languages and different versions of English and French. Some of the words, such as *obeah* and *zombi*, cannot adequately be translated into English. The culture of most of the islands' inhabitants is oral rather than literate; Christophine says: '"Read and write I don't know. Other things I know."' (p. 104) Iconoclastic local bugs have eaten their way into the canonical texts in Rochester's refuge; in it he writes letters to his father and reads about obeah, searching for some authority that will explain obeah to him, or impose judicial order on what he perceives as an anarchic situation. Nothing is what it seems. Freud, in his essay 'The Uncanny', quotes in relation to dolls Jentsch's observation 'that a particularly favourable condition for awaking uncanny feelings is created when there is intellectual uncertainty whether an object is alive or not, and when an inanimate object becomes too much like an animate one.'[10] Obeah is spirit theft, and it can reduce human beings to the state of puppets, dolls or zombis. When Rochester drinks the potion Christophine prepares for him he is overtaken by an erotic frenzy as the god of love enters and takes possession of him; after his night with Antoinette she is left bleeding and bruised, and he is brutalized. Though Antoinette caused this to happen to him through Christophine's powers, she argues that he too practises obeah: ' "Bertha is not my name. You are trying to make me into someone else, calling me by another name. I know, that's obeah too." ' (p. 94) The uncanny control he exercises over her derives from his power as a patriarchal Victorian who has stopped listening to all the islands' voices; he had begun to hear them, as he says when he describes how 'I sat for a long time listening to the waterfall, eyes half closed, drowsy and content' (p. 59), just before Daniel's letter arrives. In his fear of Christophine's obeah magic and the passion between him and Antoinette he has reduced his wife, who loves him, to a spiritless shell: 'Like a doll. Even when she threatened me with the bottle she had a marionette quality.' (p. 96) The voice of his suppressed wishes, which is heard when he speaks to the 'witch' Christophine, seems to be casting an incantatory spell: '*Marionette, Antoinette, Marionetta, Antoinetta*'. (p. 99) Christophine recognizes what he is doing and accuses him of spirit theft: ' "All you want is to break her up. [. . .] She tell me in the middle of all this you start calling her names. Marionette. [. . .] That word mean doll, eh?" ' (p. 99) He pulls the strings, but is frightened by his own creation: 'The doll had a doll's voice.' (p. 110) As puppet-master he controls her speech, but knows that he has destroyed something in himself as well as her. She tantalized him with a glimpse of something beyond his experience, something just out of reach: 'Above all I hated her. For she belonged to the magic and the loveliness. She had left me thirsty and all my life would be thirst and longing for what I had lost before I found it.' (p. 111) He loathes her otherness, and reveals himself as a practitioner of colonial obeah. With the confidence of his belief in his own cultural and racial superiority he has stolen her spirit and driven her mad, but his vindictive account of it is as unhinged as her behaviour:

Very soon she'll join all the others who know the secret and will not tell it. Or cannot. Or try and fail because they do not know enough. They can be recognized. White faces, dazed eyes, aimless gestures, high-pitched laughter. (pp. 111–12)

Rochester knows what he refuses to know; earlier in his part of the narrative, expressed typographically to suggest that he represses the knowledge, we hear Christophine's accusation that he is reducing Antoinette to a doll, with his silent acknowledgement that he meant her to suffer, and his awareness of Antoinette's agony:

'You bring that worthless girl to play with next door and you talk and laugh and love so that she hear everything. You meant her to hear.'
Yes, that didn't just happen. I meant it.
(I lay awake all night long after they were asleep, and as soon as it was light I got up and dressed and saddled Preston. And I came to you. O Christophine. O Pheena, Pheena, help me.) (p. 99)

In an uncanny doubling of her mother's story, which has been constantly prophesied by malicious neighbours, Antoinette re-enacts her mother's experience: she marries an Englishman and is driven mad by the tension between his assumptions about her and demands on her, and her precarious sense of where she belongs.

Both Antoinette and her mother are ghosts in their own lifetimes, as Rhys was in hers; she wrote to Francis Wyndham: 'I am no longer a doll, but a kind of ghost.'[11] When Rochester asks Antoinette why she told him her mother died while she was a child when she had actually died quite recently, Antoinette replies: '"She did die when I was a child. There are always two deaths, the real one and the one people know about."' (p. 81) Rochester seems to take this to mean the little death, orgasm, but Antoinette is hinting at a knowledge that Rochester, with British common sense, wants to deny. She abandons herself to him sexually because she loves him, and fears that her happiness cannot last: '"If I could die. Now, when I am happy."' (p. 57) He is so preoccupied by anxieties about incest and racial impurity that he wants to rationalize his own feelings. Though he shows tenderness for her he anxiously assures himself, in the present tense, that desire is not love and that he has no feeling for her because she is different: 'I did not love her. I was thirsty for her, but that is not love. I felt very little tenderness for her, she was a stranger to me, a stranger who did not think or feel as I did.' (p. 58) When he betrays her trust and ardour by sleeping with Amélie and being swayed by Daniel's stories he causes her 'real' death, stealing her spirit and turning her into a zombi. As Christophine says: '"Now you say you don't love her and you break her up."' (p. 102) The implication is that Rochester has also died the 'real' death; when he wakes after the obeah night he has been dreaming that he was buried alive. His instinct when he wakes is to deny what he discovered about himself and his wife that night, and to blame it on witchcraft, but he acknowledges when he leaves Granbois that he is 'wearied and empty' (p. 111) like a zombi. He sums up his own annihilation when he says that the boy who is weeping over his departure is crying 'For nothing. Nothing. . . .' (p. 112)

One of the most common experiences of the uncanny is the sense of *déjà vu*, that we are reliving an experience we have had before. The reader of *Wide Sargasso Sea* who has read *Jane Eyre* is possessed by this feeling from the moment that names like 'Mason' begin to appear, and it strengthens as Rochester plans to return to Spanish Town with Antoinette, but sketches a house with an attic that is surrounded by English trees. The narrative is both familiar and unfamiliar, made strange by being seen mostly from the perspective of the woman who laughs, yells and acts but never speaks in Brontë's novel. She herself is the Gothic secret in *Jane Eyre*; in *Wide Sargasso Sea* the secrets are whispered throughout the text, but never fully revealed. One of Freud's suggestions is that everything is uncanny 'that ought to have remained secret and hidden but has come to light.'[12] The lurking, suggested but mostly unspeakable secrets of *Wide Sargasso Sea* are glimpsed but never clearly seen. They are rooted in West Indian history; the islands' inhabitants seem to Rochester to collude in concealing their past. When he and Antoinette reach a village on the honeymoon island she tells him it is called Massacre:

'And who was massacred here? Slaves?'
'Oh no.' She sounded shocked. 'Not slaves. Something must have happened a long time ago. Nobody remembers now.' (p. 39)

A precise answer to his question could be given (see Notes: 'Islands') but a more significant one may be the willed amnesia of the descendants both of plantation owners, like Antoinette, and of slaves. It is as if both exploiters and exploited want to suppress any record of the humiliation and cruelty of slavery, as they do in the Barbados of George Lamming's *In the Castle of My Skin*, and yet the landscape is haunted by it. When Rochester is preoccupied by his recognition that his father and brother have exploited him for the sake of keeping the English estate intact, he loses his way, trips, and nearly falls. He has stumbled, literally, upon the remains of a paved road, a ruined house, and an orange tree with bunches of flowers tied with grass under it. The reader's suspicion that these must be part of an obeah ritual is strengthened when a little girl goes past and screams when she sees him; she perceives him as a zombi. Baptiste, when he finds Rochester there, denies the existence of what Rochester has seen:

> I said, 'There was a road here once, where did it lead to?'
> 'No road,' he said.
> 'But I saw it. A *pavé* road like the French made in the islands.'
> 'No road.' (p. 66)

There is a similar resolute amnesia about the transition from slavery to emancipation, when the white Creoles lost their status in comparison with new arrivals from Britain like Mason, coming to exploit the slump in trade that the loss of unpaid labour brought with it for the Creole plantation owners. Antoinette tells Rochester that '"Many died in those days, both white and black, especially the older people, but no one speaks of those days now. They are forgotten."' (pp. 83–4) They are clearly not forgotten, but memories are suppressed through guilt and shame.

Part of this guilt relates to anxiety about miscegenation. Mason buys Rochester for Antoinette because he wants the innuendoes about her and her mother to be silenced, though doubts occur to Rochester even before he hears Daniel's story. He looks at his wife as they arrive on the honeymoon island and wonders why he has refused to admit what he sees: 'Long, sad, dark alien eyes. Creole of pure English descent she may be, but they are not English or European either.' (p. 40) The gossip about old Cosway's promiscuity quickly applies to Rochester as well; after his night with Amélie he notices that 'her skin was darker, her lips thicker than I had thought' (p. 89), an ominous observation as he had an impression that Antoinette and Amélie resembled each other: 'Perhaps they are related, I thought. It's possible, it's even probable in this damned place.' (p. 81) This raises the very spectres that Mason was trying to exorcize. Unspoken fears about insanity in the family, or Pierre's apparently retarded state, combine with ideas about defining racial characteristics to suggest incest and miscegenation. Rochester again refuses to know what he knows, in that he has no qualms about having sex with Amélie but feels licensed to reject his wife when it is implied by the jealous Daniel that she may have had coloured lovers before she knew him. In the poem 'Obeah Night' that Rhys wrote in Rochester's voice as she finished the novel, Rochester half-acknowledges the link between him and the slave-owners, but makes clear that he cannot or will not confront his own situation:

> No, I'll lock that door
> Forget it. –
> The motto was 'Locked Heart I open
>   I have the heavy key'
> Written in black letters
> Under a Royal Palm Tree
> On a slave owner's gravestone
> 'Look! And look again, hypocrite' he says
>   'Before *you* judge *me*'[13]

Though the next line begins: 'I'm no damn slave owner', Rochester is in danger of failing to lock the door to recognition of the darkness in his own psyche. While he wants to disapprove of the islands' sensuous extremes ('The flowers too red' (p. 42)), the colours, perfumes and contours of the landscape seduce him and he wants to violate them:

It was a beautiful place – wild, untouched, above all untouched, with an alien, disturbing, secret loveliness. And it kept its secret. I'd find myself thinking, 'What I see is nothing – I want what it *hides* – that is not nothing.' (p. 54)

His lust for possession betrays Antoinette, who gives herself freely to him until he rejects the gift; when Christophine suggests that he and Antoinette should separate so that Antoinette can live happily with someone else 'a pang of rage and jealousy' (p. 102) shoots through Rochester and in revenge he asserts his ownership of his wife and all her belongings. Despite his sanctimonious attitude to the slave-owning planters, when he and Antoinette make love he is partly aware that he is perilously close to their excesses, and that his disorientation is rooted in uncontrollable desire for pleasure and pain. The movement between past and present tenses implies that he is reliving the intensity of the past:

Die then. Sleep. It is all that I can give you . . . . wonder if she ever guessed how near she came to dying. In her way, not in mine. It was not a safe game to play – in that place. Desire, Hatred, Life, Death came very close in the darkness. Better not know how close. Better not think, never for a moment. Not close. The same. (pp. 58–9)

The revisiting and reworking of the Gothic element in *Jane Eyre* collaborates with another aspect of rewriting in *Wide Sargasso Sea*, the response of the colonial margin to the metropolitan centre. Both Christophine and Antoinette think of England as unreal; for Antoinette it is a place of 'swans and roses and snow' (p. 70) whereas for Christophine it is ' "cold to freeze your bones and they thief your money" '. (p. 70) Edward Said, in *Culture and Imperialism*, suggests that classic realist fiction develops in Europe in the nineteenth century because the 'power to narrate, or to block other narratives from forming and emerging'[14], is a way of asserting cultural superiority. Rhys was annoyed when she read *Jane Eyre* because she thought: ' "That's only one side – the English side" '[15] and she chose to write a prequel, rather than a sequel, to *Jane Eyre* to interpret the colonial underpinning of Rochester's thought and actions, seeing from the perspective of white Creoles who have been displaced by a new wave of colonizers. The implication is that the Creoles are classified as inferior in the new society. Masters used to change their slaves' names at will; in the novel Daniel Cosway is also known as Esau, but Antoinette's name is changed from Cosway to Mason and then to her husband's name, and he alters her first name to Bertha though she pleads with him not to do so. The Creoles' identity is defined by negatives in the text. Antoinette's family adopts English food and furniture when her mother marries Mason; in this new context Antoinette looks 'at my mother, so without a doubt not English, but no white nigger either. Not my mother. Never had been. Never could be.' (p. 18) As Rochester says of Antoinette, she is not English or European either. As a child Antoinette wants to become part of her black friend Tia's family, but again her longing is expressed in negatives: 'Not to leave Coulibri. Not to go. Not.' (p. 24) Her displacement makes her more conscious of what she is not than of what she is; she envies the ex-slaves their sense of self-definition. Her only positive feeling of personal identity comes from Coulibri and Granbois, but Mason usurps the first and Rochester the second. The garden at Coulibri is fragrant and sensuous but wild, like Granbois, and Coulibri is burnt down and Granbois left to rot because Mason and Rochester want to exercise inappropriate control over them.

Mason and Rochester both demand that those around them should play the parts they would have in England, as they themselves do; Rochester says that in courting Antoinette 'I played the part I was expected to play.' (p. 46) But when the colonial subjects, including the Creoles, play the parts assigned to them a strange slippage occurs, like the slippage from a European language to Creole patois. The title of Rhys's short story 'Temps Perdi' reminds readers who have read, or know about, Proust of *A la recherche du temps perdu*, and it is nearly the same but not quite. 'Temps perdi' means wasted time, without the powerful nostalgic impetus of Proust's title, and with a reductive implication. A brilliant analysis of the ambivalence that occurs in the process of slippage can be found in Homi Bhabha's essay 'Of Mimicry and Man: The Ambivalence of Colonial Discourse'. The mimicry he describes is not a mask, like Frantz Fanon's *Black Skins, White Masks*; it is an imitation which 'radically revalues the normative knowledges of the priority of race, writing, history.'[16] The presence of the colonial other imitating the white male colonizer disrupts the authority of the colonizer's language, and can reveal an inherent absurdity in the colonial enterprise, as it does in V. S. Naipaul's *The Mimic Men*. Mimicry is pervasively present in *Wide Sargasso Sea*, in the schoolgirls modelling their behaviour on the holy martyrs and in the parodic versions of his authority that Rochester is offered by Christophine and Antoinette. When Rochester is at his most sententious, mouthing platitudes about British justice immediately after he has deliberately made love to

Amélie in Antoinette's hearing, she, drunk and dishevelled, erodes his patriarchal role by revealing him as a sham, and emphasizing it by her comments about the failure of writing to authenticate imperial abstractions:

'She won't stay here very much longer.'

'She won't stay here very much longer,' she mimicked me, 'and nor will you, nor will you. I thought you liked the black people so much,' she said, still in that mincing voice, 'but that's just a lie like everything else. You like the light brown girls better, don't you? You abused the planters and made up stories about them, but you do the same thing. [. . .]'

'Slavery was not a matter of liking or disliking,' I said, trying to speak calmly. 'It was a question of justice.'

'Justice,' she said, 'I've heard that word. It's a cold word. I tried it out [. . .] I wrote it down. I wrote it down several times and always it looked like a damn cold lie to me. There is no justice.' (p. 94)

Mimicry is emblematized in the novel in the unfortunate parrot, which seems to be anxious about its own identity. It speaks French and Creole patois, not English, and asks repeatedly in French, 'Who is there?' and replies in Creole, 'Dear Coco.' It is the English Mason who causes its death by clipping its wings; it cannot fly away from the fire. In an ironic doubling, this prefigures what will happen to Antoinette. She too wonders who she is: ' "So between you I often wonder who I am and where is my country and where do I belong and why was I ever born at all." ' (p. 64) In her final dream in the house in England she hears the parrot call again, and says the wind caught her hair and it streamed out like wings, but she has been deprived of her powers of any kind of flight by Rochester. Whether her mimicry is in earnest or subversive, it heightens the desire of the colonial master to control and break her. Grace Poole says that it is a reference to 'justice' that makes Antoinette attack Richard Mason; she flies at him with a knife, and bites him, when he says he cannot interfere 'legally' between her and her husband. She shows her awareness of the hypocrisy of 'justice' but she cannot articulate it as Christophine does. When Rochester threatens Christophine with the law she answers him directly, dismantling his coded message of imperial power: ' "No police here [. . .] No chain gang, no tread machine, no dark jail either. This is free country and I am free woman."' (p. 103) Christophine's personal life asserts her deliberate difference from Rochester, but Antoinette, who also mimics Christophine's songs in an attempt to become like her, is trapped in limbo and defined by negatives, a ghost who eventually sees herself without recognition as 'the ghost. The woman with streaming hair.' (p. 123)

Wide Sargasso Sea is a novel in which spectral presences are almost more powerful than those the reader meets. The two absent patriarchs, one dead, Antoinette's father, and one in England, her husband's father, intrude constantly into their children's lives, just as the colonial rapacity they represent marks the landscape the characters inhabit. The scarred psyches of Antoinette and her husband are mirrored in the hidden roads, decaying houses and suppressed stories of Granbois. When he wants to hold on to his increasingly tenuous resistance to the pleasures of Granbois, Rochester shuts himself away to write letters to his father. Upon receiving Daniel's letter about what he claims is his relationship to Antoinette through her father, Rochester begins to think about the suppression of the self his father taught him: 'How old was I when I learned to hide what I felt? A very small boy. Six, five, even earlier. It was necessary, I was told, and that view I have always accepted.' (p. 64) Both Rochester and Antoinette have been taught to dress up and play parts, with disastrous consequences for both, as Rochester cannot drop the role of authoritarian colonialist, even though he realizes gradually that he has been betrayed by his self-interested father, and composes scornful but apparently unsent letters to him. Rochester's relationship with his father is implied when he completes the first letter saying that he has married in obedience to the paternal edict but does not send it: 'And I wondered how they got their letters posted. I folded mine and put it into a drawer of the desk.' (p. 46) Another father figure is an absent presence in Antoinette's consciousness. When Mason prays for deliverance for himself and his family from the wrath of the people attacking them, 'God who is indeed mysterious, who had made no sign when they burned Pierre as he slept – not a clap of thunder, not a flash of lightning – mysterious God heard Mr Mason at once and answered him.' (p. 22) God the Father seems to endorse the view of the alien Englishman, and to prohibit what Antoinette loves most, the sensuous beauty of Coulibri where the tree with the secret of eternal life, rather than the Tree of Knowledge, grows:

Our garden was large and beautiful as that garden in the Bible – the tree of life grew there. But it had gone wild. The paths were overgrown and a smell of dead flowers mixed with the fresh living smell. Underneath the tree ferns, tall as forest tree ferns, the light was green. Orchids flourished out of reach [. . .] Twice a year the octopus orchid flowered – then not an inch of tentacle showed. It was a bell-shaped mass of white, mauve, deep purples, wonderful to see. The scent was very sweet and strong. I never went near it. (p. 6)

Coulibri has become a mortal paradise, both rotting and fecund, which is at once home and forbidden fruit to Antoinette, but she, like Eve, is driven out of it.

The text pivots on mirroring and doubling, reiterating the trope of the looking glass. It is almost as if Antoinette is trapped at what Lacan calls the mirror stage of infancy,[17] the moment at which a child first recognizes its image in a mirror, and is made aware of its bodily separation from its mother, but wavers about whether it is seeing itself or its mother. When Antoinette's longing for her mother's hair as 'a soft black cloak to cover me, hide me, keep me safe' (p. 9) is roughly rejected, she finds another image of possible healing for her sense of fragmentation in Tia, the black friend with whom she changes dresses. However, the doubling here confirms disruption rather than completion because Tia acts as part of the mob that Antoinette describes, in racist language, as 'like animals howling'. (p. 20) Antoinette runs towards her as Coulibri begins to burn:

When I was close I saw the jagged stone in her hand but I did not see her throw it. I did not feel it either, only something wet, running down my face. I looked at her and I saw her face crumple up as she began to cry. We stared at each other, blood on my face, tears on hers. It was as if I saw myself. Like in a looking-glass. (p. 24)

The cut and the blood signal violation and severance. This is followed immediately by another rejection by Antoinette's mother because Pierre has died in the fire; when Antoinette looks back at her childhood from the position of the madwoman in the attic she perceives how as a child she resisted self-consciousness, and the entry into the symbolic order, when she looked in the mirror. As she does so, she echoes the parrot's question: 'Long ago when I was a child and very lonely I tried to kiss her [the girl in the mirror]. But the glass was between us — hard, cold and misted over with my breath. Now they have taken everything away. What am I doing in this place and who am I?' (p. 117) A total rupture occurs in her mind; she has been constructed as the mad Creole by Rochester but she does not recognize that self when she sees it, having returned in imagination to the Caribbean world that is shut up in her, as the red dress hangs in the black press smelling of spices. In her dream she sees the woman with the streaming hair in the mirror as a framed ghost, and drops her candle in fear, setting fire to Rochester's house. The woman she sees is the one that he has created out of his own colonial prejudices, the 'red-eyed wild-haired stranger who was my wife' (p. 95) who attacked him after he had let Daniel's letter confirm what he wanted to believe.

At the end of *Wide Sargasso Sea* Antoinette has not yet done what she dreams of doing; she steps into the dark passage of the reader's imagination which may take her into *Jane Eyre*, but may not. There is no closure; as in the modernist fiction it most resembles, that of Katherine Mansfield, Virginia Woolf and Elizabeth Bowen, its ending depends on the links the reader makes. Motifs in the text, like the fires and the fireflies, or like the crowing cocks, hint at other stories; the polyphonic nature of the narrative prevents the construction of an authorized version of what happens. Rochester interrupts Antoinette's story with his account of their marriage but that is disrupted, without any explanation, by Antoinette telling of her visit to Christophine. Grace Poole, who is a cipher in *Jane Eyre*, is given a voice in the last part of *Wide Sargasso Sea*, but none of the stories quite fit together, as the two accounts of the end of Annette's marriage to Mason show. The plot is like the Sargasso Sea, where weeds tangle together and resist being unravelled; stories drift into one another inconclusively. Perhaps Sandi and Antoinette have a love affair either before or after her marriage, or both, but we can only speculate. Stories change in the telling and in the gossip; as Rochester says: 'I'd be gossiped about, sung about (but they make up songs about everything, everybody. You should hear the one about the Governor's wife).' (p. 105)

Antoinette has a nervous habit of holding her left wrist with her right hand, making a manacle for herself in an oblique reference to her ancestors' role in the islands, like her mother's significant repetition of the word 'marooned'. Rochester's attempts to own Antoinette and force her to conform make him seem as insane as he claims she is; his fragmented sentences indicate manic obsession:

Vain, silly creature. Made for loving? Yes, but she'll have no lover, for I don't want her and she'll see no other.

The tree shivers. Shivers and gathers all its strength. And waits.

(There is a cool wind blowing now – a cold wind. Does it carry the babe born to stride the blast of hurricanes?) (p. 107)

The unspeakable story of human beings claiming, without pity, to own each other, in slavery, marriage or parenthood, is the revenant that haunts the novel. As Antoinette tells Rochester, '"some things happen and are there for always even though you forget why or when."' (p. 50)

Notes

1. *Jean Rhys: Letters 1931–1966*, ed. Francis Wyndham and Diana Melly (Harmondsworth: Penguin, 1985), p. 64, 22 November 1949, to Peggy Kirkaldy.
2. *Letters*, p. 65, 6 December 1949, to Peggy Kirkaldy.
3. *Letters*, p. 50, 9 March 1949, to Peggy Kirkaldy.
4. *Letters*, p. 153, 29 March 1958, to Francis Wyndham.
5. *Letters*, p. 262, 14 April 1964, to Francis Wyndham.
6. *Wide Sargasso Sea*, p. 72. Subsequent references to *Wide Sargasso Sea* are given in brackets after the quotation.
7. Joseph Conrad, *Heart of Darkness*, Part 1.
8. Carole Angier, *Jean Rhys* (London: Penguin, 1992), p. 337.
9. Angier, p. 339.
10. Sigmund Freud, *Art and Literature*, Pelican Freud Library, vol. 14 (Harmondsworth: Penguin, 1985), p. 354.
11. *Letters*, p. 281.
12. Freud, p. 345.
13. *Letters*, p. 265.
14. Edward Said, *Culture and Imperialism* (London: Vintage, 1994), p. xiii.
15. *Letters*, p. 297.
16. In Philip Rice and Patricia Waugh (eds), *Modern Literary Theory* (London: Edward Arnold, 1989), p. 240.
17. See Jacques Lacan, *Ecrits: A Selection* (London: Tavistock, 1977).

A NOTE ON THE TEXT

The text used is that first published by André Deutsch in 1966, and by Penguin Books in 1968, with an introduction by Francis Wyndham. Earlier versions of the novel had existed but been destroyed. Sometime during the Second World War the first typed version of *Wide Sargasso Sea*, called *Le Revenant*, was burnt by Rhys, though she seems to have kept two chapters of the handwritten original. When Francis Wyndham discovered her whereabouts in May 1957 and wrote to her asking whether she was working on a new novel, she replied that she was, and offered it to him as an editor for André Deutsch. She told Diana Athill of André Deutsch that she expected to be able to submit it by the end of the year. At that stage she was considering and rejecting titles for it: she thought 'The First Mrs Rochester' and 'Creole' were not right.

The writing process was slow; her husband was ill and she found life in rural Cornwall and Devon physically and emotionally strenuous. By 1961, in a letter to Wyndham, she is debating a new list of possible titles: '*Marie Galante*', 'Sargasso Sea (The Wide) Crossing Across?', 'The Image', 'The? Question and the ?Answer?', 'All Souls'. Three years later she wonders whether it could be called 'Gold Sargasso Sea', saying that the phrase comes from a Creole song written by a cousin of hers from St Lucia. The letters she writes to Wyndham and Athill show how much she values being able to discuss the book with them; she ponders Wyndham's suggestions about problems with the narrative, and the narrative voices, and describes the novel as a demon of a book. Her reliance on Francis Wyndham's judgement and support is clear from the letters, but her obsessive anxiety about letting go of the manuscript is equally evident. Her method of working was to write on scraps of paper, crossing out and making alterations, and sometimes losing or tearing up the version that she had intended to preserve. The handwritten pages had to be typed up by friends, or employees of André Deutsch. She was eventually persuaded to publish the first part of *Wide Sargasso Sea* in a new magazine called *Art and Literature* which was published in Paris, and edited by John Ashbery, Anne Dunn, Rodrigo Moynihan and Sonia Orwell. There were twelve issues, from March 1964 to Spring 1967, with the first part of *Wide Sargasso Sea* appearing in the first issue. Her corrected proofs did not arrive with Sonia Orwell in time, and the unrevised version was published. Rhys was very distressed about this, though she did not send the alterations in time; a comparison of the two versions reveals how carefully she hones her prose. Every page has alterations, most of them not related to narrative clarification but to inflecting the nuances slightly differently. The paragraph about the garden at Coulibri (p. 6 of the text) appears in the version in *Art and Literature* like this:

Our garden was large – the largest and most beautiful in the world I thought – it was that garden in the Bible, and the tree of life grew there. But it had gone wild. Long grass grew between the flagstones, and a smell of dead flowers mixed with the fresh living smell. The tree ferns were as tall as forest tree ferns and underneath them the light was green. Some of our orchids withered but others flourished, greedy looking, snaky looking or too beautiful, not to be touched. One in particular was exactly like an octopus – its thin long brown tentacles, bare of leaves, hung from a twisted root. Twice a year it flowered – then the scent was sweeter and stronger than anything else in the garden. Not an inch of tentacle showed – it was a bell-shaped mass of white and mauve and deep purple, wonderful to see. But I never wanted to go near it. (pp. 178–9)

The power of the finished version is diminished in this. The magic of the lost place, the Eden of childhood which is also menacing because of its potent but uncomprehended sexual suggestion, is weakened by the tentative 'I thought', the prosaic phrase 'One in particular was exactly like', and the assertion that Coulibri was the garden in the Bible. The final version is more suggestive: 'the paths were overgrown' alludes to the secrets the island is attempting to conceal, unlike 'Long grass grew between the flagstones'. The balanced sentence beginning 'Some of our orchids withered' gives way to a much more trenchant sentence that introduces the Father's Law, and the young girl's perplexity within its domain, and also hints at the theme of forbidden exotic and sensuous fruit which permeates the consciousness of Rochester: 'Orchids flourished out of reach or for some reason not to be touched.' The orchid's snakiness is heightened in the finished version, and the terse sentences invite the reader to speculate about why the girl goes nowhere near what obviously entices her. The increased power to tantalize the reader is evident in the comparison between 'But I never wanted to go near it' and 'The scent was very sweet and strong. I never went near it.' The rhythms of the revised passage suggest Antoinette's state of mind, driven as she is by memories of childhood recreated by a woman with a tragic sense of what has been lost.

Even when the first part of the novel had been published in *Art and Literature*, under what became its final title, Rhys was reluctant to submit the whole manuscript for publication; nine years after she had promised it to Francis Wyndham she writes to him debating what to do with the final part. At last in March 1966 she writes to Diana Athill saying that her husband, Max, has died, that she has dreamt that she is looking at a baby in a cradle, and 'So the book must be finished, and that must be what I think about it really.' It was published on 27 October 1966, when its author was seventy-six.

Wide Sargasso Sea

PART ONE

They say when trouble comes close ranks, and so the white people did. But we were not in their ranks.[1] The Jamaican ladies had never approved of my mother, 'because she pretty like pretty self'[2] Christophine said.

She was my father's second wife, far too young for him they thought, and, worse still, a Martinique[3] girl.[4] When I asked her why so few people came to see us, she told me that the road from Spanish Town[5] to Coulibri[6] Estate where we lived was very bad and that road repairing was now a thing of the past. (My father, visitors, horses, feeling safe in bed – all belonged to the past.)

Another day I heard her talking to Mr Luttrell, our neighbour and her only friend. 'Of course they have their own misfortunes. Still waiting for this compensation the English promised when the Emancipation Act was passed.[7] Some will wait for a long time.'

How could she know that Mr Luttrell would be the first who grew tired of waiting? One calm evening he shot his dog, swam out to sea and was gone for always. No agent came from England to look after his property – Nelson's Rest[8] it was called – and strangers from Spanish Town rode up to gossip and discuss the tragedy.

'Live at Nelson's Rest? Not for love or money. An unlucky place.'

Mr Luttrell's house was left empty, shutters banging in the wind. Soon the black people said it was haunted, they wouldn't go near it. And no one came near us.

I got used to a solitary life, but my mother still planned and hoped – perhaps she had to hope every time she passed a looking glass.

She still rode about every morning not caring that the black people stood about in groups to jeer at her, especially after her riding clothes grew shabby (they notice clothes, they know about money).

Then one day, very early, I saw her horse lying down under the frangipani tree.[9] I went up to him but he was not sick, he was dead and his eyes were black with flies. I ran away and did not speak of it for I thought if I told no one it might not be true. But later that day, Godfrey found him, he had been poisoned. 'Now we are marooned,'[10] my mother said, 'now what will become of us?'

Godfrey said, 'I can't watch the horse night and day. I too old now. When the old time go, let it go. No use to grab at it. The Lord make no distinction between black and white, black and white the same for Him. Rest yourself in peace for the righteous are not forsaken.' But she couldn't. She was young. How could she not try for all the things that had gone so suddenly, so without warning. 'You're blind when you want to be blind,' she said ferociously, 'and you're deaf when you want to be deaf. The old hypocrite,' she kept saying. 'He knew what they were going to do.' 'The devil prince of this world,'[11] Godfrey said, 'but this world don't last so long for mortal man.'

She persuaded a Spanish Town doctor to visit my younger brother Pierre who staggered when he walked and couldn't speak distinctly. I don't know what the doctor told her or what she said to him but he never came again and after that she changed. Suddenly, not gradually. She grew thin and silent, and at last she refused to leave the house at all.

Our garden was large and beautiful as that garden in the Bible – the tree of life grew there.[12] But it had gone wild. The paths were overgrown and a smell of dead flowers mixed with the fresh living smell. Underneath the tree ferns,[13] tall as forest tree ferns, the light was green. Orchids flourished out of reach or for some reason not to be touched. One was snaky looking, another like an octopus with long thin brown tentacles bare of leaves hanging from a twisted root. Twice a year the octopus orchid flowered – then not an inch of tentacle showed. It was a bell-shaped mass of white, mauve, deep purples, wonderful to see. The scent was very sweet and strong. I never went near it.

All Coulibri Estate had gone wild like the garden, gone to bush. No more slavery – why should *anybody* work? This never saddened me. I did not remember the place when it was prosperous.

My mother usually walked up and down the *glacis*, a paved roofed-in terrace which ran the length of the house and sloped upwards to a clump of bamboos. Standing by the bamboos she had a clear view to the sea, but anyone passing could stare at her. They stared, sometimes they laughed. Long after the sound was far away and faint she kept her eyes shut and her hands clenched. A frown came between her black eyebrows, deep – it might have been cut with a knife. I hated this frown and once I touched her forehead trying to smooth it. But she pushed me away, not roughly but calmly, coldly, without a word, as if she had decided once and for all that I was useless to her. She wanted to sit with Pierre or walk where she pleased without being pestered, she wanted peace and quiet. I was old enough to look after myself. 'Oh, let me alone,' she would say, 'let me alone,' and after I knew that she talked aloud to herself I was a little afraid of her.

So I spent most of my time in the kitchen which was in an outbuilding some way off. Christophine slept in the little room next to it.

When evening came she sang to me if she was in the mood. I couldn't always understand her patois songs – she also came from Martinique – but she taught me the one that meant 'The little ones grow old, the children leave us, will they come back?' and the one about the cedar tree flowers which only last for a day.

The music was gay but the words were sad and her voice often quavered and broke on the high note. 'Adieu.' Not adieu as we said it, but *à dieu*,[14] which made more sense after all. The loving man was lonely, the girl was deserted, the children never came back. Adieu.

Her songs were not like Jamaican songs, and she was not like the other women.

She was much blacker – blue-black with a thin face and straight features. She wore a black dress, heavy gold earrings and a yellow handkerchief – carefully tied with the two high points in front. No other negro woman wore black, or tied her handkerchief Martinique fashion. She had a quiet voice and a quiet laugh (when she did laugh), and though she could speak good English if she wanted to, and French as well as patois, she took care to talk as they talked. But they would have nothing to do with her and she never saw her son who worked in Spanish Town. She had only one friend – a woman called Maillotte, and Maillotte was not a Jamaican.

The girls from the bayside who sometimes helped with the washing and cleaning were terrified of her. That, I soon discovered, was why they came at all – for she never paid them. Yet they brought presents of fruit and vegetables and after dark I often heard low voices from the kitchen.

So I asked about Christophine. Was she very old? Had she always been with us?

'She was your father's wedding present to me[15] – one of his presents. He thought I would be pleased with a Martinique girl. I don't know how old she was when they brought her to Jamaica, quite young. I don't know how old she is now. Does it matter? Why do you pester and bother me about all these things that happened long ago? Christophine stayed with me because she wanted to stay. She had her own very good reasons you may be sure. I dare say we would have died if she'd turned against us and that would have been a better fate. To die and be forgotten and at peace. Not to know that one is abandoned, lied about, helpless. All the ones who died – who says a good word for them now?'

'Godfrey stayed too,' I said. 'And Sass.'

'They stayed,' she said angrily, 'because they wanted somewhere to sleep and something to eat. That boy Sass! When his mother pranced off and left him here – a great deal *she* cared – why he was a little skeleton. Now he's growing into a big strong boy and away he goes. We shan't see him again. Godfrey is a rascal. These new ones[16] aren't too kind to old people and he knows it. That's why he stays. Doesn't do a thing but eats enough for a couple of horses. Pretends he's deaf. He isn't deaf – he doesn't want to hear. What a devil he is!'

'Why don't you tell him to find somewhere else to live?' I said and she laughed.

'He wouldn't go. He'd probably try to force us out. I've learned to let sleeping curs lie,' she said.

'Would Christophine go if you told her to?' I thought. But I didn't say it. I was afraid to say it.

It was too hot that afternoon. I could see the beads of perspiration on her upper lip and the dark circles under her eyes. I started to fan her, but she turned her head away. She might rest if I left her alone, she said.

Once I would have gone back quietly to watch her asleep on the blue sofa – once I made excuses to be near her when she brushed her hair, a soft black cloak to cover me, hide me, keep me safe.

But not any longer. Not any more.

These were all the people in my life – my mother and Pierre, Christophine, Godfrey, and Sass who had left us.

I never looked at any strange negro. They hated us. They called us white cockroaches.[17] Let sleeping dogs lie. One day a little girl followed me singing, 'Go away white cockroach, go away, go away.' I walked fast, but she walked faster. 'White cockroach, go away, go away. Nobody want you. Go away.'

When I was safely home I sat close to the old wall at the end of the garden. It was covered with green moss soft as velvet and I never wanted to move again. Everything would be worse if I moved. Christophine found me there when it was nearly dark, and I was so stiff she had to help me to get up. She said nothing, but next morning Tia was in the kitchen with her mother Maillotte, Christophine's friend. Soon Tia was my friend and I met her nearly every morning at the turn of the road to the river.

Sometimes we left the bathing pool at midday, sometimes we stayed till late afternoon. Then Tia would light a fire (fires always lit for her, sharp stones did not hurt her bare feet, I never saw her cry). We boiled green bananas in an old iron pot and ate them with our fingers out of a calabash[18] and after we had eaten she slept at once. I could not sleep, but I wasn't quite awake as I lay in the shade looking at the pool – deep and dark green under the trees, brown-green if it had rained, but a bright sparkling green in the sun. The water was so clear that you could see the pebbles at the bottom of the shallow part. Blue and white and striped red. Very pretty. Late or early we parted at the turn of the road. My mother never asked me where I had been or what I had done.

Christophine had given me some new pennies which I kept in the pocket of my dress. They dropped out one morning so I put them on a stone. They shone like gold in the sun and Tia stared. She had small eyes, very black, set deep in her head.

Then she bet me three of the pennies that I couldn't turn a somersault under water 'like you say you can'.

'Of course I can.'

'I never see you do it,' she said. 'Only talk.'

'Bet you all the money I can,' I said.

But after one somersault I still turned and came up choking. Tia laughed and told me that it certainly look like I drown dead that time. Then she picked up the money.

'I did do it,' I said when I could speak but she shook her head. I hadn't done it good and besides pennies didn't buy much. Why did I look at her like that?

'Keep them then, you cheating nigger,' I said, for I was tired, and the water I had swallowed made me feel sick. 'I can get more if I want to.'

That's not what she hear, she said. She hear all we poor like beggar. We ate salt fish[19] – no money for fresh fish. That old house so leaky, you run with calabash to catch water when it rain. Plenty white people in Jamaica. Real white people, they got gold money. They didn't look at us, nobody see them come near us. Old time white people nothing but white nigger now, and black nigger better than white nigger.

I wrapped myself in my torn towel and sat on a stone with my back to her, shivering cold. But the sun couldn't warm me. I wanted to go home. I looked round and Tia had gone. I searched for a long time before I could believe that she had taken my dress – not my underclothes, she never wore any – but my dress, starched, ironed, clean that morning. She had left me hers and I put it on at last and walked home in the blazing sun feeling sick, hating her. I planned to get round the back of the house to the kitchen, but passing the stables I stopped to stare at three strange horses and my mother saw me and called. She was on the *glacis* with two young ladies and a gentleman. Visitors! I dragged up the steps unwillingly – I had longed for visitors once, but that was years ago.

They were very beautiful I thought and they wore such beautiful clothes that I looked away down at the flagstones and when they laughed – the gentleman laughed the loudest – I ran into the house, into my bedroom. There I stood with my back against the door and I could feel my heart all through me. I heard them talking and I heard them leave. I came out of my room and my mother was sitting on the blue sofa. She looked at me for some time before she said that I had behaved very oddly. My dress was even dirtier than usual.

'It's Tia's dress.'

'But why are you wearing Tia's dress? Tia? Which one of them is Tia?'

Christophine, who had been in the pantry listening, came at once and was told to find a clean dress for me. 'Throw away that thing. Burn it.'

Then they quarrelled.

Christophine said I had no clean dress. 'She got two dresses, wash and wear. You want clean dress to drop from heaven? Some people crazy in truth.'

'She must have another dress,' said my mother. 'Somewhere.' But Christophine told her loudly that it shameful. She run wild, she grow up worthless. And nobody care.

My mother walked over to the window. ('Marooned,' said her straight narrow back, her carefully coiled hair. 'Marooned.')

'She has an old muslin dress. Find that.'

While Christophine scrubbed my face and tied my plaits with a fresh piece of string, she told me that those were the new people at Nelson's Rest. They called themselves Luttrell, but English or not English they were not like old Mr Luttrell. 'Old Mr Luttrell spit in their face if he see how they look at you. Trouble walk into the house this day. Trouble walk in.'

The old muslin dress was found and it tore as I forced it on. She didn't notice.

No more slavery! She had to laugh! 'These new ones have Letter of the Law. Same thing. They got magistrate. They got fine. They got jail house and chain gang.[20] They got tread machine to mash up people's feet.[21] New ones worse than old ones – more cunning, that's all.'

All that evening my mother didn't speak to me or look at me and I thought, 'She is ashamed of me, what Tia said is true.'

I went to bed early and slept at once. I dreamed that I was walking in the forest. Not alone. Someone who hated me was with me, out of sight. I could hear heavy footsteps coming closer and though I struggled and screamed I could not move. I woke crying. The covering sheet was on the floor and my mother was looking down at me.

'Did you have a nightmare?'

'Yes, a bad dream.'

She sighed and covered me up. 'You were making such a noise. I must go to Pierre, you've frightened him.'

I lay thinking, 'I am safe. There is the corner of the bedroom door and the friendly furniture. There is the tree of life in the garden and the wall green with moss. The barrier of the cliffs and the high mountains. And the barrier of the sea. I am safe. I am safe from strangers.'

The light of the candle in Pierre's room was still there when I slept again. I woke next morning knowing that nothing would be the same. It would change and go on changing.

I don't know how she got money to buy the white muslin and the pink. Yards of muslin. She may have sold her last ring, for there was one left. I saw it in her jewel box – that, and a locket with a shamrock inside. They were mending and sewing first thing in the morning and still sewing when I went to bed. In a week she had a new dress and so had I.

The Luttrells lent her a horse, and she would ride off very early and not come back till late next day – tired out because she had been to a dance or a moonlight picnic. She was gay and laughing – younger than I had ever seen her and the house was sad when she had gone.

So I too left it and stayed away till dark. I was never long at the bathing pool, I never met Tia.

I took another road, past the old sugar works and the water wheel[22] that had not turned for years. I went to parts of Coulibri that I had not seen, where there was no road, no path, no track. And if the razor grass cut my legs and arms I would think 'It's better than people.' Black ants or red ones, tall nests swarming with white ants, rain that soaked me to the skin – once I saw a snake. All better than people.

Better. Better, better than people.

Watching the red and yellow flowers in the sun thinking of nothing, it was as if a door opened and I was somewhere else, something else. Not myself any longer.

I knew the time of day when though it is hot and blue and there are no clouds, the sky can have a very black look.

I was bridesmaid when my mother married Mr Mason in Spanish Town. Christophine curled my hair. I carried a bouquet and everything

I wore was new – even my beautiful slippers. But their eyes slid away from my hating face. I had heard what all these smooth smiling people said about her when she was not listening and they did not guess I was. Hiding from them in the garden when they visited Coulibri, I listened.

'A fantastic marriage and he will regret it. Why should a very wealthy man who could take his pick of all the girls in the West Indies, and many in England too probably?' 'Why *probably*?' the other voice said. '*Certainly*.' 'Then why should he marry a widow without a penny to her name and Coulibri a wreck of a place? Emancipation troubles killed old Cosway? Nonsense – the estate was going downhill for years before that. He drank himself to death. Many's the time when – well! And all those women! She never did anything to stop him – she encouraged him. Presents and smiles for the bastards[23] every Christmas. Old customs? Some old customs are better dead and buried. Her new husband will have to spend a pretty penny before the house is fit to live in – leaks like a sieve. And what about the stables and the coach house dark as pitch, and the servants' quarters and the six-foot snake I saw with my own eyes curled up on the privy seat last time I was here. Alarmed? I screamed. Then that horrible old man she harbours came along, doubled up with laughter. As for those two children – the boy an idiot kept out of sight and mind and the girl going the same way in my opinion – a *lowering* expression.'

'Oh I agree,' the other one said, 'but Annette is such a pretty woman. And what a dancer. Reminds me of that song "light as cotton blossom on the something breeze", or is it air? I forget.'

Yes, what a dancer – that night when they came home from their honeymoon in Trinidad[24] and they danced on the *glacis* to no music. There was no need for music when she danced. They stopped and she leaned backwards over his arm, down till her black hair touched the flagstones – still down, down. Then up again in a flash, laughing. She made it look so easy – as if anyone could do it, and he kissed her – a long kiss. I was there that time too but they had forgotten me and soon I wasn't thinking of them. I was remembering that woman saying 'Dance! He didn't come to the West Indies to dance – he came to make money as they all do. Some of the big estates are going cheap,[25] and one unfortunate's loss is always a clever man's gain. No, the whole thing is a mystery. It's evidently useful to keep a Martinique obeah woman[26] on the premises.' She meant Christophine. She said it mockingly, not meaning it, but soon other people were saying it – and meaning it.

While the repairs were being done and they were in Trinidad, Pierre and I stayed with Aunt Cora in Spanish Town.

Mr Mason did not approve of Aunt Cora, an ex-slave-owner who had escaped misery, a flier in the face of Providence.

'Why did she do nothing to help you?'

I told him that her husband was English and didn't like us and he said, 'Nonsense.'

'It isn't nonsense, they lived in England and he was angry if she wrote to us. He hated the West Indies. When he died not long ago she came home, before that what could she do? *She* wasn't rich.'

'That's her story. I don't believe it. A frivolous woman. In your mother's place I'd resent her behaviour.'

'None of you understand about us,' I thought.

Coulibri looked the same when I saw it again, although it was clean and tidy, no grass between the flagstones, no leaks. But it didn't feel the same. Sass had come back and I was glad. They can *smell* money, somebody said. Mr Mason engaged new servants – I didn't like any of them excepting Mannie the groom. It was their talk about Christophine that changed Coulibri, not the repairs or the new furniture or the strange faces. Their talk about Christophine and obeah changed it.

I knew her room so well – the pictures of the Holy Family and the prayer for a happy death.[27] She had a bright patchwork counterpane, a broken-down press for her clothes, and my mother had given her an old rocking-chair.

Yet one day when I was waiting there I was suddenly very much afraid. The door was open to the sunlight, someone was whistling near the stables, but I was afraid. I was certain that hidden in the room (behind the old black press?[28]) there was a dead man's dried hand,[29] white chicken feathers, a cock with its throat cut, dying slowly, slowly. Drop by drop the blood was falling into a red basin and I imagined I could hear it. No one had ever spoken to me about obeah – but I knew what I would find if I dared to look. Then Christophine came in smiling and pleased to see me. Nothing alarming ever happened and I forgot, or told myself I had forgotten.

Mr Mason would laugh if he knew how frightened I had been. He would laugh even louder than he did when my mother told him that she wished to leave Coulibri.

This began when they had been married for over a year. They always said the same things and I seldom listened to the argument now. I knew that we were hated – but to go away . . . for once I agreed with my stepfather. That was not possible.

'You must have some reason,' he would say, and she would answer 'I need a change' or 'We could visit Richard.' (Richard, Mr Mason's son by his first marriage, was at school in Barbados. He was going to England soon and we had seen very little of him.)

'An agent could look after this place. For the time being. The people here hate us. They certainly hate me.' Straight out she said that one day and it was then he laughed so heartily.

'Annette, be reasonable. You were the widow of a slave-owner, the daughter of a slave-owner, and you had been living here alone, with two children, for nearly five years when we met. Things were at their worst then. But you were never molested, never harmed.'

'How do you know that I was not harmed?' she said. 'We were so poor then,' she told him, 'we were something to laugh at. But we are not poor now,' she said. 'You are not a poor man. Do you suppose that they don't know all about your estate in Trinidad? And the Antigua property?[30] They talk about us without stopping. They invent stories about you, and lies about me. They try to find out what we eat every day.'

'They are curious. It's natural enough. You have lived alone far too long, Annette. You imagine enmity which doesn't exist. Always one extreme or the other. Didn't you fly at me like a little wild cat when I said nigger. Not nigger, nor even Negro. Black people I must say.'

'You don't like, or even recognize, the good in them,' she said, 'and you won't believe in the other side.'

'They're too damn lazy to be dangerous,' said Mr Mason. 'I know that.'

'They are more alive than you are, lazy or not, and they can be dangerous and cruel for reasons you wouldn't understand.'

'No, I don't understand,' Mr Mason always said. 'I don't understand at all.'

But she'd speak about going away again. Persistently. Angrily.

Mr Mason pulled up near the empty huts on our way home that evening. 'All gone to one of those dances,' he said. 'Young and old. How deserted the place looks.'

'We'll hear the drums if there is a dance.' I hoped he'd ride on quickly but he stayed by the huts to watch the sun go down, the sky and the sea were on fire when we left Bertrand Bay at last. From a long way off I saw the shadow of our house high up on its stone foundations. There was a smell of ferns and river water and I felt safe again, as if I was one of the righteous. (Godfrey said that we were not righteous. One day when he was drunk he told me that we were all damned and no use praying.)

'They've chosen a very hot night for their dance,' Mr Mason said, and Aunt Cora came on to the *glacis*. 'What dance? Where?'

'There is some festivity in the neighbourhood. The huts were abandoned. A wedding perhaps?'[31]

'Not a wedding,' I said. 'There is never a wedding.' He frowned at me but Aunt Cora smiled.

When they had gone indoors I leaned my arms on the cool *glacis* railings and thought that I would never like him very much. I still called him 'Mr Mason' in my head. 'Goodnight white pappy,' I said one evening and he was not vexed, he laughed. In some ways it was better before he came though he'd rescued us from poverty and misery. 'Only just in time too.' The black people did not hate us quite so much when we were poor. We were white but we had not escaped and soon we would be dead for we had no money left. What was there to hate?

Now it had started up again and worse than before, my mother knows but she can't make him believe it. I wish I could tell him that out here is not at all like English people think it is. I wish . . .

I could hear them talking and Aunt Cora's laugh. I was glad she was staying with us. And I could hear the bamboos shiver and creak though there was no wind. It had been hot and still and dry for days. The colours had gone from the sky, the light was blue and could not last long. The *glacis* was not a good place when night was coming, Christophine said. As I went indoors my mother was talking in an excited voice.

'Very well. As you refuse to consider it, *I* will go and take Pierre with me. You won't object to that, I hope?'

'You are perfectly right, Annette,' said Aunt Cora and that did surprise me. She seldom spoke when they argued.

Mr Mason also seemed surprised and not at all pleased.

'You talk so wildly,' he said. 'And you are so mistaken. Of course you can get away for a change if you wish it. I promise you.'

'You have promised that before,' she said. 'You don't keep your promises.'

He sighed. 'I feel very well here. However, we'll arrange something. Quite soon.'

'I will not stay at Coulibri any longer,' my mother said. 'It is not safe. It is not safe for Pierre.'

Aunt Cora nodded.

As it was late I ate with them instead of by myself as usual. Myra, one of the new servants, was standing by the sideboard, waiting to change the plates. We ate English food now, beef and mutton, pies and puddings.

I was glad to be like an English girl but I missed the taste of Christophine's cooking.

My stepfather talked about a plan to import labourers – coolies he called them – from the East Indies.[32] When Myra had gone out Aunt Cora said, 'I shouldn't discuss that if I were you. Myra is listening.'

'But the people here won't work.[33] They don't want to work. Look at this place – it's enough to break your heart.'

'Hearts have been broken,' she said. 'Be sure of that. I suppose you all know what you are doing.'

'Do you mean to say –'

'I said nothing, except that it would be wiser not to tell that woman your plans – necessary and merciful no doubt. I don't trust her.'

'Live here most of your life and know nothing about the people. It's astonishing. They are children – they wouldn't hurt a fly.'

'Unhappily children do hurt flies,'[34] said Aunt Cora.

Myra came in again looking mournful as she always did though she smiled when she talked about hell. Everyone went to hell, she told me, you had to belong to her sect to be saved[35] and even then – just as well not to be too sure. She had thin arms and big hands and feet and the handkerchief she wore round her head was always white. Never striped or a gay colour.

So I looked away from her at my favourite picture, 'The Miller's Daughter', a lovely English girl with brown curls and blue eyes and a dress slipping off her shoulders. Then I looked across the white table-cloth and the vase of yellow roses[36] at Mr Mason, so sure of himself, so without a doubt English. And at my mother, so without a doubt not English, but no white nigger either. Not my mother. Never had been. Never could be. Yes, she would have died, I thought, if she had not met him. And for the first time I was grateful and liked him. There are more ways than one of being happy, better perhaps to be peaceful and contented and protected, as I feel now, peaceful for years and long years, and afterwards I may be saved whatever Myra says. (When I asked Christophine what happened when you died, she said, 'You want to know too much.') I remembered to kiss my stepfather good-night. Once Aunt Cora had told me, 'He's very hurt because you never kiss him.'

'He does not look hurt,' I argued. 'Great mistake to go by looks,' she said, 'one way or the other.'

I went into Pierre's room which was next to mine, the last one in the house. The bamboos were outside his window. You could almost touch them. He still had a crib and he slept more and more, nearly all the time. He was so thin that I could lift him easily. Mr Mason had promised to take him to England later on, there he would be cured, made like other people. 'And how will you like that?' I thought, as I kissed him. 'How will you like being made exactly like other people?' He looked happy asleep. But that will be later on. Later on. Sleep now. It was then I heard the bamboos creak again and a sound like whispering. I forced myself to look out of the window. There was a full moon but I saw nobody, nothing but shadows.

I left a light on the chair by my bed and waited for Christophine, for I liked to see her last thing. But she did not come, and as the candle burned down, the safe peaceful feeling left me. I wished I had a big Cuban dog to lie by my bed and protect me, I wished I had not heard a noise by the bamboo clump, or that I was very young again, for then I believed in my stick. It was not a stick, but a long narrow piece of wood, with two nails sticking out at the end, a shingle, perhaps. I picked it up soon after they killed our horse and I thought I can fight with this, if the worst comes to the worst I can fight to the end though the best ones fall and that is another song. Christophine knocked the nails out, but she let me keep the shingle and I grew very fond of it, I believed that no one could harm me when it was near me, to lose it would be a great misfortune. All this was long ago, when I was still babyish and sure that everything was alive, not only the river or the rain, but chairs, looking-glasses, cups, saucers, everything.

I woke up and it was still night and my mother was there. She said, 'Get up and dress yourself, and come downstairs quickly.' She was dressed, but she had not put up her hair and one of her plaits was loose. 'Quickly,' she said again, then she went into Pierre's room, next door. I heard her speak to Myra and I heard Myra answer her. I lay there, half asleep, looking at the lighted candle on the chest of drawers, till I heard a noise as though a chair had fallen over in the little room, then I got up and dressed.

The house was on different levels. There were three steps down from my bedroom and Pierre's to the dining-room and then three steps from the dining-room to the rest of the house, which we called 'downstairs'. The folding doors of the dining-room were not shut and I could see that the big drawing-room was full of people. Mr Mason, my mother, Christophine and Mannie and Sass. Aunt Cora was sitting on the blue sofa in the corner now, wearing a black silk dress, her ringlets were carefully arranged. She looked very haughty, I thought. But Godfrey was not there, or Myra, or the cook, or any of the others.

'There is no reason to be alarmed,' my stepfather was saying as I came in. 'A handful of drunken negroes.' He opened the door leading to the *glacis* and walked out. 'What is all this,' he shouted. 'What do you want?' A horrible noise swelled up, like animals howling, but worse. We heard stones falling on to the *glacis*. He was pale when he came in again, but he tried to smile as he shut and bolted the door. 'More of them than I thought, and in a nasty mood too. They will repent in the morning. I foresee gifts of tamarinds[37] in syrup and ginger sweets tomorrow.'

'Tomorrow will be too late,' said Aunt Cora, 'too late for ginger sweets or anything else.' My mother was not listening to either of them. She said, 'Pierre is asleep and Myra is with him, I thought it better to leave him in his own room, away from this horrible noise. I don't know. Perhaps.' She was twisting her hands together, her wedding ring fell off and rolled into a corner near the steps. My stepfather and Mannie both stooped for it, then Mannie straightened up and said, 'Oh, my God, they get at the back, they set fire to the back of the house.'[38] He pointed to my bedroom door which I had shut after me, and smoke was rolling out from underneath.

I did not see my mother move she was so quick. She opened the door of my room and then again I did not see her, nothing but smoke. Mannie ran after her, so did Mr Mason but more slowly. Aunt Cora put her arms round me. She said, 'Don't be afraid, you are quite safe. We are all quite safe.' Just for a moment I shut my eyes and rested my head against her shoulder. She smelled of vanilla, I remember. Then there was another smell, of burned hair, and I looked and my mother was in the room carrying Pierre. It was her loose hair that had burned and was smelling like that.

I thought, Pierre is dead. He looked dead. He was white and he did not make a sound, but his head hung back over her arm as if he had no life at all and his eyes were rolled up so that you only saw the whites. My stepfather said, 'Annette, you are hurt – your hands . . .' But she did not even look at him. 'His crib was on fire,' she said to Aunt Cora. 'The little room is on fire and Myra was not there. She has gone. She was not there.'

'That does not surprise me at all,' said Aunt Cora. She laid Pierre on the sofa, bent over him, then lifted up her skirt, stepped out of her white petticoat and began to tear it into strips.

'She left him, she ran away and left him alone to die,' said my mother, still whispering. So it was all the more dreadful when she began to scream abuse at Mr Mason, calling him a fool, a cruel stupid fool. 'I told you,' she said, 'I told you what would happen again and again.' Her voice broke, but still she screamed, 'You would not listen, you sneered at me, you grinning hypocrite, you ought not to live either, you know so much, don't you? Why don't you go out and ask them to let you go? Say how innocent you are. Say you have always trusted them.'

I was so shocked that everything was confused. And it happened quickly. I saw Mannie and Sass staggering along with two large earthenware jars of water which were kept in the pantry. They threw the water into the bedroom and it made a black pool on the floor, but the smoke rolled over the pool. Then Christophine, who had run into my mother's bedroom for the pitcher there, came back and spoke to my aunt. 'It seems they have fired the other side of the house,' said Aunt Cora. 'They must have climbed that tree outside. This place is going to burn like tinder and there is nothing we can do to stop it. The sooner we get out the better.'

Mannie said to the boy, 'You frightened?' Sass shook his head. 'Then come on,' said Mannie. 'Out of my way,' he said and pushed Mr Mason aside. Narrow wooden stairs led down from the pantry to the outbuildings, the kitchen, the servants' rooms, the stables. That was where they were going. 'Take the child,' Aunt Cora told Christophine, 'and come.'

It was very hot on the *glacis* too, they roared as we came out, then there was another roar behind us. I had not seen any flames, only smoke and sparks, but now I saw tall flames shooting up to the sky, for the bamboos had caught. There were some tree ferns near, green and damp, one of those was smouldering too.

'Come quickly,' said Aunt Cora, and she went first, holding my hand. Christophine followed, carrying Pierre, and they were quite silent as we went down the *glacis* steps. But when I looked round for my mother I saw that Mr Mason, his face crimson with heat, seemed to be dragging her along and she was holding back, struggling. I heard him say, 'It's impossible, too late now.'

'Wants her jewel case?' Aunt Cora said.

'Jewel case? Nothing so sensible,' bawled Mr Mason. 'She wanted to go back for her damned parrot. I won't allow it.' She did not answer, only fought him silently, twisting like a cat and showing her teeth.

Our parrot was called Coco, a green parrot. He didn't talk very well, he could say *Qui est là? Qui est là?*[39] and answer himself *Ché Coco, Ché Coco.*[40] After Mr Mason clipped his wings he grew very bad tempered, and though he would sit quietly on my mother's shoulder, he darted at everyone who came near her and pecked their feet.

'Annette,' said Aunt Cora. 'They are laughing at you, do not allow them to laugh at you.' She stopped fighting then and he half supported, half pulled her after us, cursing loudly.

Still they were quiet and there were so many of them I could hardly see any grass or trees. There must have been many of the bay people but I recognized no one. They all looked the same, it was the same face repeated over and over, eyes gleaming, mouth half open to shout. We were past the mounting stone when they saw Mannie driving the carriage round the corner. Sass followed, riding one horse and leading another. There was a ladies' saddle on the one he was leading.

Somebody yelled, 'But look the black Englishman! Look the white niggers!', and then they were all yelling. 'Look the white niggers! Look the damn white niggers!' A stone just missed Mannie's head, he cursed back at them and they cleared away from the rearing, frightened horses. 'Come on, for God's sake,' said Mr Mason. 'Get to the carriage, get to the horses.' But we could not move for they pressed too close round us. Some of them were laughing and waving sticks, some of the ones at the back were carrying flambeaux[41] and it was light as day. Aunt Cora held my hand very tightly and her lips moved but I could not hear because of the noise. And I was afraid, because I knew that the ones who laughed would be the worst. I shut my eyes and waited. Mr Mason stopped swearing and began to pray in a loud pious voice. The prayer ended, 'May Almighty God defend us.' And God who is indeed mysterious, who had made no sign when they burned Pierre as he slept – not a clap of thunder, not a flash of lightning – mysterious God heard Mr Mason at once and answered him. The yells stopped.

I opened my eyes, everybody was looking up and pointing at Coco on the *glacis* railings with his feathers alight. He made an effort to fly down but his clipped wings failed him and he fell screeching. He was all on fire.

I began to cry. 'Don't look,' said Aunt Cora. 'Don't look.' She stooped and put her arms round me and I hid my face, but I could feel that they were not so near. I heard someone say something about bad luck and remembered that it was very unlucky to kill a parrot,[42] or even to see a parrot die. They began to go then, quickly, silently, and those that were left drew aside and watched us as we trailed across the grass. They were not laughing any more.

'Get to the carriage, get to the carriage,' said Mr Mason. 'Hurry!' He went first, holding my mother's arm, then Christophine carrying Pierre, and Aunt Cora was last, still with my hand in hers. None of us looked back.

Mannie had stopped the horses at the bend of the cobblestone road and as we got closer we heard him shout, 'What all you are, eh? Brute beasts?' He was speaking to a group of men and a few women who were standing round the carriage. A coloured man with a machete[43] in his hand was holding the bridle. I did not see Sass or the other two horses. 'Get in,' said Mr Mason. 'Take no notice of him, get in.' The man with the machete said no. We would go to police and tell a lot of damn lies. A woman said to let us go. All this an accident and they had plenty witness. 'Myra she witness for us.'

'Shut your mouth,' the man said. 'You mash centipede, mash it, leave one little piece and it grow again . . . [44] What you think police believe, eh? You, or the white nigger?'

Mr Mason stared at him. He seemed not frightened, but too astounded to speak. Mannie took up the carriage whip but one of the blacker men wrenched it out of his hand, snapped it over his knee and threw it away. 'Run away, black Englishman, like the boy run. Hide in the bushes. It's better for you.' It was Aunt Cora who stepped forward and said, 'The little boy is very badly hurt. He will die if we cannot get help for him.'

The man said, 'So black and white, they burn the same, eh?'

'They do,' she said. 'Here and hereafter, as you will find out. Very shortly.'

He let the bridle go and thrust his face close to hers. He'd throw her on the fire, he said, if she put bad luck on him. Old white jumby,[45] he called her. But she did not move an inch, she looked straight into his eyes and threatened him with eternal fire in a calm voice. 'And never a drop of sangoree[46] to cool your burning tongue,' she said. He cursed her again but he backed away. 'Now get in,' said Mr Mason. 'You, Christophine, get in with the child.' Christophine got in. 'Now you,' he said to my mother. But she had turned and was looking back at the house and when he put his hand on her arm, she screamed.

One woman said she only come to see what happen. Another woman began to cry. The man with the cutlass said, 'You cry for her – when she ever cry for you? Tell me that.'

But now I turned too. The house was burning, the yellow-red sky was like sunset and I knew that I would never see Coulibri again. Nothing would be left, the golden ferns and the silver ferns, the orchids, the ginger lilies and the roses, the rocking-chairs and the blue sofa, the jasmine and the honeysuckle, and the picture of the Miller's Daughter. When they had finished, there would be nothing left but blackened walls and the mounting stone. That was always left. That could not be stolen or burned.

Then, not so far off, I saw Tia and her mother and I ran to her, for she was all that was left of my life as it had been. We had eaten the same food, slept side by side, bathed in the same river. As I ran, I thought, I will live with Tia and I will be like her. Not to leave Coulibri. Not to go. Not. When I was close I saw the jagged stone in her hand but I did not see her throw it. I did not feel it either, only something wet, running down my face. I looked at her and I saw her face crumple up as she began to cry. We stared at each other, blood on my face, tears on hers. It was as if I saw myself. Like in a looking-glass.

*

'I saw my plait, tied with red ribbon, when I got up,' I said. 'In the chest of drawers. I thought it was a snake.'

'Your hair had to be cut. You've been very ill, my darling,' said Aunt Cora. 'But you are safe with me now. We are all safe as I told you we would be. You must stay in bed though. Why are you wandering about the room? Your hair will grow again,' she said. 'Longer and thicker.'

'But darker,' I said.

'Why not darker?'

She picked me up and I was glad to feel the soft mattress and glad to be covered with a cool sheet.

'It's time for your arrowroot,' she said and went out. When that was finished she took the cup away and stood looking down at me.

'I got up because I wanted to know where I was.'

'And you do know, don't you?' she said in an anxious voice.

'Of course. But how did I get to your house?'

'The Luttrells were very good. As soon as Mannie got to Nelson's Rest they sent a hammock[47] and four men. You were shaken about a good deal though. But they did their best. Young Mr Luttrell rode alongside you all the way. Wasn't that kind?'

'Yes,' I said. She looked thin and old and her hair wasn't arranged prettily so I shut my eyes, not wanting to see her.

'Pierre is dead, isn't he?'

'He died on the way down, the poor little boy,' she said.

'He died before that,' I thought but was too tired to speak.

'You mother is in the country. Resting. Getting well again. You will see her quite soon.'

'I didn't know,' I said. 'Why did she go away?'

'You've been very ill for nearly six weeks. You didn't know anything.'

What was the use of telling her that I'd been awake before and heard my mother screaming '*Qui est là? Qui est là?*' then 'Don't touch me. I'll kill you if you touch me. Coward. Hypocrite. I'll kill you.' I'd put my hands over my ears, her screams were so loud and terrible. I slept and when I woke up everything was quiet.

Still Aunt Cora stayed by my bed looking at me.

'My head is bandaged up. It's so hot,' I said. 'Will I have a mark on my forehead?'

'No, no.' She smiled for the first time. 'That is healing very nicely. It won't spoil you on your wedding day,' she said.

She bent down and kissed me. 'Is there anything you want? A cool drink to sip?'

'No, not a drink. Sing to me. I like that.'

She began in a shaky voice.

25

'Every night at half past eight
Comes tap tap tapping –'

'Not that one. I don't like that one. Sing *Before I was set free*.'

She sat near me and sang very softly, 'Before I was set free'. I heard as far as 'The sorrow that my heart feels for –' I didn't hear the end but I heard that before I slept, 'The sorrow that my heart feels for.'

I was going to see my mother. I had insisted that Christophine must be with me, no one else, and as I was not yet quite well they had given way. I remember the dull feeling as we drove along for I did not expect to see her. She was part of Coulibri, that had gone, so she had gone, I was certain of it. But when we reached the tidy pretty little house where she lived now (they said) I jumped out of the carriage and ran as fast as I could across the lawn. One door was open on to the veranda. I went in without knocking and stared at the people in the room. A coloured man, a coloured woman, and a white woman sitting with her head bent so low that I couldn't see her face. But I recognized her hair, one plait much shorter than the other. And her dress. I put my arms round her and kissed her. She held me so tightly that I couldn't breathe and I thought, 'It's not her.' Then, 'It must be her.' She looked at the door, then at me, then at the door again. I could not say, 'He is dead,' so I shook my head. 'But I am here, I am here,' I said, and she said, 'No,' quietly. Then 'No no no' very loudly and flung me from her. I fell against the partition and hurt myself. The man and the woman were holding her arms and Christophine was there. The woman said, 'Why you bring the child to make trouble, trouble, trouble? Trouble enough without that.'

All the way back to Aunt Cora's house we didn't speak.

The first day I had to go to the convent, I clung to Aunt Cora as you would cling to life if you loved it. At last she got impatient, so I forced myself away from her and through the passage, down the steps into the street and, as I knew they would be, they were waiting for me under the sandbox tree. There were two of them, a boy and a girl. The boy was about fourteen and tall and big for his age, he had a white skin,[48] a dull ugly white covered with freckles, his mouth was a negro's mouth and he had small eyes, like bits of green glass. He had the eyes

of a dead fish. Worst, most horrible of all, his hair was crinkled, a
negro's hair, but bright red, and his eyebrows and eyelashes were red.
The girl was very black and wore no head handkerchief. Her hair had
been plaited and I could smell the sickening oil she had daubed on it,
from where I stood on the steps of Aunt Cora's dark, clean, friendly
house, staring at them. They looked so harmless and quiet, no one
would have noticed the glint in the boy's eyes.

Then the girl grinned and began to crack the knuckles of her fingers.
At each crack I jumped and my hands began to sweat. I was holding
some school books in my right hand and I shifted them to under my
arm, but it was too late, there was a mark on the palm of my hand
and a stain on the cover of the book. The girl began to laugh, very
quietly, and it was then that hate came to me and courage with the
hate so that I was able to walk past without looking at them.

I knew they were following, I knew too that as long as I was in
sight of Aunt Cora's house they would do nothing but stroll along
some distance after me. But I knew when they would draw close. It
would be when I was going up the hill. There were walls and gardens
on each side of the hill and no one would be there at this hour of the
morning.

Half-way up they closed in on me and started talking. The girl said,
'Look the crazy girl, you crazy like your mother. Your aunt frightened
to have you in the house. She send you for the nuns to lock up. Your
mother walk about with no shoes and stockings on her feet, she *sans
culottes*.[49] She try to kill her husband and she try to kill you too that
day you go to see her. She have eyes like zombi[50] and you have eyes
like zombi too. Why you won't look at me.' The boy only said, 'One
day I catch you alone, you wait, one day I catch you alone.' When I
got to the top of the hill they were jostling me, I could smell the girl's
hair.

A long empty street stretched away to the convent, the convent
wall and a wooden gate. I would have to ring before I could get
in. The girl said, 'You don't want to look at me, eh, I make you
look at me.' She pushed me and the books I was carrying fell to the
ground.

I stooped to pick them up and saw that a tall boy who was walking
along the other side of the street had stopped and looked towards us.

Then he crossed over, running. He had long legs, his feet hardly touched the ground. As soon as they saw him, they turned and walked away. He looked after them, puzzled. I would have died sooner than run when they were there, but as soon as they had gone, I ran. I left one of my books on the ground and the tall boy came after me.

'You dropped this,' he said, and smiled. I knew who he was, his name was Sandi, Alexander Cosway's son. Once I would have said 'my cousin Sandi' but Mr Mason's lectures had made me shy about my coloured relatives. I muttered, 'Thank you.'

'I'll talk to that boy,' he said. 'He won't bother you again.'

In the distance I could see my enemy's red hair as he pelted along, but he hadn't a chance. Sandi caught him up before he reached the corner. The girl had disappeared. I didn't wait to see what happened but I pulled and pulled at the bell.

At last the door opened. The nun was a coloured woman and she seemed displeased. 'You must not ring the bell like that,' she said. 'I come as quick as I can.' Then I heard the door shut behind me.

I collapsed and began to cry. She asked me if I was sick, but I could not answer. She took my hand, still clicking her tongue and muttering in an ill-tempered way, and led me across the yard, past the shadow of the big tree, not into the front door but into a big, cool, stoneflagged room. There were pots and pans hanging on the wall and a stone fireplace. There was another nun at the back of the room and when the bell rang again, the first one went to answer it. The second nun, also a coloured woman, brought a basin and water but as fast as she sponged my face, so fast did I cry. When she saw my hand she asked if I had fallen and hurt myself. I shook my head and she sponged the stain away gently. 'What is the matter, what are you crying about? What has happened to you?' And still I could not answer. She brought me a glass of milk, I tried to drink it, but I choked. 'Oh la la,' she said, shrugging her shoulders and went out.

When she came in again, a third nun was with her who said in a calm voice, 'You have cried quite enough now, you must stop. Have you got a handkerchief?'

I remembered that I had dropped it. The new nun wiped my eyes with a large handkerchief, gave it to me and asked my name.

'Antoinette,' I said.

'Of course,' she said. 'I know. You are Antoinette Cosway, that is to say Antoinette Mason. Has someone frightened you?'

'Yes.'

'Now look at me,' she said. 'You will not be frightened of me.'

I looked at her. She had large brown eyes, very soft, and was dressed in white, not with a starched apron like the others had. The band round her face was of linen and above the white linen a black veil of some thin material, which fell in folds down her back. Her cheeks were red, she had a laughing face and two deep dimples. Her hands were small but they looked clumsy and swollen, not like the rest of her. It was only afterwards that I found out that they were crippled with rheumatism. She took me into a parlour furnished stiffly with straight-backed chairs and a polished table in the middle. After she had talked to me I told her a little of why I was crying and that I did not like walking to school alone.

'That must be seen to,' she said. 'I will write to your aunt. Now Mother St Justine will be waiting for you. I have sent for a girl who has been with us for nearly a year. Her name is Louise – Louise de Plana. If you feel strange, she will explain everything.'

Louise and I walked along a paved path to the classroom. There was grass on each side of the path and trees and shadows of trees and sometimes a bright bush of flowers. She was very pretty and when she smiled at me I could scarcely believe I had ever been miserable. She said, 'We always call Mother St Justine, Mother Juice of a Lime. She is not very intelligent, poor woman. You will see.'

Quickly, while I can, I must remember the hot classroom. The hot classroom, the pitchpine desks, the heat of the bench striking up through my body, along my arms and hands. But outside I could see cool, blue shadow on a white wall. My needle is sticky, and creaks as it goes in and out of the canvas. 'My needle is swearing,' I whisper to Louise, who sits next to me. We are cross-stitching silk roses on a pale background. We can colour the roses as we choose and mine are green, blue and purple. Underneath, I will write my name in fire red, Antoinette Mason, née Cosway, Mount Calvary Convent, Spanish Town, Jamaica, 1839.

As we work, Mother St Justine reads us stories from the lives of the Saints, St Rose, St Barbara, St Agnes. But we have our own Saint, the skeleton of a girl of fourteen under the altar of the convent chapel. The Relics.[51] But how did the nuns get them out here, I ask myself? In a cabin trunk? Specially packed for the hold? How? But here she is, and St Innocenzia is her name. We do not know her story, she is not in the book. The saints we hear about were all very beautiful and wealthy. All were loved by rich and handsome young men.

'. . . more lovely and more richly dressed than he had ever seen her in life,' drones Mother St Justine. 'She smiled and said, "Here Theophilus is a rose from the garden of my Spouse,[52] in whom you did not believe." The rose he found by his side when he awoke has never faded. It still exists.' (Oh, but where? Where?) 'And Theophilus was converted to Christianity,' says Mother St Justine, reading very rapidly now, 'and became one of the Holy Martyrs.' She shuts the book with a clap and talks about pushing down the cuticles of our nails when we wash our hands. Cleanliness, good manners and kindness to God's poor. A flow of words. ('It is her time of life,' said Hélène de Plana, 'she cannot help it, poor old Justine.') 'When you insult or injure the unfortunate or the unhappy, you insult Christ Himself and He will not forget, for they are His chosen ones.' This remark is made in a casual and perfunctory voice and she slides on to order and chastity, that flawless crystal that, once broken, can never be mended. Also deportment. Like everyone else, she has fallen under the spell of the de Plana sisters and holds them up as an example to the class. I admire them. They sit so poised and imperturbable while she points out the excellence of Miss Hélène's coiffure, achieved without a looking-glass.

'Please, Hélène, tell me how you do your hair, because when I grow up I want mine to look like yours.'

'It's very easy. You comb it upwards, like this and then push it a little forward, like that, and then you pin it here and here. Never too many pins.'

'Yes, but Hélène, mine does not look like yours, whatever I do.'

Her eyelashes flickered, she turned away, too polite to say the obvious thing. We have no looking-glass in the dormitory, once I saw the new young nun from Ireland looking at herself in a cask of water, smiling to see if her dimples were still there. When she noticed me, she blushed and I thought, now she will always dislike me.

Sometimes it was Miss Hélène's hair and sometimes Miss Germaine's impeccable deportment, and sometimes it was the care Miss Louise took of her beautiful teeth. And if we were never envious, they never seemed vain. Hélène and Germaine, a little disdainful, aloof perhaps, but Louise, not even that. She took no part in it – as if she knew that she was born for other things. Hélène's brown eyes could snap, Germaine's grey eyes were beautiful, soft and cow-like, she spoke slowly and, unlike most Creole girls, was very even-tempered. It is easy to imagine what happened to those two, bar accidents. Ah but Louise! Her small waist, her thin brown hands, her black curls which smelled of vetiver,[53] her high sweet voice, singing so carelessly in Chapel about death. Like a bird would sing. Anything might have happened to you, Louise, anything at all, and I wouldn't be surprised.

Then there was another saint, said Mother St Justine, she lived later on but still in Italy, or was it in Spain. Italy is white pillars and green water. Spain is hot sun on stones, France is a lady with black hair wearing a white dress because Louise was born in France fifteen years ago, and my mother, whom I must forget and pray for as though she were dead, though she is living, liked to dress in white.

No one spoke of her now that Christophine had left us to live with her son. I seldom saw my stepfather. He seemed to dislike Jamaica, Spanish Town in particular, and was often away for months.

One hot afternoon in July my aunt told me that she was going to England for a year. Her health was not good and she needed a change. As she talked she was working at a patchwork counterpane. The diamond-shaped pieces of silk melted one into the other, red, blue, purple, green, yellow, all one shimmering colour. Hours and hours she had spent on it and it was nearly finished. Would I be lonely? she asked and I said 'No', looking at the colours. Hours and hours and hours I thought.

This convent was my refuge, a place of sunshine and of death where very early in the morning the clap of a wooden signal woke the nine of us who slept in the long dormitory. We woke to see Sister Marie Augustine sitting, serene and neat, bolt upright in a wooden chair.

The long brown room was full of gold sunlight and shadows of trees moving quietly. I learnt to say very quickly as the others did, 'offer up all the prayers, works and sufferings of this day.' But what about happiness, I thought at first, is there no happiness? There must be. Oh happiness of course, happiness, well.

But I soon forgot about happiness, running down the stairs to the big stone bath where we splashed about wearing long grey cotton chemises[54] which reached to our ankles. The smell of soap as you cautiously soaped yourself under the chemise, a trick to be learned, dressing with modesty, another trick. Great splashes of sunlight as we ran up the wooden steps of the refectory. Hot coffee and rolls and melting butter. But after the meal, now and at the hour of our death, and at midday and at six in the evening, now and at the hour of our death.[55] Let perpetual light shine on them.[56] This is for my mother, I would think, wherever her soul is wandering, for it has left her body. Then I remembered how she hated a strong light and loved the cool and the shade. It is a different light they told me. Still, I would not say it. Soon we were back in the shifting shadows outside, more beautiful than any perpetual light could be, and soon I learnt to gabble without thinking as the others did. About changing now and the hour of our death for that is all we have.

Everything was brightness, or dark. The walls, the blazing colours of the flowers in the garden, the nuns' habits were bright, but their veils, the Crucifix hanging from their waists, the shadow of the trees, were black. That was how it was, light and dark, sun and shadow, Heaven and Hell, for one of the nuns knew all about Hell and who does not? But another one knew about Heaven and the attributes of the blessed, of which the least is transcendent beauty. The very least. I could hardly wait for all this ecstasy and once I prayed for a long time to be dead. Then remembered that this was a sin. It's presumption or despair, I forget which, but a mortal sin. So I prayed for a long time about that too, but the thought came, so many things are sins, why? Another sin, to think that. However, happily, Sister Marie Augustine says thoughts are not sins, if they are driven away at once. You say Lord save me, I perish. I find it very comforting to know exactly what must be done. All the same, I did not pray so often after that and soon, hardly at all. I felt bolder, happier, more free. But not so safe.

During this time, nearly eighteen months, my stepfather often came to see me. He interviewed Mother Superior first, then I would go into the parlour dressed ready for a dinner or a visit to friends. He gave me presents when we parted, sweets, a locket, a bracelet, once a very pretty dress which, of course, I could not wear.

The last time he came was different. I knew that as soon as I got into the room. He kissed me, held me at arm's length looking at me carefully and critically, then smiled and said that I was taller than he thought. I reminded him that I was over seventeen, a grown woman. 'I've not forgotten your present,' he said.

Because I felt shy and ill at ease I answered coldly, 'I can't wear all these things you buy for me.'

'You can wear what you like when you live with me,' he said.

'Where? In Trinidad?'

'Of course not. Here, for the time being. With me and your Aunt Cora who is coming home at last. She says another English winter will kill her. And Richard. You can't be hidden away all your life.'

'Why not?' I thought.

I suppose he noticed my dismay because he began to joke, pay me compliments, and ask me such absurd questions that soon I was laughing too. How would I like to live in England? Then, before I could answer, had I learnt dancing, or were the nuns too strict?

'They are not strict at all,' I said. 'The Bishop who visits them every year says they are lax. Very lax. It's the climate he says.'

'I hope they told him to mind his own business.'

'She did. Mother Superior did. Some of the others were frightened. They are not strict but no one has taught me to dance.'

'That won't be the difficulty. I want you to be happy, Antoinette, secure, I've tried to arrange it, but we'll have time to talk about that later.'

As we were going out of the convent gate he said in a careless voice, 'I have asked some English friends to spend next winter here. You won't be dull.'

'Do you think they'll come?' I said doubtfully.

'One of them will. I'm certain of that.'

It may have been the way he smiled, but again a feeling of dismay, sadness, loss, almost choked me. This time I did not let him see it.

It was like that morning when I found the dead horse. Say nothing and it may not be true.

But they all knew at the convent. The girls were very curious but I would not answer their questions and for the first time I resented the nuns' cheerful faces.

They are safe. How can they know what it can be like *outside*?

This was the second time I had my dream.

Again I have left the house at Coulibri. It is still night and I am walking towards the forest. I am wearing a long dress and thin slippers, so I walk with difficulty, following the man who is with me and holding up the skirt of my dress. It is white and beautiful and I don't wish to get it soiled. I follow him, sick with fear but I make no effort to save myself; if anyone were to try to save me, I would refuse. This must happen. Now we have reached the forest. We are under the tall dark trees and there is no wind. 'Here?' He turns and looks at me, his face black with hatred, and when I see this I begin to cry. He smiles slyly. 'Not here, not yet,' he says, and I follow him, weeping. Now I do not try to hold up my dress, it trails in the dirt, my beautiful dress. We are no longer in the forest but in an enclosed garden surrounded by a stone wall and the trees are different trees. I do not know them. There are steps leading upwards. It is too dark to see the wall or the steps, but I know they are there and I think, 'It will be when I go up these steps. At the top.' I stumble over my dress and cannot get up. I touch a tree and my arms hold on to it. 'Here, here.' But I think I will not go any further. The tree sways and jerks as if it is trying to throw me off. Still I cling and the seconds pass and each one is a thousand years. 'Here, in here,' a strange voice said, and the tree stopped swaying and jerking.

Now Sister Marie Augustine is leading me out of the dormitory, asking if I am ill, telling me that I must not disturb the others and though I am still shivering I wonder if she will take me behind the mysterious curtains to the place where she sleeps. But no. She seats me in a chair, vanishes, and after a while comes back with a cup of hot chocolate.

I said, 'I dreamed I was in Hell.'

'That dream is evil. Put it from your mind – never think of it again,' and she rubbed my cold hands to warm them.

She looks as usual, composed and neat, and I want to ask her if she gets up before dawn or hasn't been to bed at all.

'Drink your chocolate.'

While I am drinking it I remember that after my mother's funeral, very early in the morning, almost as early as this, we went home to drink chocolate and eat cakes. She died last year, no one told me how, and I didn't ask. Mr Mason was there and Christophine, no one else. Christophine cried bitterly but I could not. I prayed, but the words fell to the ground meaning nothing.

Now the thought of her is mixed up with my dream.

I saw her in her mended habit riding a borrowed horse, trying to wave at the head of the cobblestoned road at Coulibri, and tears came to my eyes again. 'Such terrible things happen,' I said. 'Why? Why?'

'You must not concern yourself with that mystery,' said Sister Marie Augustine. 'We do not know why the devil must have his little day. Not yet.'

She never smiled as much as the others, now she was not smiling at all. She looked sad.

She said, as if she was talking to herself, 'Now go quietly back to bed. Think of calm, peaceful things and try to sleep. Soon I will give the signal. Soon it will be tomorrow morning.'

PART TWO

So it was all over, the advance and retreat, the doubts and hesitations. Everything finished, for better or for worse.[1] There we were, sheltering from the heavy rain under a large mango[2] tree, myself, my wife Antoinette and a little half-caste servant who was called Amélie. Under a neighbouring tree I could see our luggage covered with sacking, the two porters and a boy holding fresh horses, hired to carry us up 2,000 feet to the waiting honeymoon house.

The girl Amélie said this morning, 'I hope you will be very happy, sir, in your sweet honeymoon house.' She was laughing at me I could see. A lovely little creature but sly, spiteful, malignant perhaps, like much else in this place.

'It's only a shower,' Antoinette said anxiously. 'It will soon stop.'

I looked at the sad leaning coconut palms, the fishing boats drawn up on the shingly beach, the uneven row of whitewashed huts, and asked the name of the village.

'Massacre.'[3]

'And who was massacred here? Slaves?'

'Oh no.' She sounded shocked. 'Not slaves. Something must have happened a long time ago. Nobody remembers now.'

The rain fell more heavily, huge drops sounded like hail on the leaves of the tree, and the sea crept stealthily forwards and backwards.

So this is Massacre. Not the end of the world, only the last stage of our interminable journey from Jamaica, the start of our sweet honeymoon. And it will all look very different in the sun.

It had been arranged that we would leave Spanish Town immediately after the ceremony and spend some weeks in one of the Windward Islands,[4] at a small estate which had belonged to Antoinette's mother. I agreed. As I had agreed to everything else.

The windows of the huts were shut, the doors opened into silence and dimness. Then three little boys came to stare at us. The smallest wore nothing but a religious medal round his neck and the brim of a large fisherman's hat. When I smiled at him, he began to cry. A woman called from one of the huts and he ran away, still howling.

The other two followed slowly, looking back several times.

As if this was a signal a second woman appeared at her door, then a third.

'It's Caro,' Antoinette said. 'I'm sure it's Caro. Caroline,' she called, waving, and the woman waved back. A gaudy old creature in a brightly flowered dress, a striped head handkerchief and gold ear-rings.

'You'll get soaked, Antoinette,' I said.

'No, the rain is stopping.' She held up the skirt of her riding habit and ran across the street. I watched her critically. She wore a tricorne hat[5] which became her. At least it shadowed her eyes which are too large and can be disconcerting. She never blinks at all it seems to me. Long, sad, dark alien eyes. Creole of pure English descent she may be, but they are not English or European either.[6] And when did I begin to notice all this about my wife Antoinette? After we left Spanish Town I suppose. Or did I notice it before and refuse to admit what I saw? Not that I had much time to notice anything. I was married a month after I arrived in Jamaica and for nearly three weeks of that time I was in bed with fever.

The two women stood in the doorway of the hut gesticulating, talking not English but the debased French patois[7] they use in this island. The rain began to drip down the back of my neck adding to my feeling of discomfort and melancholy.

I thought about the letter which should have been written to England a week ago. Dear Father . . .

'Caroline asks if you will shelter in her house.'

This was Antoinette. She spoke hesitatingly as if she expected me to refuse, so it was easy to do so.

'But you are getting wet,' she said.

'I don't mind that.' I smiled at Caroline and shook my head.

'She will be very disappointed,' said my wife, crossed the street again and went into the dark hut.

Amélie, who had been sitting with her back to us, turned round.

Her expression was so full of delighted malice, so intelligent, above all so intimate that I felt ashamed and looked away.

'Well,' I thought. 'I have had fever. I am not myself yet.'

The rain was not so heavy and I went to talk to the porters. The first man was not a native of the island. 'This a very wild place – not civilized.[8] Why you come here?' He was called the Young Bull he told me, and he was twenty-seven years of age. A magnificent body and a foolish conceited face. The other man's name was Emile, yes, he was born in the village, he lived there. 'Ask him how old he is,' suggested the Young Bull. Emile said in a questioning voice, 'Fourteen? Yes I have fourteen years master.'

'Impossible,' I said. I could see the grey hairs in his sparse beard.

'Fifty-six years perhaps.' He seemed anxious to please.

The Young Bull laughed loudly. 'He don't know how old he is, he don't think about it. I tell you sir these people are not civilized.'

Emile muttered, 'My mother she know, but she dead.' Then he produced a blue rag which he twisted into a pad and put on his head.[9]

Most of the women were outside their doors looking at us but without smiling. Sombre people in a sombre place. Some of the men were going to their boats. When Emile shouted, two of them came towards him. He sang in a deep voice. They answered, then lifted the heavy wicker basket and swung it on to his head-pad singing. He tested the balance with one hand and strode off, barefooted on the sharp stones, by far the gayest member of the wedding party. As the Young Bull was loaded up he glanced at me sideways boastfully and he too sang to himself in English.

The boy brought the horses to a large stone and I saw Antoinette coming from the hut. The sun blazed out and steam rose from the green behind us. Amélie took her shoes off, tied them together and hung them round her neck. She balanced her small basket on her head and swung away as easily as the porters. We mounted, turned a corner and the village was out of sight. A cock crowed loudly[10] and I remembered the night before which we had spent in the town. Antoinette had a room to herself, she was exhausted. I lay awake listening to cocks crowing all night, then got up very early and saw the women with trays covered with white cloths on their heads going to the kitchen. The woman with small hot loaves for sale, the woman with cakes, the woman with sweets. In the street another called *Bon sirop, Bon sirop*,[11] and I felt peaceful.

The road climbed upward. On one side the wall of green, on the other a steep drop to the ravine below. We pulled up and looked at the hills, the mountains and the blue-green sea. There was a soft warm wind blowing but I understood why the porter had called it a wild place. Not only wild but menacing. Those hills would close in on you.

'What an extreme green,' was all I could say, and thinking of Emile calling to the fishermen and the sound of his voice, I asked about him.

'They take short cuts. They will be at Granbois long before we are.'

Everything is too much, I felt as I rode wearily after her. Too much blue, too much purple, too much green. The flowers too red, the mountains too high, the hills too near. And the woman is a stranger. Her pleading expression annoys me. I have not bought her, she has bought me, or so she thinks. I looked down at the coarse mane of the horse . . . Dear Father. The thirty thousand pounds[12] have been paid to me without question or condition. No provision made for her[13] (that must be seen to). I have a modest competence now. I will never be a disgrace to you or to my dear brother the son you love. No begging letters, no mean requests. None of the furtive shabby manoeuvres of a younger son. I have sold my soul[14] or you have sold it, and after all is it such a bad bargain? The girl is thought to be beautiful, she is beautiful. And yet . . .

Meanwhile the horses jogged along a very bad road. It was getting cooler. A bird whistled, a long sad note. 'What bird is that?' She was too far ahead and did not hear me. The bird whistled again. A mountain bird. Shrill and sweet. A very lonely sound.

She stopped and called, 'Put your coat on now.' I did so and realized that I was no longer pleasantly cool but cold in my sweat-soaked shirt.

We rode on again, silent in the slanting afternoon sun, the wall of trees on one side, a drop on the other. Now the sea was a serene blue, deep and dark.

We came to a little river. 'This is the boundary of Granbois.' She smiled at me. It was the first time I had seen her smile simply and naturally. Or perhaps it was the first time I had felt simple and natural with her. A bamboo spout jutted from the cliff, the water coming from it was silver blue. She dismounted quickly, picked a large shamrock-shaped leaf to make a cup, and drank. Then she picked another leaf, folded it and brought it to me. 'Taste. This is mountain water.' Looking up smiling, she might have been any pretty English girl and to please her I drank. It was cold, pure and sweet, a beautiful colour against the thick green leaf.

She said, 'After this we go down then up again. Then we are there.'

Next time she spoke she said, 'The earth is red here, do you notice?'

'It's red in parts of England too.'

'Oh England, England,' she called back mockingly, and the sound went on and on like a warning I did not choose to hear.

Soon the road was cobblestoned and we stopped at a flight of stone steps. There was a large screw pine[15] to the left and to the right what looked like an imitation of an English summer house – four wooden posts and a thatched roof. She dismounted and ran up the steps. At the top a badly cut, coarse-grained lawn and at the end of the lawn a shabby white house. 'Now you are at Granbois.' I looked at the mountains purple against a very blue sky.

Perched up on wooden stilts the house seemed to shrink from the forest behind it and crane eagerly out to the distant sea. It was more awkward than ugly, a little sad as if it knew it could not last. A group of negroes were standing at the foot of the veranda steps. Antoinette ran across the lawn and as I followed her I collided with a boy coming in the opposite direction. He rolled his eyes, looking alarmed and went on towards the horses without a word of apology. A man's voice said, 'Double up now double up. Look sharp.' There were four of them. A woman, a girl and a tall, dignified man were together. Antoinette was standing with her arms round another woman. 'That was Bertrand who nearly knocked you down. That is Rose and Hilda. This is Baptiste.'

The servants grinned shyly as she named them.

'And here is Christophine who was my da,[16] my nurse long ago.'

Baptiste said that it was a happy day and that we'd brought fine weather with us. He spoke good English, but in the middle of his address of welcome Hilda began to giggle. She was a young girl of about twelve or fourteen, wearing a sleeveless white dress which just reached her knees. The dress was spotless but her uncovered hair, though it was oiled and braided into many small plaits, gave her a savage appearance. Baptiste frowned at her and she giggled more loudly, then put her hand over her mouth and went up the wooden steps into the house. I could hear her bare feet running along the veranda.

'*Doudou, ché cocotte,*'[17] the elderly woman said to Antoinette. I looked at her sharply but she seemed insignificant. She was blacker than most and her clothes, even the handkerchief round her head, were subdued in colour. She looked at me steadily, not with approval, I thought. We stared at each other for quite a minute. I looked away first and she smiled to herself, gave Antoinette a little push forward and disappeared into the shadows at the back of the house. The other servants had gone.

Standing on the veranda I breathed the sweetness of the air. Cloves I could smell and cinnamon, roses and orange blossom. And an intoxicating freshness as if all this had never been breathed before. When Antoinette said 'Come, I will show you the house' I went with her unwillingly for the rest of the place seemed neglected and deserted. She led me into a large unpainted room. There was a small shabby sofa, a mahogany table in the middle, some straight-backed chairs and an old oak chest with brass feet like lion's claws.

Holding my hand she went up to the sideboard where two glasses of rum punch were waiting for us. She handed me one and said, 'To happiness.'

'To happiness,' I answered.

The room beyond was larger and emptier. There were two doors, one leading to the veranda, the other very slightly open into a small room. A big bed, a round table by its side, two chairs, a surprising dressing-table with a marble top and a large looking-glass. Two wreaths of frangipani lay on the bed.

'Am I expected to wear one of these? And when?'

I crowned myself with one of the wreaths and made a face in the glass. 'I hardly think it suits my handsome face, do you?'

'You look like a king, an emperor.'

'God forbid,' I said and took the wreath off. It fell on the floor and

44

as I went towards the window I stepped on it. The room was full of the scent of crushed flowers. I saw her reflection in the glass fanning herself with a small palm-leaf fan coloured blue and red at the edges. I felt sweat on my forehead and sat down, she knelt near me and wiped my face with her handkerchief.

'Don't you like it here? This is my place and everything is on our side. Once,' she said, 'I used to sleep with a piece of wood by my side so that I could defend myself if I were attacked. That's how afraid I was.'

'Afraid of what?'

She shook her head. 'Of nothing, of everything.'

Someone knocked and she said, 'It's only Christophine.'

'The old woman who was your nurse? Are you afraid of her?'

'No, how could I be?'

'If she were taller,' I said, 'one of these strapping women dressed up to the nines, I might be afraid of her.'

She laughed. 'That door leads into your dressing-room.'

I shut it gently after me.

It seemed crowded after the emptiness of the rest of the house. There was a carpet, the only one I had seen, a press made of some beautiful wood I did not recognize. Under the open window a small writing-desk with paper, pens, and ink. 'A refuge' I was thinking when someone said, 'This was Mr Mason's room, sir, but he did not come here often. He did not like the place.' Baptiste, standing in the doorway to the veranda, had a blanket over his arm.

'It's all very comfortable,' I said. He laid the blanket on the bed.

'It can be cold here at night,' he said. Then went away. But the feeling of security had left me. I looked round suspiciously. The door into her room could be bolted, a stout wooden bar pushed across the other. This was the last room in the house. Wooden steps from the veranda led on to another rough lawn, a Seville orange tree grew by the steps. I went back into the dressing-room and looked out of the window. I saw a clay road, muddy in places, bordered by a row of tall trees. Beyond the road various half-hidden outbuildings. One was the kitchen. No chimney but smoke was pouring out of the window. I sat on the soft narrow bed and listened. Not a sound except the river. I might have been alone in the house. There was a crude bookshelf made of three shingles[18] strung together over the desk and I looked at the books, Byron's poems, novels by Sir Walter Scott, *Confessions of an Opium Eater*,[19] some shabby brown volumes, and on the last shelf, *Life and Letters of* . . . The rest was eaten away.

Dear Father, we have arrived from Jamaica after an uncomfortable few days. This little estate in the Windward Islands is part of the family property and Antoinette is much attached to it. She wished to get here as soon as possible. All is well and has gone according to your plans and wishes. I dealt of course with Richard Mason.[20] His father died soon after I left for the West Indies as you probably know. He is a good fellow, hospitable and friendly; he seemed to become attached to me and trusted me completely. This place is very beautiful but my illness has left me too exhausted to appreciate it fully. I will write again in a few days' time.

I reread this letter and added a postscript:

I feel that I have left you too long without news for the bare announcement of my approaching marriage was hardly news. I was down with fever for two weeks after I got to Spanish Town. Nothing serious but I felt wretched enough. I stayed with the Frasers, friends of the Masons. Mr Fraser is an Englishman, a retired magistrate, and he insisted on telling me at length about some of his cases. It was difficult to think or write coherently. In this cool and remote place it is called Granbois (the High Woods I suppose) I feel better already and my next letter will be longer and more explicit.

A cool and remote place . . . And I wondered how they got their letters posted. I folded mine and put it into a drawer of the desk.

As for my confused impressions they will never be written. There are blanks in my mind that cannot be filled up.

*

It was all very brightly coloured, very strange, but it meant nothing to me. Nor did she, the girl I was to marry. When at last I met her I bowed, smiled, kissed her hand, danced with her. I played the part I was expected to play. She never had anything to do with me at all. Every movement I made was an effort of will and sometimes I wondered that no one noticed this. I would listen to my own voice and marvel at it, calm, correct but toneless, surely. But I must have given a faultless performance. If I saw an expression of doubt or curiosity it was on a black face not a white one.

I remember little of the actual ceremony. Marble memorial tablets on the walls commemorating the virtues of the last generation of planters. All benevolent. All slave-owners. All resting in peace. When we came out of the church I took her hand. It was cold as ice in the hot sun.

Then I was at a long table in a crowded room. Palm leaf fans, a mob of servants, the women's head handkerchiefs striped red and yellow, the men's dark faces. The strong taste of punch, the cleaner taste of champagne, my bride in white but I hardly remember what she looked like. Then in another room women dressed in black. Cousin Julia, Cousin Ada, Aunt Lina. Thin or fat they all looked alike. Gold ear-rings in pierced ears. Silver bracelets jangling on their wrists. I said to one of them, 'We are leaving Jamaica tonight,' and she answered after a pause, 'Of course, Antoinette does not like Spanish Town. Nor did her mother.' Peering at me. (Do their eyes get smaller as they grow older? Smaller, beadier, more inquisitive?) After that I thought I saw the same expression on all their faces. Curiosity? Pity? Ridicule? But why should they pity me. I who have done so well for myself?

The morning before the wedding Richard Mason burst into my room at the Frasers' as I was finishing my first cup of coffee. 'She won't go through with it!'

'Won't go through with what?'

'She won't marry you.'

'But why?'

'She doesn't say why.'

'She must have some reason.'

'She won't give a reason. I've been arguing with the little fool for an hour.'

We stared at each other.

'Everything arranged, the presents, the invitations. What shall I tell your father?' He seemed on the verge of tears.

I said, 'If she won't, she won't. She can't be dragged to the altar. Let me get dressed. I must hear what she has to say.'

He went out meekly and while I dressed I thought that this would indeed make a fool of me. I did not relish going back to England in the role of rejected suitor jilted by this Creole girl. I must certainly know why.

She was sitting in a rocking-chair with her head bent. Her hair was in two long plaits over her shoulders. From a little distance I spoke gently. 'What is the matter, Antoinette? What have I done?'

She said nothing.

'You don't wish to marry me?'

'No.' She spoke in a very low voice.

'But why?'

'I'm afraid of what may happen.'

'But don't you remember last night I told you that when you are my wife there would not be any more reason to be afraid?'

'Yes,' she said. 'Then Richard came in and you laughed. I didn't like the way you laughed.'

'But I was laughing at myself, Antoinette.'

She looked at me and I took her in my arms and kissed her.

'You don't know anything about me,' she said.

'I'll trust you if you'll trust me. Is that a bargain? You will make me very unhappy if you send me away without telling me what I have done to displease you. I will go with a sad heart.'

'Your sad heart,' she said, and touched my face. I kissed her fervently, promising her peace, happiness, safety, but when I said, 'Can I tell poor Richard that it was a mistake? He is sad too,' she did not answer me. Only nodded.

*

Thinking of all this, of Richard's angry face, her voice saying, 'Can you give me peace?', I must have slept.

I woke to the sound of voices in the next room, laughter and water being poured out. I listened, still drowsy. Antoinette said, 'Don't put any more scent on my hair. He doesn't like it.' The other: 'The man don't like scent? I never hear that before.' It was almost dark.

The dining-room was brilliantly lit. Candles on the table, a row on the sideboard, three-branch candlesticks on the old sea-chest. The two doors on to the veranda stood open but there was no wind. The flames burned straight. She was sitting on the sofa and I wondered why I had never realized how beautiful she was. Her hair was combed away from her face and fell smoothly far below her waist. I could see the red and gold lights in it. She seemed pleased when I complimented her on her dress and told me she had it made in St Pierre, Martinique. 'They call the fashion *à la Joséphine*.'[21]

'You talk of St Pierre as though it were Paris,' I said.

'But it is the Paris of the West Indies.'

There were trailing pink flowers on the table and the name echoed pleasantly in my head. Coralita Coralita.[22] The food, though too highly seasoned, was lighter and more appetizing than anything I had tasted in Jamaica. We drank champagne. A great many moths and beetles found their way into the room, flew into the candles and fell dead on the tablecloth. Amélie swept them up with a crumb brush. Uselessly. More moths and beetles came.

'Is it true,' she said, 'that England is like a dream? Because one of my friends who married an Englishman wrote and told me so. She said this place London is like a cold dark dream sometimes. I want to wake up.'

'Well,' I answered annoyed, 'that is precisely how your beautiful island seems to me, quite unreal and like a dream.'

'But how can rivers and mountains and the sea be unreal?'

'And how can millions of people, their houses and their streets be unreal?'

'More easily,' she said, 'much more easily. Yes a big city must be like a dream.'

'No, this is unreal and like a dream,' I thought.

The long veranda was furnished with canvas chairs, two hammocks, and a wooden table on which stood a tripod telescope. Amélie brought out candles with glass shades but the night swallowed up the feeble light. There was a very strong scent of flowers – the flowers by the river that open at night she told me – and the noise, subdued in the inner room, was deafening. 'Crac-cracs,'[23] she explained, 'they make a sound like their name, and crickets and frogs.'

I leaned on the railing and saw hundreds of fireflies – 'Ah yes, fireflies in Jamaica, here they call a firefly La belle.'[24]

A large moth, so large that I thought it was a bird, blundered into

one of the candles, put it out and fell to the floor. 'He's a big fellow,'
I said.

'Is it badly burned?'

'More stunned than hurt.'

I took the beautiful creature up in my handkerchief and put it on
the railing. For a moment it was still and by the dim candlelight I
could see the soft brilliant colours, the intricate pattern on the wings.
I shook the handkerchief gently and it flew away.

'I hope that gay gentleman will be safe,' I said.

'He will come back if we don't put the candles out. It's light enough
by the stars.'

Indeed the starlight was so bright that shadows of the veranda posts
and the trees outside lay on the floor.

'Now come for a walk,' she said, 'and I will tell you a story.'

We walked along the veranda to the steps which led to the lawn.

'We used to come here to get away from the hot weather in
June, July and August. I came three times with my Aunt Cora who
is ill. That was after . . .' She stopped and put her hand up to her
head.

'If this is a sad story, don't tell it to me tonight.'

'It is not sad,' she said. 'Only some things happen and are there for
always even though you forget why or when. It was in that little
bedroom.'

I looked where she was pointing but could only see the outline of a
narrow bed and one or two chairs.

'This night I can remember it was very hot. The window was shut
but I asked Christophine to open it because the breeze comes from the
hills at night. The land breeze. Not from the sea. It was so hot that
my night chemise was sticking to me but I went to sleep all the same.
And then suddenly I was awake. I saw two enormous rats, as big as
cats, on the sill staring at me.'

'I'm not astonished that you were frightened.'

'But I was not frightened. That was the strange thing. I stared at
them and they did not move. I could see myself in the looking-glass
the other side of the room, in my white chemise with a frill round the
neck, staring at those rats and the rats quite still, staring at me.'

'Well, what happened?'

'I turned over, pulled up the sheet and went to sleep instantly.'

'And is that the story?'

'No, I woke up again suddenly like the first time and the rats were not there but I felt very frightened. I got out of bed quickly and ran on to the veranda. I lay down in this hammock. This one.' She pointed to a flat hammock, a rope at each of the four corners.

'There was a full moon that night – and I watched it for a long time. There were no clouds chasing it, so it seemed to be standing still and it shone on me. Next morning Christophine was angry. She said that it was very bad to sleep in the moonlight when the moon is full.'[25]

'And did you tell her about the rats?'

'No, I never told anyone till now. But I have never forgotten them.'

I wanted to say something reassuring but the scent of the river flowers was overpoweringly strong. I felt giddy.

'Do you think that too,' she said, 'that I have slept too long in the moonlight?'

Her mouth was set in a fixed smile but her eyes were so withdrawn and lonely that I put my arms round her, rocked her like a child and sang to her. An old song I thought I had forgotten:

> 'Hail to the queen of the silent night,
> Shine bright, shine bright Robin as you die.'

She listened, then sang with me:

> 'Shine bright, shine bright Robin as you die.'

There was no one in the house and only two candles in the room which had been so brilliantly lit. Her room was dim, with a shaded candle by the bed and another on the dressing-table. There was a bottle of wine on the round table. It was very late when I poured out two glasses and told her to drink to our happiness, to our love and the day without end which would be tomorrow. I was young then. A short youth mine was.

I woke next morning in the green-yellow light, feeling uneasy as though someone were watching me. She must have been awake for some time. Her hair was plaited and she wore a fresh white chemise.

I turned to take her in my arms, I meant to undo the careful plaits, but as I did so there was a soft discreet knock.

She said, 'I have sent Christophine away twice. We wake very early here. The morning is the best time.'

'Come in,' she called and Christophine came in with our coffee on a tray. She was dressed up and looking very imposing. The skirt of her flowered dress trailed after her making a rustling noise as she walked and her yellow silk turban was elaborately tied. Long heavy gold ear-rings pulled down the lobes of her ears. She wished us good morning smiling and put the tray of coffee, cassava[26] cakes and guava[27] jelly on the round table. I got out of bed and went into the dressing-room. Someone had laid my dressing-gown on the narrow bed. I looked out of the window. The cloudless sky was a paler blue than I'd imagined but as I looked I thought I saw the colour changing to a deeper blue. At noon I knew it would be gold, then brassy in the heat. Now it was fresh and cool and the air itself was blue. At last I turned away from the light and space and went back into the bedroom, which was still in the half dark. Antoinette was leaning back against the pillows with her eyes closed. She opened them and smiled when I came in. It was the black woman hovering over her who said, 'Taste my bull's blood, master.' The coffee she handed me was delicious and she had long-fingered hands, thin and beautiful I suppose.

'Not horse piss like the English madams drink,' she said. 'I know them. Drink, drink their yellow horse piss, talk, talk their lying talk.' Her dress trailed and rustled as she walked to the door. There she turned. 'I send the girl to clear up the mess you make with the frangipani, it bring cockroach in the house. Take care not to slip on the flowers, young master.' She slid through the door.

'Her coffee is delicious but her language is horrible and she might hold her dress up. It must get very dirty, yards of it trailing on the floor.'

'When they don't hold their dress up it's for respect,' said Antoinette. 'Or for feast days or going to Mass.'

'And is this feast day?'

'She wanted it to be a feast day.'

'Whatever the reason it is not a clean habit.'

'It is. You don't understand at all. They don't care about getting a dress dirty because it shows it isn't the only dress they have. Don't you like Christophine?'

'She is a very worthy person no doubt. I can't say I like her language.'

'It doesn't mean anything,' said Antoinette.

'And she looks so lazy. She dawdles about.'

'Again you are mistaken. She seems slow, but every move she makes is right so it's quick in the end.'

I drank another cup of bull's blood. (Bull's blood, I thought. The Young Bull.)

'How did you get that dressing-table up here?'

'I don't know. It's always been here ever since I can remember. A lot of the furniture was stolen, but not that.'

There were two pink roses on the tray, each in a small brown jug. One was full blown and as I touched it the petals dropped.

'*Rose elle a vécu*,'[28] I said and laughed. 'Is that poem true? Have all beautiful things sad destinies?'

'No, of course not.'

Her little fan was on the table, she took it up laughing, lay back and shut her eyes. 'I think I won't get up this morning.'

'Not get up. Not get up at all?'

'I'll get up when I wish to. I'm very lazy you know. Like Christophine. I often stay in bed all day.' She flourished her fan. 'The bathing pool is quite near. Go before it gets hot, Baptiste will show you. There are two pools, one we call the champagne pool because it has a waterfall, not a big one you understand, but it's good to feel it on your shoulders. Underneath is the nutmeg pool, that's brown and shaded by a big nutmeg tree. It's just big enough to swim in. But be careful. Remember to put your clothes on a rock and before you dress again shake them very well. Look for the red ant, that is the worst. It is very small but bright red so you will be able to see it easily if you look. Be careful,' she said and waved her little fan.

One morning soon after we arrived, the row of tall trees outside my window was covered with small pale flowers too fragile to resist the wind. They fell in a day, and looked like snow on the rough grass – snow with a faint sweet scent. Then they were blown away.

The fine weather lasted longer. It lasted all that week and the next and the next and the next. No sign of a break. My fever weakness left me, so did all misgiving.

I went very early to the bathing pool and stayed there for hours, unwilling to leave the river, the trees shading it, the flowers that opened at night. They were tightly shut, drooping, sheltering from the sun under their thick leaves.

It was a beautiful place – wild, untouched, above all untouched, with an alien, disturbing, secret loveliness. And it kept its secret. I'd find myself thinking, 'What I see is nothing – I want what it *hides* – that is not nothing.'

In the late afternoon when the water was warmer she bathed with me. She'd spend some time throwing pebbles at a flat stone in the middle of the pool. 'I've seen him. He hasn't died or gone to any other river. He's still there. The land crabs are harmless. People *say* they are harmless. I wouldn't like to –'

'Nor would I. Horrible looking creatures.'

She was undecided, uncertain about facts – any fact. When I asked her if the snakes we sometimes saw were poisonous, she said, 'Not those. The *fer de lance*[29] of course, but there are none here,' and added, 'but how can they be sure? Do you think they know?' Then, 'Our snakes are not poisonous. Of course not.'

However, she was certain about the monster crab and one afternoon when I was watching her, hardly able to believe she was the pale silent creature I had married, watching her in her blue chemise, blue with white spots, hitched up far above her knees, she stopped laughing, called a warning and threw a large pebble. She threw like a boy, with a sure graceful movement, and I looked down at very long pincer claws, jagged-edged and sharp, vanishing.

'He won't come after you if you keep away from that stone. He lives there. Oh it's another sort of crab. I don't know the name in English. Very big, very old.'

As we were walking home I asked her who had taught her to aim so well. 'Oh, Sandi taught me, a boy you never met.'

Every evening we saw the sun go down from the thatched shelter she called the *ajoupa*,[30] I the summer house. We watched the sky and the distant sea on fire – all colours were in that fire and the huge clouds fringed and shot with flame. But I soon tired of the display. I was waiting for the scent of the flowers by the river – they opened when darkness came and it came quickly. Not night or darkness as I knew it but night with blazing stars, an alien moon – night full of strange noises. Still night, not day.

'The man who owns Consolation Estate is a hermit,' she was saying. 'He never sees anyone – hardly ever speaks, they say.'

'A hermit neighbour suits me. Very well indeed.'

'There are four hermits in this island,' she said. 'Four real ones. Others pretend but they leave when the rainy season comes. Or else they are drunk all the time. That's when sad things happen.'

'So this place is as lonely as it feels?' I asked her.

'Yes it is lonely. Are you happy here?'

'Who wouldn't be?'

'I love it more than anywhere in the world. As if it were a person. More than a person.'

'But you don't know the world,' I teased her.

'No, only here, and Jamaica of course. Coulibri, Spanish Town. I don't know the other islands at all. Is the world more beautiful, then?'

And how to answer that? 'It's different,' I said.

She told me that for a long time they had not known what was happening at Granbois. 'When Mr Mason came' (she always called her stepfather Mr Mason) 'the forest was swallowing it up.' The overseer drank, the house was dilapidated, all the furniture had been stolen, then Baptiste was discovered. A butler. In St Kitts. But born in this island and willing to come back. 'He's a very good overseer,' she'd say, and I'd agree, keeping my opinion of Baptiste, Christophine and all the others to myself. 'Baptiste says . . . Christophine wants . . .'

She trusted them and I did not. But I could hardly say so. Not yet.

We did not see a great deal of them. The kitchen and the swarming kitchen life were some way off. As for the money which she handed out so carelessly, not counting it, not knowing how much she gave, or the unfamiliar faces that appeared then disappeared, though never without a large meal eaten and a shot of rum I discovered – sisters, cousins, aunts and uncles – if she asked no questions how could I?

The house was swept and dusted very early, usually before I woke.

Hilda brought coffee and there were always two roses on the tray. Sometimes she'd smile a sweet childish smile, sometimes she would giggle very loudly and rudely, bang the tray down and run away.

'Stupid little girl,' I'd say.

'No, no. She is shy. The girls here are very shy.'

After breakfast at noon there'd be silence till the evening meal which was served much later than in England. Christophine's whims and fancies, I was sure. Then we were left alone. Sometimes a sidelong look or a sly knowing glance disturbed me, but it was never for long. 'Not now,' I would think. 'Not yet.'

It was often raining when I woke during the night, a light capricious shower, dancing playful rain, or hushed, muted, growing louder, more persistent, more powerful, an inexorable sound. But always music, a music I had never heard before.

Then I would look at her for long minutes by candlelight, wonder why she seemed sad asleep, and curse the fever or the caution that had made me so blind, so feeble, so hesitating. I'd remember her effort to escape. (*No, I am sorry, I do not wish to marry you.*) Had she given way to that man Richard's arguments, threats probably, I wouldn't trust him far, or to my half-serious blandishments and promises? In any case she had given way, but coldly, unwillingly, trying to protect herself with silence and a blank face. Poor weapons, and they had not served her well or lasted long. If I have forgotten caution, she has forgotten silence and coldness.

Shall I wake her up and listen to the things she says, whispers, in darkness. Not by day.

'I never wished to live before I knew you. I always thought it would be better if I died. Such a long time to wait before it's over.'

'And did you ever tell anyone this?'

'There was no one to tell, no one to listen. Oh you can't imagine Coulibri.'

'But after Coulibri?'

'After Coulibri it was too late. I did not change.'

All day she'd be like any other girl, smile at herself in her looking-glass (*do you like this scent?*), try to teach me her songs, for they haunted me.

Adieu foulard, adieu madras,[31] or *Ma belle ka di maman li.*[32] My beautiful girl said to her mother (*No it is not like that. Now listen. It is this way*). She'd be silent, or angry for no reason, and chatter to Christophine in patois.

'Why do you hug and kiss Christophine?' I'd say.

'Why not?'

'*I* wouldn't hug and kiss them,' I'd say, 'I couldn't.'

At this she'd laugh for a long time and never tell me why she laughed.

But at night how different, even her voice was changed. Always this talk of death. (Is she trying to tell me that is the secret of this place? That there is no other way? She knows. She knows.)

'Why did you make me want to live? Why did you do that to me?'

'Because I wished it. Isn't that enough?'

'Yes, it is enough. But if one day you didn't wish it. What should I do then? Suppose you took this happiness away when I wasn't looking . . .'

'And lose my own? Who'd be so foolish?'

'I am not used to happiness,' she said. 'It makes me afraid.'

'Never be afraid. Or if you are tell no one.'

'I understand. But trying does not help me.'

'What would?' She did not answer that, then one night whispered, 'If I could die. Now, when I am happy.[33] Would you do that? You wouldn't have to kill me. Say die and I will die. You don't believe me? Then try, try, say die and watch me die.'

'Die then! Die!' I watched her die many times.[34] In my way, not in hers. In sunlight, in shadow, by moonlight, by candlelight. In the long afternoons when the house was empty. Only the sun was there to keep us company. We shut him out. And why not? Very soon she was as eager for what's called loving as I was — more lost and drowned afterwards.

She said, 'Here I can do as I like,' not I, and then I said it too. It seemed right in that lonely place. 'Here I can do as I like.'

We seldom met anyone when we left the house. If we did they'd greet us and go on their way.

I grew to like these mountain people, silent, reserved, never servile, never curious (or so I thought), not knowing that their quick sideways looks saw everything they wished to see.

It was at night that I felt danger and would try to forget it and push it away.

'You are safe,' I'd say. She'd liked that – to be told 'you are safe.' Or I'd touch her face gently and touch tears. Tears – nothing! Words – less than nothing. As for the happiness I gave her, that was worse than nothing. I did not love her. I was thirsty for her, but that is not love. I felt very little tenderness for her, she was a stranger to me, a stranger who did not think or feel as I did.

One afternoon the sight of a dress which she'd left lying on her bedroom floor made me breathless and savage with desire. When I was exhausted I turned away from her and slept, still without a word or a caress. I woke and she was kissing me – soft light kisses. 'It is late,' she said and smiled. 'You must let me cover you up – the land breeze can be cold.'

'And you, aren't you cold?'

'Oh I will be ready quickly. I'll wear the dress you like tonight.'

'Yes, do wear it.'

The floor was strewn with garments, hers and mine. She stepped over them carelessly as she walked to her clothes press. 'I was thinking, I'll have another made exactly like it,' she promised happily. 'Will you be pleased?'

'Very pleased.'

If she was a child she was not a stupid child but an obstinate one. She often questioned me about England and listened attentively to my answers, but I was certain that nothing I said made much difference. Her mind was already made up. Some romantic novel, a stray remark never forgotten, a sketch, a picture, a song, a waltz, some note of music, and her ideas were fixed. About England and about Europe. I could not change them and probably nothing would. Reality might disconcert her, bewilder her, hurt her, but it would not be reality. It would be only a mistake, a misfortune, a wrong path taken, her fixed ideas would never change.

Nothing that I told her influenced her at all.

Die then. Sleep. It is all that I can give you . . . wonder if she ever guessed how near she came to dying. In her way, not in mine. It was not a safe game to play – in that place. Desire, Hatred, Life, Death came very close in the darkness. Better not know how close. Better not think, never for a moment. Not close. The same . . . 'You are safe,' I'd say to her and to myself. 'Shut your eyes. Rest.'

Then I'd listen to the rain, a sleepy tune that seemed as if it would go on for ever . . . Rain, for ever raining. Drown me in sleep. And soon.

Next morning there would be very little sign of these showers. If some of the flowers were battered, the others smelt sweeter, the air was bluer and sparkling fresh. Only the clay path outside my window was muddy. Little shallow pools of water glinted in the hot sun, red earth does not dry quickly.

*

'It came for you this morning early, master,' Amélie said. 'Hilda take it.' She gave me a bulky envelope addressed in careful copperplate. '*By hand. Urgent*' was written in the corner.

'One of our hermit neighbours,' I thought. 'And an enclosure for Antoinette.' Then I saw Baptiste standing near the veranda steps, put the letter in my pocket and forgot it.

I was later than usual that morning but when I was dressed I sat for a long time listening to the waterfall, eyes half closed, drowsy and content. When I put my hand in my pocket for my watch, I touched the envelope and opened it.

Dear Sir. I take up my pen after long thought and meditation but in the end the truth is better than a lie. I have this to say. You have been shamefully deceived by the Mason family. They tell you perhaps that your wife's name is Cosway, the English gentleman Mr Mason being her stepfather only, but they don't tell you what sort of people were these Cosways. Wicked and detestable slave-owners since generations – yes everybody hate them in Jamaica and also in this beautiful island where I hope your stay will be long and pleasant in spite of all, for some not worth sorrow. Wickedness is not the worst. There is madness in that family. Old Cosway die raving like his father before him.

You ask what proof I have and why I mix myself up in your affairs. I will answer you. I am your wife's brother by another lady, half-way house as we say. Her father and mine was a shameless man and of all his illegitimates I am the most unfortunate and poverty stricken.

My momma die when I was quite small and my godmother take care of me. The old mister hand out some money for that though he don't like me. No, that old devil don't like me at all, and when I grow older I see it and I think, Let him wait my day will come. Ask the older people sir about his disgusting goings on, some will remember.

When Madam his wife die the reprobate marry again quick, to a young girl from Martinique – it's too much for him. Dead drunk from morning till night and he die raving and cursing.

Then comes the glorious Emancipation Act and trouble for some of the high and mighties. Nobody would work for the young woman and her two children and that place Coulibri goes quickly to bush as all does out here when nobody toil and labour on the land. She have no money and she have no friends, for French and English like cat and dog in these islands since long time. Shoot, Kill, Everything.

The woman called Christophine also from Martinique stay with her and an old man Godfrey, too silly to know what happen. Some like that. This young Mrs Cosway is worthless and spoilt, she can't lift a hand for herself and soon the madness that is in her, and in all these white Creoles, come out. She shut herself away, laughing and talking to nobody as many can bear witness. As for the little girl, Antoinetta, as soon as she can walk she hide herself if she see anybody.

We all wait to hear the woman jump over a precipice '*fini batte'e*' as we say here which mean 'finish to fight'.

But no. She marry again to the rich Englishman Mr Mason, and there is much I could say about that but you won't believe so I shut my mouth. They say he love her so much that if he have the world on a plate he give it to her – but no use.

The madness gets worse and she has to be shut away for she try to kill her husband – madness not being all either.

That sir is your wife's mother – that was her father. I leave Jamaica. I don't know what happen to the woman. Some say she is dead, other deny it. But old Mason take a great fancy for the girl Antoinetta and give her half his money when he die.

As for me I wander high and low, not much luck but a little money put by and I get to know of a house for sale in this island near Massacre. It's going very cheap so I buy it. News travel even to this wild place and next thing I hear from Jamaica is that old Mason is dead and that family plan to marry the girl to a young Englishman who know nothing of her. Then it seems to me that it is my Christian duty to warn the gentleman that she is no girl to marry with the bad blood she have from both sides. But they are white, I am coloured. They are rich, I am poor. As I think about these things they do it quick while you still weak with fever at the magistrate's, before you can ask questions. If this is true or not you must know for yourself.

Then you come to this island for your honeymoon and it's certain that the Lord put the thing on my shoulders and that it is I must speak the truth to you. Still I hesitate.

I hear you young and handsome with a kind word for all, black, white, also coloured. But I hear too that the girl is beautiful like her mother was beautiful, and you bewitch with her. She is in your blood and your bones. By night and by day. But you, an honourable man, know well that for marriage more is needed than all this. Which does not last. Old Mason bewitch so with her mother and look what happen to him. Sir I pray I am in time to warn you what to do.

Sir ask yourself how I can make up this story and for what reason. When I leave Jamaica I can read write and cypher a little. The good man in Barbados teach me more, he give me books, he tell me read the Bible every day and I pick up knowledge without effort. He is surprise how quick I am. Still I remain an ignorant man and I do not make up this story. I cannot. It is true.

I sit at my window and the words fly past me like birds – with God's help I catch some.

A week this letter take me. I cannot sleep at night thinking what to say. So quickly now I draw to a close and cease my task.

Still you don't believe me? Then ask that devil of a man Richard Mason three questions and make him answer you. Is your wife's mother shut away, a raging lunatic and worse besides? Dead or alive I do not know.

Was your wife's brother an idiot from birth, though God mercifully take him early on?

Is your wife herself going the same way as her mother and all knowing it?

Richard Mason is a sly man and he will tell you a lot of nancy stories,[35] which is what we call lies here, about what happen at Coulibri and this and that. Don't listen. Make him answer – yes or no.

If he keep his mouth shut ask others for many think it shameful how that family treat you and your relatives.

I beg you sir come to see me for there is more that you should know. But my hand ache, my head ache and my heart is like a stone for the grief I bring you. Money is good but no money can pay for a crazy wife in your bed. Crazy and worse besides.

I lay down my pen with one last request. Come and see me quickly. Your obt servant. Daniel Cosway.

Ask the girl Amélie where I live. She knows, and she knows me. She belongs to this island.

I folded the letter carefully and put it into my pocket. I felt no surprise. It was as if I'd expected it, been waiting for it. For a time, long or short I don't know, I sat listening to the river. At last I stood up, the sun was hot now. I walked stiffly nor could I force myself to think. Then I passed an orchid with long sprays of golden-brown flowers. One of them touched my cheek and I remembered picking some for her one day. 'They are like you,' I told her. Now I stopped, broke a spray off and trampled it into the mud. This brought me to my senses. I leaned against a tree, sweating and trembling. 'Far too hot today,' I said aloud, 'far too hot.' When I came in sight of the house I began to walk silently. No one was about. The kitchen door was shut and the place looked deserted. I went up the steps and along the veranda and when I heard voices stopped behind the door which led into Antoinette's room. I could see it reflected in the looking-glass. She was in bed and the girl Amélie was sweeping.

'Finish quickly,' said Antoinette, 'and go and tell Christophine I want to see her.'

Amélie rested her hands on the broom handle. 'Christophine is going,' she said.

'Going?' repeated Antoinette.

'Yes, going,' said Amélie. 'Christophine don't like this sweet honeymoon house.' Turning round she saw me and laughed loudly. 'Your husban' he outside the door and he look like he see zombi. Must be he tired of the sweet honeymoon too.'

Antoinette jumped out of bed and slapped her face.

'I hit you back white cockroach, I hit you back,' said Amélie. And she did.

Antoinette gripped her hair. Amélie, whose teeth were bared, seemed to be trying to bite.

'Antoinette, for God's sake,' I said from the doorway.

She swung round, very pale. Amélie buried her face in her hands and pretended to sob, but I could see her watching me through her fingers.

'Go away, child,' I said.

'You call her child,' said Antoinette. 'She is older than the devil himself, and the devil is not more cruel.'

'Send Christophine up,' I said to Amélie.

'Yes master, yes master,' she answered softly, dropping her eyes. But as soon as she was out of the room she began to sing:

> 'The white cockroach she marry
> The white cockroach she marry
> The white cockroach she buy young man
> The white cockroach she marry.'

Antoinette took a few steps forward. She walked unsteadily. I went to help her but she pushed me away, sat on the bed and with clenched teeth pulled at the sheet, then made a clicking sound of annoyance. She took a pair of scissors from the round table, cut through the hem and tore the sheet in half, then each half into strips.

The noise she made prevented me from hearing Christophine come in, but Antoinette heard her.

'You're not leaving?' she said.

'Yes,' said Christophine.

'And what will become of me?' said Antoinette.

'Get up, girl, and dress yourself. Women must have spunks[36] to live in this wicked world.'

She had changed into a drab cotton dress and taken off her heavy gold ear-rings.

'I see enough trouble,' she said. 'I have right to my rest. I have my house that your mother give me so long ago and I have my garden and my son to work for me. A lazy boy but I make him work. Too besides the young master don't like me, and perhaps I don't like him so much. If I stay here I bring trouble and bone of contention in your house.'

'If you are not happy here then go,' said Antoinette.

Amélie came into the room with two jugs of hot water. She looked at me sideways and smiled.

Christophine said in a soft voice, 'Amélie. Smile like that once more, just once more, and I mash your face like I mash plantain.[37] You hear me? Answer me, girl.'

'Yes, Christophine,' Amélie said. She looked frightened.

'And too besides I give you bellyache like you never see bellyache. Perhaps you lie a long time with the bellyache I give you. Perhaps you don't get up again with the bellyache I give you. So keep yourself quiet and decent. You hear me?'

'Yes, Christophine,' Amélie said and crept out of the room.

'She worthless and good for nothing,' said Christophine with contempt. 'She creep and crawl like centipede.'

She kissed Antoinette on the cheek. Then she looked at me, shook her head, and muttered in patois before she went out.

'Did you hear what that girl was singing?' Antoinette said.

'I don't always understand what they say or sing.' Or anything else.

'It was a song about a white cockroach. That's me. That's what they call all of us who were here before their own people in Africa sold them to the slave traders. And I've heard English women call us white niggers. So between you I often wonder who I am and where is my country and where do I belong and why was I ever born at all. Will you go now please. I must dress like Christophine said.'

After I had waited half an hour I knocked at her door. There was no answer so I asked Baptiste to bring me something to eat. He was sitting under the Seville orange tree at the end of the veranda. He served the food with such a mournful expression that I thought these people are very vulnerable. How old was I when I learned to hide what I felt? A very small boy. Six, five, even earlier. It was necessary, I was told, and that view I have always accepted. If these mountains challenge me, or Baptiste's face, or Antoinette's eyes, they are mistaken, melodramatic, unreal (England must be quite unreal and like a dream she said).

The rum punch I had drunk was very strong and after the meal was over I had a great wish to sleep. And why not? This is the time when everyone sleeps. I imagined the dogs the cats the cocks and hens all sleeping, even the water in the river running more slowly.

I woke up, thought at once of Antoinette and opened the door into her room, but she was sleeping too. Her back was towards me and she was quite still. I looked out of the window. The silence was disturbing, absolute. I would have welcomed the sound of a dog barking, a man sawing wood. Nothing. Silence. Heat. It was five minutes to three.

I went out following the path I could see from my window. It must have rained heavily during the night for the red clay was very muddy. I passed a sparse plantation of coffee trees, then straggly guava bushes. As I walked I remembered my father's face and his thin lips, my brother's round conceited eyes. They knew. And Richard the fool, he knew too. And the girl with her blank smiling face. They all knew.

I began to walk very quickly, then stopped because the light was different. A green light. I had reached the forest and you cannot mistake the forest. It is hostile. The path was overgrown but it was possible to follow it. I went on without looking at the tall trees on either side. Once I stepped over a fallen log swarming with white ants. How can one discover truth I thought and that thought led me nowhere. No one would tell me the truth. Not my father nor Richard Mason, certainly not the girl I had married. I stood still, so sure I was being watched that I looked over my shoulder. Nothing but the trees and the green light under the trees. A track was just visible and I went on, glancing from side to side and sometimes quickly behind me. This was why I stubbed my foot on a stone and nearly fell. The stone I had tripped on was not a boulder but part of a paved road. There had been a paved road through this forest. The track led to a large clear space. Here were the ruins of a stone house and round the ruins rose trees that had grown to an incredible height. At the back of the ruins a wild orange tree covered with fruit, the leaves a dark green. A beautiful place. And calm – so calm that it seemed foolish to think or plan. What had I to think about and how could I plan? Under the orange tree I noticed little bunches of flowers tied with grass.

I don't know how long it was before I began to feel chilly. The light had changed and the shadows were long. I had better get back before dark, I thought. Then I saw a little girl carrying a large basket on her head. I met her eye and to my astonishment she screamed loudly, threw up her arms and ran. The basket fell off, I called after her, but she screamed again and ran faster. She sobbed as she ran, a small frightened sound. Then she disappeared. I must be within a few minutes of the path I thought, but after I had walked for what seemed a long time I found that the undergrowth and creepers caught at my legs and the trees closed over my head. I decided to go back to the clearing and start again, with the same result. It was getting dark. It was useless to tell myself that I was not far from the house. I was lost and afraid among these enemy trees, so certain of danger that when I heard footsteps and a shout I did not answer. The footsteps and the voice came nearer. Then I shouted back. I did not recognize Baptiste at first. He was wearing blue cotton trousers pulled up above his knees and a broad ornamented belt round his slim waist. His machete was in his hand and the light caught the razor-sharp blue-white edge. He did not smile when he saw me.

'We look for you a long time,' he said.

'I got lost.'

He grunted in answer and led the way, walking in front of me very quickly and cutting off any branch or creeper that stopped us with an easy swing of his machete.

I said, 'There was a road here once, where did it lead to?'

'No road,' he said.

'But I saw it. A *pavé* road like the French made in the islands.'

'No road.'

'Who lived in that house?'

'They say a priest. Père Lilièvre. He lived here a long time ago.'

'A child passed,' I said. 'She seemed very frightened when she saw me. Is there something wrong about the place?' He shrugged his shoulders.

'Is there a ghost, a zombi there?' I persisted.

'Don't know nothing about all that foolishness.'

'There was a road here sometime.'

'No road,' he repeated obstinately.

It was nearly dark when we were back on the red clay path. He walked more slowly, turned and smiled at me. It was as if he'd put his service mask on the savage reproachful face I had seen.

'You don't like the woods at night?'

He did not answer, but pointed to a light and said, 'It's a long time

I've been looking for you. Miss Antoinette frightened you come to harm.'

When we reached the house I felt very weary.

'You like you catch fever,' he said.

'I've had that already.'

'No limit to times you catch fever.'

There was no one on the veranda and no sound from the house. We both stood in the road looking up, then he said, 'I send the girl to you, master.'

Hilda brought me a large bowl of soup and some fruit. I tried the door into Antoinette's room. It was bolted and there was no light. Hilda giggled. A nervous giggle.

I told her that I did not want anything to eat, to bring me the decanter of rum and a glass. I drank, then took up the book I had been reading, *The Glittering Coronet of Isles* it was called, and I turned to the chapter 'Obeah':

'A zombi is a dead person who seems to be alive or a living person who is dead. A zombi can also be the spirit of a place, usually malignant but sometimes to be propitiated with sacrifices or offerings of flowers and fruit.' [I thought at once of the bunches of flowers at the priest's ruined house.] ' "They cry out in the wind that is their voice, they rage in the sea that is their anger."

'So I was told, but I have noticed that negroes as a rule refuse to discuss the black magic in which so many believe. Voodoo as it is called in Haiti – Obeah in some of the islands, another name in South America. They confuse matters by telling lies if pressed. The white people, sometimes credulous, pretend to dismiss the whole thing as nonsense. Cases of sudden or mysterious death are attributed to a poison known to the negroes which cannot be traced. It is further complicated by . . .'

*

I did not look up though I saw him at the window but rode on without thinking till I came to the rocks[38]. People here call them Mounes Mors (the Dead Ones). Preston shied at them, they say horses always do. Then he stumbled badly, so I dismounted and walked along with the bridle over my arm. It was getting hot and I was tired when I reached the path to Christophine's two-roomed house, the roof shingled, not thatched. She was sitting on a box under her mango tree, smoking a white clay pipe and she called out, 'It's you, Antoinette? Why you come up here so early?'

'I just wanted to see you,' I said.

She helped me loosen Preston's girth and led him to a stream near by. He drank as if he were very thirsty, then shook himself and snorted. Water flew out of his nostrils. We left him cropping grass and went back to the mango tree. She sat on her box and pushed another towards me, but I knelt close to her touching a thin silver bangle that she always wore.

'You smell the same,' I said.

'You come all this long way to tell me that?' she said. Her clothes smelled of clean cotton, starched and ironed. I had seen her so often standing knee deep in the river at Coulibri, her long skirt hitched up, washing her dresses and her white shifts, then beating them against the stones.[39] Sometimes there would be other women all bringing their washing down on the stones again and again, a gay busy noise. At last they would spread the wet clothes in the sun, wipe their foreheads, start laughing and talking. She smelled too, of their smell, so warm and comforting to me (but he does not like it). The sky was dark blue through the dark green mango leaves, and I thought, 'This is my place and this is where I belong and this is where I wish to stay.' Then I thought, 'What a beautiful tree, but it is too high up here for mangoes and it may never bear fruit,' and I thought of lying alone in my bed with the soft silk cotton mattress and fine sheets, listening. At last I said, 'Christophine, he does not love me, I think he hates me. He always sleeps in his dressing-room now and the servants know. If I get angry he is scornful and silent, sometimes he does not speak to me for hours and I cannot endure it any more, I cannot. What shall I do? He was not like that at first,' I said.

Pink and red hibiscus[40] grew in front of her door, she lit her pipe and did not answer.

'Answer me,' I said. She puffed out a cloud of smoke.

'You ask me a hard thing, I tell you a hard thing, pack up and go.'

'Go, go where? To some strange place where I shall never see him? No, I will not, then everyone, not only the servants, will laugh at me.'

'It's not you they laugh at if you go, they laugh at him.'

'I will not do that.'

'Why you ask me, if when I answer you say no? Why you come up here if when I tell you the truth, you say no?'

'But there must be something else I can do.'

She looked gloomy. 'When man don't love you, more you try, more he hate you, man like that. If you love them they treat you bad, if you don't love them they after you night and day bothering your soul case out. I hear about you and your husband,' she said.

'But I cannot go. He is my husband after all.'

She spat over her shoulder. 'All women, all colours, nothing but fools. Three children I have. One living in this world, each one a different father, but no husband, I thank my God. I keep my money. I don't give it to no worthless man.'

'When must I go, where must I go?'

'But look me trouble, a rich white girl like you and more foolish than the rest. A man don't treat you good, pick up your skirt and walk out. Do it and he come after you.'

'He will not come after me. And you must understand I am not rich now, I have no money of my own at all, everything I had belongs to him.'

'What you tell me there?' she said sharply.

'That is English law.'

'Law! The Mason boy fix it, that boy worse than Satan and he burn in Hell one of these fine nights. Listen to me now and I advise you what to do. Tell your husband you feeling sick, you want to visit your cousin in Martinique. Ask him pretty for some of your own money, the man not bad-hearted, he give it. When you get away, stay away. Ask more. He give again and well satisfy. In the end he come to find out what you do, how you get on without him, and if he see you fat and happy he want you back. Men like that. Better not stay in that old house. Go from that house, I tell you.'

'You think I must leave him?'

'You ask me so I answer.'

'Yes,' I said. 'After all I could, but why should I go to Martinique? I wish to see England, I might be able to borrow money for that. Not from him but I know how I might get it. I must travel far, if I go.'

I have been too unhappy, I thought, it cannot last, being so unhappy, it would kill you. I will be a different person when I live in England and different things will happen to me . . . England, rosy pink in the geography book map, but on the page opposite the words are closely crowded, heavy looking. Exports, coal, iron, wool. Then Imports and Character of Inhabitants. Names, Essex, Chelmsford on the Chelmer. The Yorkshire and Lincolnshire wolds.[41] Wolds? Does that mean hills? How high? Half the height of ours, or not even that? Cool green leaves in the short cool summer. Summer. There are fields of corn like sugar-cane fields, but gold colour and not so tall. After summer the trees are bare, then winter and snow. White feathers falling? Torn pieces of paper falling? They say frost makes flower patterns on the window panes. I must know more than I know already. For I know that house where I will be cold and not belonging, the bed I shall lie in has red curtains and I have slept there many times before, long ago. How long ago? In that bed I will dream the end of my dream. But my dream had nothing to do with England and I must not think like this, I must remember about chandeliers and dancing, about swans and roses and snow. And snow.

'England,' said Christophine, who was watching me. 'You think there is such a place?'

'How can you ask that? You know there is.'

'I never see the damn place, how I know?'

'You do not believe that there is a country called England?'

She blinked and answered quickly, 'I don't say I don't *believe*, I say I don't *know*, I know what I see with my eyes and I never see it. Besides I ask myself is this place like they tell us? Some say one thing, some different, I hear it cold to freeze your bones and they thief your money, clever like the devil. You have money in your pocket, you look again and bam! No money. Why you want to go to this cold thief place? If there is this place at all, I never see it, that is one thing sure.'

I stared at her, thinking, 'but how can she know the best thing for me to do, this ignorant, obstinate old negro woman, who is not certain if there is such a place as England?' She knocked out her pipe and stared back at me, her eyes had no expression at all.

'Christophine,' I said, 'I may do as you advise. But not yet.' (Now,

I thought, I must say what I came to say.) 'You knew what I wanted as soon as you saw me, and you certainly know now. Well, don't you?' I heard my voice getting high and thin.

'Hush up,' she said. 'If the man don't love you, I can't make him love you.'

'Yes you can, I know you can. That is what I wish and that is why I came here. You can make people love or hate. Or . . . or die,' I said.

She threw back her head and laughed loudly. (But she never laughs loudly and why is she laughing at all?)

'So you believe in that tim-tim[42] story about obeah, you hear when you so high? All that foolishness and folly. Too besides, that is not for *béké*.[43] Bad, bad trouble come when *béké* meddle with that.'

'You must,' I said. 'You must.'

'Hush up. Jo-jo my son coming to see me, if he catch you crying, he tell everybody.'

'I will be quiet, I will not cry. But Christophine, if he, my husband, could come to me one night. Once more. I would make him love me.'

'No *doudou*.[44] No.'

'Yes, Christophine.'

'You talk foolishness. Even if I can make him come to your bed, I cannot make him love you. Afterward he hate you.'

'No. And what do I care if he does? He hates me now. I hear him every night walking up and down the veranda. Up and down. When he passes my door he says. "Good-night, Bertha." He never calls me Antoinette now. He has found out it was my mother's name. "I hope you will sleep well, Bertha" – it cannot be worse,' I said. 'That one night he came I might sleep afterwards. I sleep so badly now. And I dream.'

'No, I don't meddle with that for you.'

Then I beat my fist on a stone, forcing myself to speak calmly.

'Going away to Martinique or England or anywhere else, that is the lie. He would never give me any money to go away and he would be furious if I asked him. There would be a scandal if I left him and he hates scandal. Even if I got away (and how?) he would force me back. So would Richard. So would everybody else. Running away from him, from this island, is the lie. What reason could I give for going and who would believe me?'

When she bent her head she looked old and I thought, 'Oh Christophine, do not grow old. You are the only friend I have, do not go away from me into being old.'

'Your husband certainly love money,' she said. 'That is no lie. Money have pretty face for everybody, but for that man money pretty like pretty self, he can't see nothing else.'

'Help me then.'

'Listen *doudou ché*.[45] Plenty people fasten bad words on you and on your mother. I know it. I know who is talking and what they say. The man not a bad man, even if he love money, but he hear so many stories he don't know what to believe. That is why he keep away. I put no trust in none of those people round you. Not here, not in Jamaica.'

'Not Aunt Cora?'

'Your aunty old woman now, she turn her face to the wall.'

'*How do you know?*' I said. For that is what happened.

When I passed her room, I heard her quarrelling with Richard and I knew it was about my marriage. 'It's disgraceful,' she said. 'It's shameful. You are handing over everything the child owns to a perfect stranger. Your father would never have allowed it. She should be protected, legally. A settlement can be arranged and it should be arranged. That was his intention.'

'You are talking about an honourable gentleman, not a rascal,' Richard said. 'I am not in a position to make conditions, as you know very well. She is damn lucky to get him, all things considered. Why should I insist on a lawyer's settlement when I trust him? I would trust him with my life,' he went on in an affected voice.

'You are trusting him with her life, not yours,' she said.

He told her for God's sake shut up you old fool and banged the door when he left. So angry that he did not notice me standing in the passage. She was sitting up in bed when I went into her room. 'Halfwit that the boy is, or pretends to be. I do not like what I have seen of this honourable gentleman. Stiff. Hard as a board and stupid as a foot, in my opinion, except where his own interests are concerned.'

She was very pale and shaking all over, so I gave her the smelling salts on the dressing-table. They were in a red glass bottle with a gilt top. She put the bottle to her nose but her hand dropped as though she were too tired to hold it steady. Then she turned away from the window, the sky, the looking-glass, the pretty things on the dressing-table. The red and gilt bottle fell to the floor. She turned her face to the wall. 'The Lord has forsaken us,' she said, and shut her eyes. She did not speak again, and after a while I thought she was asleep. She was too ill to come to my wedding and I went to say good-bye, I was excited and happy thinking now it is my honeymoon. I kissed her and she gave me a little silk bag. 'My rings. Two are valuable. Don't show it to him. Hide it away. Promise me.'

I promised, but when I opened it, one of the rings was plain gold. I thought I might sell another yesterday but who will buy what I have to sell here? . . .

Christophine was saying, 'Your aunty too old and sick, and that Mason boy worthless. Have spunks and do battle for yourself. Speak to your husband calm and cool, tell him about your mother and all what happened at Coulibri and why she get sick and what they do to her. Don't bawl at the man and don't make crazy faces. Don't cry either. Crying no good with him. Speak nice and make him understand.'

'I have tried,' I said, 'but he does not believe me. It is too late for that now' (it is always too late for truth, I thought). 'I will try again if you will do what I ask. Oh Christophine, I am so afraid,' I said, 'I do not know why, but so afraid. All the time. Help me.'

She said something I did not hear. Then she took a sharp stick and drew lines and circles on the earth under the tree, then rubbed them out with her foot.

'If you talk to him first I do what you ask me.'

'Now?'

'Yes,' she said. 'Now look at me. Look in my eyes.'

I was giddy when I stood up, and she went into the house muttering and came out with a cup of coffee.

'Good shot of white rum in that,' she said. 'Your face like dead woman and your eyes red like *soucriant*.[46] Keep yourself quiet – look, Jo-jo coming, he talk to everybody about what he hear. Nothing but leaky calabash that boy.'

When I had drunk the coffee I began to laugh. 'I have been so unhappy for nothing, nothing,' I said.

Her son was carrying a large basket on his head. I watched his strong brown legs swinging along the path so easily. He seemed surprised and inquisitive when he saw me, but he asked politely in patois, was I well, was the master in good health?

'Yes, Jo-jo, thank you, we are both well.'

Christophine helped him with the basket, then she brought out the bottle of white rum and poured out half a tumblerful. He swallowed it quickly. Then she filled the glass with water and he drank that like they do.

She said in English, 'The mistress is going, her horse at the back there. Saddle him up.'

I followed her into the house. There was a wooden table in the outer room, a bench and two broken-down chairs. Her bedroom was large and dark. She still had her bright patchwork counterpane, the palm leaf from Palm Sunday and the prayer for a happy death. But after I noticed a heap of chicken feathers in one corner, I did not look round any more.

'So already you frightened eh?' And when I saw her expression I took my purse from my pocket and threw it on the bed.

'You don't have to give me money. I do this foolishness because you beg me – not for money.'

'Is it foolishness?' I said, whispering and she laughed again, but softly.

'If *béké* say it foolishness, then it foolishness. *Béké* clever like the devil. More clever than God. Ain't so? Now listen and I will tell you what to do.'

When we came out into the sunlight, Jo-jo was holding Preston near a big stone. I stood on it and mounted.

'Good-bye, Christophine; good-bye, Jo-jo.'

'Good-bye, mistress.'

'You will come and see me very soon, Christophine?'

'Yes, I will come.'

I looked back at the end of the path. She was talking to Jo-jo and he seemed curious and amused. Nearby a cock crowed and I thought, 'That is for betrayal, but who is the traitor?' She did not want to do this. I forced her with my ugly money. And what does anyone know about traitors, or why Judas did what he did?[47]

I can remember every second of that morning, if I shut my eyes I can see the deep blue colour of the sky and the mango leaves, the pink and red hibiscus, the yellow handkerchief she wore round her head, tied in the Martinique fashion with the sharp points in front, but now I see everything still, fixed for ever like the colours in a stained-glass window. Only the clouds move. It was wrapped in a leaf, what she had given me, and I felt it cool and smooth against my skin.

*

'The mistress pay a visit,' Baptiste told me when he brought my coffee that morning.[48] 'She will come back tonight or tomorrow. She make up her mind in a hurry and she has gone.'

In the afternoon Amélie brought me a second letter.

Why you don't answer. You don't believe me? Then ask someone else – everybody in Spanish Town know. Why you think they bring you to this place? You want me to come to your house and bawl out your business before everybody? You come to me or I come –

At this point I stopped reading. The child Hilda came into the room and I asked her, 'Is Amélie here?'

'Yes, master.'

'Tell her I wish to speak to her.'

'Yes, master.'

She put her hand over her mouth as if to stifle laughter, but her eyes, which were the blackest I had ever seen, so black that it was impossible to distinguish the pupils from the iris, were alarmed and bewildered.

I sat on the veranda with my back to the sea and it was as if I had done it all my life. I could not imagine different weather or a different sky. I knew the shape of the mountains as well as I knew the shape of the two brown jugs filled with white sweet-scented flowers on the wooden table. I knew that the girl would be wearing a white dress. Brown and white she would be, her curls, her white girl's hair she called it, half covered with a red handkerchief, her feet bare. There would be the sky and the mountains, the flowers and the girl and the feeling that all this was a nightmare, the faint consoling hope that I might wake up.

She leaned lightly against the veranda post, indifferently graceful, just respectful enough, and waited.

'Was this letter given to you?' I asked.

'No, master. Hilda take it.'

'And is this man who writes a friend of yours?'

'Not my friend,' she said.

'But he knows you – or says he does.'

'Oh yes, I know Daniel.'

'Very well then. Will you tell him that his letters annoy me, and that he'd better not write again for his own sake. If he brings a letter give it back to him. Understand?'

'Yes, master. I understand.'

Still leaning against the post she smiled at me, and I felt that at any moment her smile would become loud laughter. It was to stop this that I went on, 'Why does he write to me?'

She answered innocently, 'He don't tell you that? He write you two letters and he don't say why he is writing? If you don't know then I don't know.'

'But you know him?' I said. 'Is his name Cosway?'

'Some people say yes, some people say no. That's what he calls himself.'

She added thoughtfully that Daniel was a very superior man, always reading the Bible and that he lived like white people. I tried to find out what she meant by this, and she explained that he had a house like white people, with one room only for sitting. That he had two pictures on the wall of his father and his mother.

'White people?'

'Oh no, coloured.'

'But he told me in his first letter that his father was a white man.'

She shrugged her shoulders. 'All that too long ago for me.' It was easy to see her contempt for long ago. 'I tell him what you say, master.' Then she added, 'Why you don't go and see him? It is much better. Daniel is a bad man and he will come here and make trouble for you. It's better he don't come. They say one time he was a preacher in Barbados, he talk like a preacher, and he have a brother in

Jamaica in Spanish Town, Mr Alexander. Very wealthy man. He own
three rum shops and two dry goods stores.' She flicked a look at me
as sharp as a knife. 'I hear one time that Miss Antoinette and his son
Mr Sandi get married, but that all foolishness. Miss Antoinette a white
girl with a lot of money, she won't marry with a coloured man even
though he don't look like a coloured man. You ask Miss Antoinette,
she tell you.'

Like Hilda she put her hand over her mouth as though she could
not stop herself from laughing and walked away.

Then turned and said in a very low voice, 'I am sorry for you.'

'What did you say?'

'I don't say nothing, master.'

A large table covered with a red fringed cloth made the small room
seem hotter; the only window was shut.

'I put your chair near the door,' Daniel said, 'a breeze come in
from underneath.' But there was no breeze, not a breath of air, this
place was lower down the mountain almost at sea-level.

'When I hear you coming I take a good shot of rum, and then I take
a glass of water to cool me down, but it don't cool me down, it run
out of my eyes in tears and lamentations. Why don't you give me an
answer when I write to you the first time?' He went on talking, his
eyes fixed on a framed text hanging on the dirty white wall, 'Vengeance
is Mine'.

'You take too long, Lord,' he told it. 'I hurry you up a bit.' Then
he wiped his thin yellow face and blew his nose on a corner of the
tablecloth.

'They call me Daniel,' he said, still not looking at me, 'but my
name is Esau.[49] All I get is curses and get-outs from that damn devil
my father. My father old Cosway, with his white marble tablet in the
English church at Spanish Town for all to see. It have a crest on it and
a motto in Latin and words in big black letters.[50] I never know such
lies. I hope that stone tie round his neck and drag him down to Hell
in the end. "Pious," they write up. "Beloved by all". Not a word about
the people he buy and sell like cattle. "Merciful to the weak", they
write up. Mercy! The man have a heart like stone. Sometimes when
he get sick of a woman which is quickly, he free her like he free my

mother, even he give her a hut and a bit of land for herself (a garden some call that), but it is no mercy, it's for wicked pride he do it. I never put my eyes on a man haughty and proud like that – he walk like he own the earth. "I don't give a damn," he says. Let him wait . . . I can still see that tablet before my eyes because I go to look at it often. I know by heart all the lies they tell – no one to stand up and say, Why you write lies in the church? . . . I tell you this so you can know what sort of people you mix up with. The heart know its own bitterness but to keep it lock up all the time, that is hard. I remember it like yesterday the morning he put a curse on me. Sixteen years old I was and anxious. I start very early. I walk all the way to Coulibri – five six hours it take. He don't refuse to see me; he receive me very cool and calm and first thing he tell me is I'm always pestering him for money. This because sometimes I ask help to buy a pair of shoes and such. Not to go barefoot like a nigger. Which I am not. He look at me like I was dirt and I get angry too. "I have my rights after all," I tell him and you know what he do? He laugh in my face. When he finished laughing he call me what's-your-name. "I can't remember all their names – it's too much to expect of me," he says, talking to himself. Very old he look in the bright sunshine that morning. "It's you yourself call me Daniel," I tell him. "I'm no slave like my mother was."

'"Your mother was a sly-boots if ever there was one," he says, "and I'm not a fool. However the woman's dead and that's enough. But if there's one drop of my blood in your spindly carcass I'll eat my hat." By this time my own blood at boiling point, I tell you, so I bawl back at him, "Eat it then. Eat it. You haven't much time. Not much time either to kiss and love your new wife. She too young for you." "Great God!" he said and his face go red and then a kind of grey colour. He try to get up but he falls back in his chair. He have a big silver inkstand on his desk, he throw it at my head and he curse me, but I duck and the inkstand hit the door. I have to laugh but I go off quick. He send me some money – not a word, only the money. It's the last time I see him.'

Daniel breathed deeply and wiped his face again and offered me some rum. When I thanked him and shook my head he poured himself half a glassful and swallowed it.

'All that long time ago,' he said.

'Why did you wish to see me, Daniel?'

The last drink seemed to have sobered him. He looked at me directly and spoke more naturally.

'I insist because I have this to say. When you ask if what I tell you is true, you will ask though you don't like me, I see that; but you know well my letter was no lie. Take care who you talk to. Many people like to say things behind your back, to your face they get frightened, or they don't want to mix up. The magistrate now, he know a lot, but his wife very friendly with the Mason family and she stop him if she can. Then there is my half brother Alexander, coloured like me but not unlucky like me, he will want to tell you all sorts of lies. He was the old man's favourite and he prosper right from the start. Yes, Alexander is a rich man now but he keep quiet about it. Because he prosper he is two-faced, he won't speak against white people. There is that woman up at your house, Christophine. She is the worst. She have to leave Jamaica because she go to jail: you know that?'

'Why was she sent to jail? What did she do?'

His eyes slid away from mine. 'I tell you I leave Spanish Town, I don't know all that happen. It's something very bad. She is obeah woman and they catch her. I don't believe in all that devil business but many believe. Christophine is a bad woman and she will lie to you worse than your wife. Your own wife she talks sweet talk and she lies.'

The black and gilt clock on a shelf struck four.

I must go. I must get away from his yellow sweating face and his hateful little room. I sat still, numb, staring at him.

'You like my clock?' said Daniel. 'I work hard to buy it. But it's to please myself. I don't have to please no woman. Buy me this and buy me that – demons incarnate in my opinion. Alexander now, he can't keep away from them, and in the end he marry a very fair-coloured girl, very respectable family. His son Sandi is like a white man, but more handsome than any white man, and received by many white people they say. Your wife know Sandi since long time. Ask her and she tell you. But not everything I think.' He laughed. 'Oh no, not everything. I see them when they think nobody see them. I see her when she . . . You going eh?' He darted to the doorway.

'No you don't go before I tell you the last thing. You want me to shut my mouth about what I know. She start with Sandi. They fool you well about that girl. She look you straight in the eye and talk sweet talk – and it's lies she tell you. Lies. Her mother was so. They say she worse than her mother, and she hardly more than a child. Must be you deaf you don't hear people laughing when you marry her. Don't waste your anger on me, sir. It's not I fool you, it's I wish to open your eyes . . . A tall fine English gentleman like you, you don't want to touch a little yellow rat like me eh? Besides I understand well. You believe me, but you want to do everything quiet like the English can. All right. But if I keep my mouth shut it seems to me you owe me something. What is five hundred pounds to you? To me it's my life.'

Now disgust was rising in me like sickness. Disgust and rage.

'All right,' he yelled, and moved away from the door. 'Go then . . . get out. Now it's me to say it. Get out. Get out. And if I don't have the money I want you will see what I can do.'

'Give my love to your wife – my sister,' he called after me venomously. 'You are not the first to kiss her pretty face. Pretty face, soft skin, pretty colour – not yellow like me. But my sister just the same . . .'

At the end of the path out of sight and sound of the house I stopped. The world was given up to heat and to flies, the light was dazzling after his little dark room. A black and white goat tethered near by was staring at me and for what seemed minutes I stared back into its slanting yellow-green eyes. Then I walked to the tree where I'd left my horse and rode away as quickly as I could.

The telescope was pushed to one side of the table making room for a decanter half full of rum and two glasses on a tarnished silver tray. I listened to the ceaseless night noises outside, and watched the procession of small moths and beetles fly into the candle flames, then poured out a drink of rum and swallowed. At once the night noises drew away, became distant, bearable, even pleasant.

'Will you listen to me for God's sake,' Antoinette said. She had said this before and I had not answered, now I told her, 'Of course. I'd be the brute you doubtless think me if I did not do that.'

'Why do you hate me?' she said.

'I do not hate you, I am most distressed about you, I am distraught,' I said. But this was untrue, I was not distraught, I was calm, it was the first time I had felt calm or self-possessed for many a long day.

She was wearing the white dress I had admired, but it had slipped untidily over one shoulder and seemed too large for her. I watched her holding her left wrist with her right hand, an annoying habit.

'Then why do you never come near me?' she said. 'Or kiss me, or talk to me. Why do you think I can bear it, what reason have you for treating me like that? Have you any reason?'

'Yes,' I said, 'I have a reason,' and added very softly, 'My God.'

'You are always calling on God,' she said. 'Do you believe in God?'

'Of course, of course I believe in the power and wisdom of my creator.'

She raised her eyebrows and the corners of her mouth turned down in a questioning mocking way. For a moment she looked very much like Amélie. Perhaps they are related,[51] I thought. It's possible, it's even probable in this damned place.

'And you,' I said. 'Do you believe in God?'

'It doesn't matter,' she answered calmly, 'what I believe or you believe, because we can do nothing about it, we are like these.' She flicked a dead moth off the table. 'But I asked you a question, you remember. Will you answer that?'

I drank again and my brain was cold and clear.

'Very well, but question for question. Is your mother alive?'

'No, she is dead, she died.'

'When?'

'Not long ago.'

'Then why did you tell me that she died when you were a child?'

'Because they told me to say so and because it is true. She did die when I was a child. There are always two deaths, the real one and the one people know about.'

'Two at least,' I said, 'for the fortunate.' We were silent for a moment, then I went on, 'I had a letter from a man who calls himself Daniel Cosway.'

'He has no right to that name,' she said quickly. 'His real name, if he has one, is Daniel Boyd. He hates all white people, but he hates me the most. He tells lies about us and he is sure that you will believe him and not listen to the other side.'

'Is there another side?' I said.

'There is always the other side, always.'

'After his second letter, which was threatening, I thought it best to go and see him.'

'You saw him,' she said. 'I know what he told you. That my mother was mad and an infamous woman and that my little brother who died was born a cretin, an idiot, and that I am a mad girl too. That is what he told you, isn't it?'

'Yes, that was his story, and is any of it true?' I said, cold and calm.

One of the candles flared up and I saw the hollows under her eyes, her drooping mouth, her thin, strained face.

'We won't talk about it now,' I said. 'Rest tonight.'

'But we must talk about it.' Her voice was high and shrill.

'Only if you promise to be reasonable.'

But this is not the place or the time, I thought, not in this long dark veranda with the candles burning low and the watching, listening night outside. 'Not tonight,' I said again. 'Some other time.'

'I might never be able to tell you in any other place or at any other time. No other time, now. You frightened?' she said, imitating a Negro's voice, singing and insolent.

Then I saw her shiver and remembered that she had been wearing a yellow silk shawl. I got up (my brain so clear and cold, my body so weighted and heavy). The shawl was on a chair in the next room, there were candles on the sideboard and I brought them on to the veranda, lit two, and put the shawl around her shoulders. 'But why not tell me tomorrow, in the daylight?'

'You have no right,' she said fiercely. 'You have no right to ask questions about my mother and then refuse to listen to my answer.'

'Of course I will listen, of course we can talk now, if that's what you wish.' But the feeling of something unknown and hostile was very strong. 'I feel very much a stranger here,' I said. 'I feel that this place is my enemy and on your side.'

'You are quite mistaken,' she said. 'It is not for you and not for me. It has nothing to do with either of us. That is why you are afraid of it, because it is something else. I found that out long ago when I was a child. I loved it because I had nothing else to love, but it is as indifferent as this God you call on so often.'

'We can talk here or anywhere else,' I said, 'just as you wish.'

The decanter of rum was nearly empty so I went back into the dining-room, and brought out another bottle of rum. She had eaten nothing and refused wine, now she poured herself a drink, touched it with her lips then put it down again.

'You want to know about my mother, I will tell you about her, the truth, not lies.' Then she was silent for so long that I said gently, 'I know that after your father died, she was very lonely and unhappy.'

'And very poor,' she said. 'Don't forget that. For five years. Isn't it quick to say. And isn't it long to live. And lonely. She was so lonely that she grew away from other people. That happens. It happened to me too but it was easier for me because I hardly remembered anything else. For her it was strange and frightening. And then she was so lovely. I used to think that every time she looked in the glass she must have hoped and pretended. I pretended too. Different things of course. You can pretend for a long time, but one day it all falls away and you are alone. We were alone in the most beautiful place in the world, it is not possible that there can be anywhere else so beautiful as Coulibri. The sea was not far off but we never heard it, we always heard the river. No sea. It was an old-time house and once there was an avenue of royal palms but a lot of them had fallen and others had been cut down and the ones that were left looked lost. Lost trees. Then they poisoned her horse and she could not ride about any more. She worked in the garden even when the sun was very hot and they'd say "You go in now, mistress." '

'And who were they?'

'Christophine was with us, and Godfrey the old gardener stayed, and a boy, I forget his name. Oh yes,' she laughed. 'His name was Disastrous because his godmother thought it such a pretty word. The parson said, "I cannot christen this child Disastrous, he must have another name," so his name was Disastrous Thomas, we called him Sass. It was Christophine who bought our food from the village and persuaded some girls to help her sweep and wash clothes. We would have died, my mother always said, if she had not stayed with us. Many died in those days, both white and black, especially the older people, but no one speaks of those days now. They are forgotten, except the lies. Lies are never forgotten, they go on and they grow.'

'And you,' I said. 'What about you?'

'I was never sad in the morning,' she said, 'and every day was a fresh day for me. I remember the taste of milk and bread and the sound of the grandfather clock ticking slowly and the first time I had my hair tied with string because there was no ribbon left and no money to buy any. All the flowers in the world were in our garden and sometimes when I was thirsty I licked raindrops from the Jasmine leaves after a shower. If I could make you see it, because they destroyed it and it is only here now.' She struck her forehead. 'One of the best things was a curved flight of shallow steps that went down from the *glacis* to the mounting stone, the handrail was ornamented iron.'

'Wrought iron,' I said.

'Yes, wrought iron, and at the end of the last step it was curved like a question mark and when I put my hand on it, the iron was warm and I was comforted.'

'But you said you were always happy.'

'No, I said I was always happy in the morning, not always in the afternoon and never after sunset, for after sunset the house was haunted, some places are. Then there was that day when she saw I was growing up like a white nigger and she was ashamed of me, it was after that day that everything changed. Yes, it was my fault, it was my fault that she started to plan and work in a frenzy, in a fever to change our lives. Then people came to see us again and though I still hated them and was afraid of their cool, teasing eyes, I learned to hide it.'

'No,' I said.

'Why no?'

'You have never learned to hide it,' I said.

'I learned to try,' said Antoinette. Not very well, I thought.

'And there was that night when they destroyed it.' She lay back in the chair, very pale. I poured some rum out and offered it to her, but she pushed the glass away so roughly that it spilled over her dress. 'There is nothing left now. They trampled on it. It was a sacred place. It was sacred to the sun!' I began to wonder how much of all this was true, how much imagined, distorted. Certainly many of the old estate houses were burned. You saw ruins all over the place.

As if she'd guessed my thoughts she went on calmly, 'But I was telling you about my mother. Afterwards I had fever. I was at Aunt Cora's house in Spanish Town. I heard screams and then someone laughing very loud. Next morning Aunt Cora told me that my mother was ill and had gone to the country. This did not seem strange to me for she was part of Coulibri, and if Coulibri had been destroyed and gone out of my life, it seemed natural that she should go too. I was ill for a long time. My head was bandaged because someone had thrown a stone at me. Aunt Cora told me that it was healing up and that it wouldn't spoil me on my wedding day. But I think it did spoil me for my wedding day and all the other days and nights.'

I said, 'Antoinette, your nights are not spoiled, or your days, put the sad things away. Don't think about them and nothing will be spoiled, I promise you.'

But my heart was heavy as lead.

'Pierre died,' she went on as if she had not heard me, 'and my mother hated Mr Mason. She would not let him go near her or touch her. She said she would kill him, she tried to, I think. So he bought her a house and hired a coloured man and woman to look after her. For a while he was sad but he often left Jamaica and spent a lot of time in Trinidad. He almost forgot her.'

'And you forgot her too,' I could not help saying.

'I am not a forgetting person,' said Antoinette. 'But she – she didn't want me. She pushed me away and cried when I went to see her. They told me I made her worse. People talked about her, they would not leave her alone, they would be talking about her and stop if they saw me. One day I made up my mind to go to her, by myself. Before I reached her house I heard her crying. I thought I will kill anyone who is hurting my mother. I dismounted and ran quickly on to the veranda where I could look into the room. I remember the dress she was wearing – an evening dress cut very low, and she was barefooted. There was a fat black man with a glass of rum in his hand. He said, "Drink it and you will forget." She drank it without stopping. He poured her some more and she took the glass and laughed and threw it over her shoulder. It smashed to pieces. "Clean it up," the man said to the woman, "or she'll walk in it."

'"If she walk in it a damn good thing," the woman said. "Perhaps she keep quiet then." However she brought a pan and brush and swept up the broken glass. All this I saw. My mother did not look at them.

She walked up and down and said, "But this is a very pleasant surprise, Mr Luttrell. Godfrey, take Mr Luttrell's horse." Then she seemed to grow tired and sat down in the rocking-chair. I saw the man lift her up out of the chair and kiss her. I saw his mouth fasten on hers and she went all soft and limp in his arms and he laughed. The woman laughed too, but she was angry. When I saw that I ran away. Christophine was waiting for me when I came back crying. "What you want to go up there for?" she said, and I said, "You shut up devil, damned black devil from Hell." Christophine said, "Aie Aie Aie! Look me trouble, look me cross!"'

After a long time I heard her say as if she were talking to herself, 'I have said all I want to say. I have tried to make you understand. But nothing has changed.' She laughed.

'Don't laugh like that, Bertha.'

'My name is not Bertha; why do you call me Bertha?'

'Because it is a name I'm particularly fond of. I think of you as Bertha.'

'It doesn't matter,' she said.

I said, 'When you went off this morning where did you go?'

'I went to see Christophine,' she said. 'I will tell you anything you wish to know, but in a few words because words are no use, I know that now.'

'Why did you go to see her?'

'I went to ask her to do something for me.'

'And did she do it?'

'Yes.' Another long pause.

'You wanted to ask her advice, was that it?'

She did not answer.

'What did she say?'

'She said that I ought to go away – to leave you.'

'Oh did she?' I said, surprised.

'Yes, that was her advice.'

'I want to do the best for both of us,' I said. 'So much of what you tell me is strange, different from what I was led to expect. Don't you feel that perhaps Christophine is right? That if you went away from this place or I went away – exactly as you wish of course – for a time, it might be the wisest thing we could do?' Then I said sharply, 'Bertha, are you asleep, are you ill, why don't you answer me?' I got up, went over to her chair and took her cold hands in mine. 'We've been sitting here long enough, it is very late.'

'You go,' she said. 'I wish to stay here in the dark . . . where I belong,' she added.

'Oh nonsense,' I said. I put my arms round her to help her up, I kissed her, but she drew away.

'Your mouth is colder than my hands,' she said. I tried to laugh. In the bedroom, I closed the shutters. 'Sleep now, we will talk things over tomorrow.'

'Yes,' she said, 'of course, but will you come in and say goodnight to me?'

'Certainly I will, my dear Bertha.'[52]

'Not Bertha tonight,' she said.

'Of course, on this of all nights, you must be Bertha.'

'As you wish,' she said.

As I stepped into her room I noticed the white powder strewn on the floor. That was the first thing I asked her – about the powder. I asked what it was. She said it was to keep cockroaches away.

'Haven't you noticed that there are no cockroaches in this house and no centipedes? If you knew how horrible these things can be.' She had lit all the candles and the room was full of shadows. There were six on the dressing-table and three on the table near her bed. The light changed her. I had never seen her look so gay or so beautiful. She poured wine into two glasses and handed me one but I swear it was before I drank that I longed to bury my face in her hair as I used to do. I said, 'We are letting ghosts trouble us. Why shouldn't we be happy?' She said, 'Christophine knows about ghosts too, but that is not what she calls them.' She need not have done what she did to me. I will always swear that, she need not have done it. When she handed me the glass she was smiling. I remember saying in a voice that was not like my own that it was too light. I remember putting out the candles on the table near the bed and that is all I remember. All I will remember of the night.

I woke in the dark after dreaming that I was buried alive, and when I was awake the feeling of suffocation persisted. Something was lying across my mouth; hair with a sweet heavy smell. I threw it off but still I could not breathe. I shut my eyes and lay without moving for a few seconds. When I opened them I saw the candles burnt down on that abominable dressing-table, then I knew where I was. The door on to the veranda was open and the breeze was so cold that I knew it must be very early in the morning, before dawn. I was cold too, deathly cold and sick and in pain. I got out of bed without looking at her, staggered into my dressing-room and saw myself in the glass. I turned away at once. I could not vomit. I only retched painfully.

I thought, I have been poisoned. But it was a dull thought, like a child spelling out the letters of a word which he cannot read, and which if he could would have no meaning or context. I was too giddy to stand and fell backwards on to the bed, looking at the blanket which was of a peculiar shade of yellow. After looking at it for some time I was able to go over to the window and vomit. It seemed like hours before this stopped. I would lean up against the wall and wipe my face, then the retching and sickness would start again. When it was over I lay on the bed too weak to move.

I have never made a greater effort in my life than I made then. I longed to lie there and sleep but forced myself up. I was weak and giddy but no longer sick or in pain. I put on my dressing-gown and splashed water on my face, then I opened the door into her room.

The cold light was on her and I looked at the sad droop of her lips, the frown between her thick eyebrows,[53] deep as if it had been cut with a knife. As I looked she moved and flung her arm out. I thought coldly, yes, very beautiful, the thin wrist, the sweet swell of the forearm, the rounded elbow, the curve of her shoulder into her upper arm. All present, all correct. As I watched, hating, her face grew smooth and very young again, she even seemed to smile. A trick of the light perhaps. What else?

She may wake at any moment, I told myself. I must be quick. Her torn shift was on the floor, I drew the sheet over her gently as if I covered a dead girl. One of the glasses was empty, she had drained hers. There was some wine left in the other which was on the dressing-table. I dipped my finger into it and tasted it. It was bitter. I didn't look at her again, but holding the glass went on to the veranda. Hilda was there with a broom in her hand. I put my finger to my lips and she looked at me with huge eyes, then imitated me, putting her own finger to her lips.

As soon as I had dressed and got out of the house I began to run.

I do not remember that day clearly, where I ran or how I fell or wept or lay exhausted. But I found myself at last near the ruined house and the wild orange tree. Here with my head in my arms I must have slept and when I woke it was getting late and the wind was chilly. I got up and found my way back to the path which led to the house. I knew how to avoid every creeper, and I never stumbled once. I went to my dressing-room and if I passed anyone I did not see them and if they spoke I did not hear them.

There was a tray on the table with a jug of water, a glass and some brown fish cakes. I drank almost all the water, for I was very thirsty, but I did not touch the food. I sat on the bed waiting, for I knew that Amélie would come, and I knew what she would say: 'I am sorry for you.'

She came soundlessly on bare feet. 'I get you something to eat,' she said. She brought cold chicken, bread, fruit and a bottle of wine, and I drank a glass without speaking, then another. She cut some of the food up and sat beside me and fed me as if I were a child. Her arm behind my head was warm but the outside when I touched it was cool, almost cold. I looked into her lovely meaningless face, sat up and pushed the plate away. Then she said, 'I am sorry for you.'

'You've told me so before, Amélie. Is that the only song you know?'

There was a spark of gaiety in her yes, but when I laughed she put her hand over my mouth apprehensively. I pulled her down beside me and we were both laughing. That is what I remember most about that encounter. She was so gay, so natural and something of this gaiety she must have given to me, for I had not one moment of remorse. Nor was I anxious to know what was happening behind the thin partition which divided us from my wife's bedroom.

In the morning, of course, I felt differently.

Another complication. Impossible. And her skin was darker, her lips thicker than I had thought.

She was sleeping very soundly and quietly but there was awareness in her eyes when she opened them, and after a moment suppressed laughter. I felt satisfied and peaceful, but not gay as she did, no, by God, not gay. I had no wish to touch her and she knew it, for she got up at once and began to dress.

'A very graceful dress,' I said and she showed me the many ways it could be worn, trailing on the floor, lifted to show a lace petticoat, or hitched up far above the knee.

I told her that I was leaving the island soon but that before I left I wanted to give her a present. It was a large present but she took it with no thanks and no expression on her face. When I asked her what she meant to do she said, 'It's long time I know what I want to do and I know I don't get it here.'

'You are beautiful enough to get anything you want,' I said.

'Yes,' she agreed simply. 'But not here.'

She wanted, it seemed, to join her sister who was a dressmaker in Demerara, but she would not stay in Demerara,[54] she said. She wanted to go to Rio.[55] There were rich men in Rio.

'And when will you start all this?' I said, amused.

'I start now.' She would catch one of the fishing boats at Massacre and get into town.

I laughed and teased her. She was running away from the old woman Christophine, I said.

She was unsmiling when she answered, 'I have malice to no one but I don't stay here.'

I asked her how she would get to Massacre. 'I don't want no horse or mule,' she said. 'My legs strong enough to carry me.'

As she was going I could not resist saying, half longing, half triumphant, 'Well, Amélie, are you still sorry for me?'

'Yes,' she said, 'I am sorry for you. But I find it in my heart to be sorry for her too.'

She shut the door gently. I lay and listened for the sound I knew I should hear, the horse's hoofs as my wife left the house.

I turned over and slept till Baptiste woke me with coffee. His face was gloomy.

'The cook is leaving,' he announced.

'Why?'

He shrugged his shoulders and spread his hands open.

I got up, looked out of the window and saw her stride out of the kitchen, a strapping woman. She couldn't speak English, or said she couldn't. I forgot this when I said, 'I must talk to her. What is the huge bundle on her head?'

'Her mattress,' said Baptiste. 'She will come back for the rest. No good to talk to her. She won't stay in this house.'

I laughed.

'Are you leaving too?'

'No,' said Baptiste. 'I am overseer here.'

I noticed that he did not call me 'sir' or 'master'.

'And the little girl, Hilda?'

'Hilda will do as I tell her. Hilda will stay.'

'Capital,' I said. 'Then why are you looking so anxious? Your mistress will be back soon.'

He shrugged again and muttered, but whether he was talking about my morals or the extra work he would have to do I couldn't tell, for he muttered in patois.

I told him to sling one of the veranda hammocks under the cedar trees and there I spent the rest of that day.

Baptiste provided meals, but he seldom smiled and never spoke except to answer a question. My wife did not return. Yet I was not lonely or unhappy. Sun, sleep and the cool water of the river were enough. I wrote a cautious letter to Mr Fraser on the third day.

I told him that I was considering a book about obeah and had remembered his story of the case he had come across. Had he any idea of the whereabouts of the woman now? Was she still in Jamaica?

This letter was sent down by the twice weekly messenger and he must have answered at once for I had his reply in a few days:[56]

I have often thought of your wife and yourself. And was on the point of writing to you. Indeed I have not forgotten the case. The woman in question was called Josephine or Christophine Dubois, some such name and she had been one of the Cosway servants. After she came out of jail she disappeared, but it was common knowledge that old Mr Mason befriended her. I heard that she owned or was given a small house and a piece of land near Granbois. She is intelligent in her way and can express herself well, but I did not like the look of her at all, and consider her a most dangerous person. My wife insisted that she had gone back to Martinique her native island, and was very upset that I had mentioned the matter even in such a roundabout fashion. I happen to know now that she has not returned to Martinique, so I have written very discreetly to Hill, the white inspector of police in your town. If she lives near you and gets up to any of her nonsense let him know at once. He'll send a couple of policemen up to your place and she won't get off lightly this time.[57] I'll make sure of that . . .

So much for you, Josephine or Christophine, I thought. So much for you, Pheena.

It was that half-hour after the sunset, the blue half-hour I called it to myself. The wind drops, the light is very beautiful, the mountains sharp, every leaf on every tree is clear and distinct. I was sitting in the hammock, watching, when Antoinette rode up. She passed me without looking at me, dismounted and went into the house. I heard her bedroom door slam and her handbell ring violently. Baptiste came running along the veranda. I got out of the hammock and went to the sitting-room. He had opened the chest and taken out a bottle of rum. Some of this he poured into a decanter which he put on a tray with a glass.

'Who is that for?' I said. He didn't answer.

'No road?' I said and laughed.

'I don't want to know nothing about all this,' he said.

'Baptiste!' Antoinette called in a high voice.

'Yes, mistress.' He looked straight at me and carried the tray out.

As for the old woman, I saw her shadow before I saw her. She too passed me without turning her head. Nor did she go into Antoinette's room or look towards it. She walked along the veranda, down the steps the other side, and went into the kitchen. In that short time the dark had come and Hilda came in to light the candles. When I spoke to her she gave me an alarmed look and ran away. I opened the chest and looked at the rows of bottles inside. Here was the rum that kills you in a hundred years, the brandy, the red and white wine smuggled, I suppose, from St Pierre, Martinique[58] — the Paris of the West Indies. It was rum I chose to drink. Yes, it was mild in the mouth, I waited a second for the explosion of heat and light in my chest, the strength and warmth running through my body. Then I tried the door into Antoinette's room. It yielded very slightly. She must have pushed some piece of furniture against it, that round table probably. I pushed again and it opened enough for me to see her. She was lying on the bed on her back. Her eyes were closed and she breathed heavily. She had pulled the sheet up to her chin. On a chair beside the bed there was the empty decanter, a glass with some rum left in it and a small brass handbell.

I shut the door and sat down with my elbows on the table for I thought I knew what would happen and what I must do. I found the room oppressively hot, so I blew out most of the candles and waited in the half darkness. Then I went on to the veranda to watch the door of the kitchen where a light was showing.

Soon the little girl came out followed by Baptiste. At the same time the handbell in the bedroom rang. They both went into the sitting-room and I followed. Hilda lit all the candles with a frightened roll of the eyes in my direction. The handbell went on ringing.

'Mix me a good strong one, Baptiste. Just what I feel like.'

He took a step away from me and said, 'Miss Antoinette –'

'Baptiste, where are you?' Antoinette called. 'Why don't you come?'

'I come as quick as I can,' Baptiste said. But as he reached for the bottle I took it away from him.

Hilda ran out of the room. Baptiste and I stared at each other. I thought that his large protuberant eyes and his expression of utter bewilderment were comical.

Antoinette shrieked from the bedroom, 'Baptiste! Christophine! Pheena, Pheena!'

'*Que komesse!*'[59] Baptiste said. 'I get Christophine.'

He ran out almost as fast as the little girl had done.

The door of Antoinette's room opened. When I saw her I was too shocked to speak. Her hair hung uncombed and dull into her eyes which were inflamed and staring, her face was very flushed and looked swollen. Her feet were bare. However when she spoke her voice was low, almost inaudible.

'I rang the bell because I was thirsty. Didn't anybody hear?'

Before I could stop her she darted to the table and seized the bottle of rum.

'Don't drink any more,' I said.

'And what right have you to tell me what I'm to do? Christophine!' she called again, but her voice broke.

'Christophine is an evil old woman and you know it as well as I do,' I said. 'She won't stay here very much longer.'

'She won't stay here very much longer,' she mimicked me, 'and nor will you, nor will you. I thought you liked the black people so much,' she said, still in that mincing voice, 'but that's just a lie like everything else. You like the light brown girls better, don't you? You abused the planters and made up stories about them, but you do the same thing. You send the girl away quicker, and with no money or less money, and that's all the difference.'

'Slavery was not a matter of liking or disliking,' I said, trying to speak calmly. 'It was a question of justice.'

'Justice,' she said. 'I've heard that word. It's a cold word. I tried it out,' she said, still speaking in a low voice. 'I wrote it down. I wrote it down several times and always it looked like a damn cold lie to me. There is no justice.' She drank some more rum and went on, 'My mother whom you all talk about, what justice did she have? My mother sitting in the rocking-chair speaking about dead horses and dead grooms and a black devil kissing her sad mouth. Like you kissed mine,' she said.

The room was now unbearably hot. 'I'll open the window and let a little air in,' I said.

'It will let the night in too,' she said, 'and the moon and the scent of those flowers you dislike so much.'

When I turned from the window she was drinking again.

'Bertha,' I said.

'Bertha is not my name. You are trying to make me into someone else, calling me by another name. I know, that's obeah too.'

Tears streamed from her eyes.

'If my father, my real father, was alive you wouldn't come back here in a hurry after he'd finished with you. If he was alive. Do you know what you've done to me? It's not the girl, not the girl. But I loved this place and you have made it into a place I hate. I used to think that if everything else went out of my life I would still have this, and now you have spoilt it. It's just somewhere else where I have been unhappy, and all the other things are nothing to what has happened here. I hate it now like I hate you and before I die I will show you how much I hate you.'

Then to my astonishment she stopped crying and said, 'Is she so much prettier than I am? Don't you love me at all?'

'No, I do not,' I said (at the same time remembering Amélie saying, 'Do you like my hair? Isn't it prettier than hers?'). 'Not at this moment,' I said.

She laughed at that. A crazy laugh.

'You see. That's how you are. A stone. But it serves me right because didn't Aunt Cora say to me don't marry him. Not if he were stuffed with diamonds. And a lot of other things she told me. Are you talking about England, I said, and what about Grandpappy passing his glass over the water decanter[60] and the tears running down his face for all the friends dead and gone, whom he would never see again. That was nothing to do with England that I ever heard, she said. On the contrary:

> A Benky foot and a Benky leg
> For Charlie over the water.
> Charlie, Charlie,'[61]

she sang in a hoarse voice. And lifted the bottle to drink again.

I said, and my voice was not very calm, 'No.'

I managed to hold her wrist with one hand and the rum with the other, but when I felt her teeth in my arm I dropped the bottle. The smell filled the room. But I was angry now and she saw it. She smashed another bottle against the wall and stood with the broken glass in her hand and murder in her eyes.

'Just you touch me once. You'll soon see if I'm a dam' coward like you are.'

Then she cursed me comprehensively, my eyes, my mouth, every member of my body, and it was like a dream in the large unfurnished room with the candles flickering and this red-eyed wild-haired stranger who was my wife shouting obscenities at me. It was at this nightmare moment that I heard Christophine's calm voice.

'You hush up and keep yourself quiet. And don't cry. Crying's no good with him. I told you before. Crying's no good.'

Antoinette collapsed on the sofa and went on sobbing. Christophine looked at me and her small eyes were very sad. 'Why you do that eh? Why you don't take that worthless good-for-nothing girl somewhere else? But she love money like you love money — must be why you come together. Like goes to like.'

I couldn't bear any more and again I went out of the room and sat on the veranda.

My arm was bleeding and painful and I wrapped my handkerchief round it, but it seemed to me that everything round me was hostile. The telescope drew away and said don't touch me. The trees were threatening and the shadows of the trees moving slowly over the floor menaced me. That green menace. I had felt it ever since I saw this place. There was nothing I knew, nothing to comfort me.

I listened. Christophine was talking softly. My wife was crying. Then a door shut. They had gone into the bedroom. Someone was singing 'Ma belle ka di',[62] or was it the song about one day and a thousand years? But whatever they were singing or saying was dangerous. I must protect myself. I went softly along the dark veranda. I could see Antoinette stretched on the bed quite still. Like a doll. Even when she threatened me with the bottle she had a marionette quality. 'Ti moun,'[63] I heard and 'Doudou ché,'[64] and the end of a head handkerchief made a finger on the wall. 'Do do l'enfant do.'[65] Listening, I began to feel sleepy and cold.

I stumbled back into the big candlelit room which still smelt strongly of rum. In spite of this I opened the chest and got out another bottle. That was what I was thinking when Christophine came in. I was thinking of a last strong drink in my room, fastening both doors, and sleeping.

'I hope you satisfy, I hope you well satisfy,' she said, 'and no good to start your lies with me. I know what you do with that girl as well as you know. Better. Don't think I frightened of you either.'

'So she ran off to tell you I'd ill-treated her, did she? I ought to have guessed that.'

'She don't tell me a thing,' said Christophine. 'Not one single thing. Always the same. Nobody is to have any pride but you. She have more pride than you and she say nothing. I see her standing at my door with that look on her face and I know something bad happen to her. I know I must act quick and I act.'

'You seem to have acted, certainly. And what did you do before you brought her back in her present condition?'

'What did I do! Look! Don't you provoke me more than I provoke already. Better not I tell you. You want to know what I do? I say *doudou*, if you have trouble you are right to come to me. And I kiss her. It's when I kiss her she cry – not before. It's long time she hold it back, I think. So I let her cry. That is the first thing. Let them cry – it eases the heart. When she can't cry no more I give her a cup of milk – it's lucky I have some. She won't eat, she won't talk. So I say, "Lie down on the bed *doudou* and try to sleep, for me I can sleep on the floor, don't matter for me." She isn't going to sleep natural that's certain, but I can make her sleep. That's what I do. As for what you do – you pay for it one day.

'When they get like that,' she said, 'first they must cry, then they must sleep. Don't talk to me about doctor, I know more than any doctor. I undress Antoinette so she can sleep cool and easy; it's then I see you very rough with her eh?'

At this point she laughed – a hearty merry laugh. 'All that is a little thing – it's nothing. If you see what I see in this place with the machete bright and shining in the corner, you don't have such a long face for such a little thing. You make her love you more if that's what you want. It's not for that she have the look of death on her face. Oh no.

'One night,' she went on, 'I hold on a woman's nose because her husband nearly chop it off with his machete. I hold it on, I send a boy running for the doctor and the doctor come galloping at dead of night to sew up the woman. When he finish he tell me, "Christophine you have a great presence of mind." That's what he tell me. By this time the man crying like a baby. He says, "Doctor I don't mean it. It just happened." "I know, Rupert," the doctor says, "but it mustn't happen again. Why don't you keep the damn machete in the other room?" he says. They have two small rooms only so I say, "No, doctor – it much worse near the bed. They chop each other up in no time at all." The doctor he laugh and laugh. Oh he was a good doctor. When he finished with that woman nose I won't say it look like before but I will say it don't notice much. Rupert that man's name was. Plenty Ruperts here you notice? One is Prince Rupert, and one who makes songs is Rupert the Rine. You see him? He sells his songs down by the bridge there in town. It's in the town I live when I first leave Jamaica. It's a pretty name eh – Rupert – but where they get it from? I think it's from old time they get it.[66]

'That doctor an old-time doctor. These new ones I don't like them. First word in their mouth is police. Police – that's something I don't like.'

'I'm sure you don't,' I said. 'But you haven't told me yet what happened when my wife was with you. Or exactly what you did?'

'*Your wife!*' she said. 'You make me laugh. I don't know all you did but I know some. Everybody know that you marry her for her money and you take it all. And then you want to break her up, because you jealous of her. She is more better than you, she have better blood in her and she don't care for money – it's nothing for her. Oh I see that first time I look at you. You young but already you hard. You fool the girl. You make her think you can't see the sun for looking at her.'

It was like that, I thought. It was like that. But better to say nothing. Then surely they'll both go and it will be my turn to sleep – a long deep sleep, mine will be, and very far away.

'And then,' she went on in her judge's voice, 'you make love to her till she drunk with it, no rum could make her drunk like that, till she can't do without it. It's *she* can't see the sun any more. Only you she see. But all you want is to break her up.'

(*Not the way you mean, I thought*)

'But she hold out eh? She hold out.'

(*Yes, she held out. A pity*)

'So you pretend to believe all the lies that damn bastard tell you.'

(*That damn bastard tell you*)

Now every word she said was echoed, echoed loudly in my head.

'So that you can leave her alone.'

(*Leave her alone*)

'Not telling her why.'

(*Why?*)

'No more love, eh?'

(*No more love*)

'And that,' I said coldly, 'is where you took charge, isn't it? You tried to poison me.'

'Poison you? But look me trouble, the man crazy! She come to me and ask me for something to make you love her again and I tell her no I don't meddle in that for *béké*. I tell her it's foolishness.'

(*Foolishness foolishness*)

'And even if it's no foolishness, it's too strong for *béké*.'

(*Too strong for* béké. *Too strong*)

'But she cry and she beg me.'

(*She cry and she beg me*)

'So I give her something for love.'

(*For love*)

'But you don't love. All you want is to break her up. And it help you break her up.'

(*Break her up*)

'She tell me in the middle of all this you start calling her names. Marionette. Some word so.'

'Yes, I remember, I did.'

(*Marionette, Antoinette, Marionetta, Antoinetta*)

'That word mean doll, eh? Because she don't speak. You want to force her to cry and to speak.'

(*Force her to cry and to speak*)

'But she won't. So you think up something else. You bring that worthless girl to play with next door and you talk and laugh and love so that she hear everything. You meant her to hear.'

Yes, that didn't just happen. I meant it.

(*I lay awake all night long after they were asleep, and as soon as it was light I got up and dressed and saddled Preston. And I came to you. Oh Christophine. O Pheena, Pheena, help me.*)

'You haven't yet told me exactly what you did with my – with Antoinette.'

'Yes I tell you. I make her sleep.'

'What? All the time?'

'No, no. I wake her up to sit in the sun, bathe in the cool river. Even if she dropping with sleep. I make good strong soup. I give her milk if I have it, fruit I pick from my own trees. If she don't want to eat I say, "Eat it up for my sake, *doudou*." And she eat it up, then she sleep again.'

'And why did you do all this?'

There was a long silence. Then she said, 'It's better she sleep. She must sleep while I work for her – to make her well again. But I don't speak of all that to you.'

'Unfortunately your cure was not successful. You didn't make her well. You made her worse.'

'Yes I succeed,' she said angrily. 'I succeed. But I get frightened that she sleep too much, too long. She is not *béké* like you, but she is *béké*, and not like us either. There are mornings when she can't wake, or when she wake it's as if she still sleeping. I don't want to give her any more of – of what I give. So,' she went on after another pause, 'I let her have rum instead. I know that won't hurt her. Not much. As soon as she has the rum she starts raving that she must go back to you and I can't quiet her. She says she'll go alone if I don't come but she beg me to come. And I hear well when you tell her that you don't love her – quite calm and cool you tell her so, and undo all the good I do.'

'The good you did! I'm very weary of your nonsense, Christophine. You seem to have made her dead drunk on bad rum and she's a wreck. I scarcely recognized her. Why you did it I can't say – hatred of me I suppose. And as you heard so much perhaps you were listening to all she admitted – boasted about, and to the vile names she called me. Your *doudou* certainly knows some filthy language.'

'I tell you no. I tell you it's nothing. You make her so unhappy she don't know what she is saying. Her father old Mister Cosway swear like half past midnight[67] – she pick it up from him. And once, when she was little she run away to be with the fishermen and the sailors on the bayside. Those men!' She raised her eyes to the ceiling. 'Never would you think they was once innocent babies. She come back copying them. She don't understand what she says.'

'I think she understood every word, and meant what she said too. But you are right, Christophine – it was all a very little thing. It was nothing. No machete here, so no machete damage. No damage at all by this time. I'm sure you took care of that however drunk you made her.'

'You are a damn hard man for a young man.'

'So you say, so you say.'

'I tell her so. I warn her. I say this is not a man who will help you when he sees you break up. Only the best can do that. The best – and sometimes the worst.'

'But you think I'm one of the worst, surely?'

'No,' she said indifferently, 'to me you are not the best, not the worst. You are –' she shrugged '– you will not help her. I tell her so.'

Nearly all the candles were out. She didn't light fresh ones – nor did I. We sat in the dim light. I should stop this useless conversation, I thought, but could only listen, hypnotized, to her dark voice coming from the darkness.

'I know that girl. She will never ask you for love again, she will die first. But I Christophine I beg you. She love you so much. She thirsty for you. Wait, and perhaps you can love her again. A little, like she say. A little. Like you can love.'

I shook my head and went on shaking it mechanically.

'It's lies all that yellow bastard tell you. He is no Cosway either. His mother was a no-good woman and she try to fool the old man but the old man isn't fooled. "One more or less" he says, and laughs. He was wrong. More he do for those people, more they hate him. The hate in that man Daniel – he can't rest with it. If I know you coming here I stop you. But you marry quick, you leave Jamaica quick. No time.'

'She told me that all he said was true. She wasn't lying then.'

'Because you hurt her she want to hurt you back, that's why.'

'And that her mother was mad. Another lie?'

Christophine did not answer me at once. When she did her voice was not so calm.

'They drive her to it. When she lose her son she lose herself for a while and they shut her away. They tell her she is mad, they act like she is mad. Question, question. But no kind word, no friends, and her husban' he go off, he leave her. They won't let me see her. I try, but no. They won't let Antoinette see her. In the end – mad I don't know – she give up, she care for nothing. That man who is in charge of her he take her whenever he want and his woman talk. That man, and others. Then they have her. Ah there is no God.'

'Only your spirits,' I reminded her.

'Only my spirits,' she said steadily. 'In your Bible it say God is a spirit – it don't say no others. Not at all. It grieve me what happen to her mother, and I can't see it happen again. You call her a doll? She don't satisfy you? Try her once more, I think she satisfy you now. If you forsake her they will tear her in pieces – like they did her mother.'

'I will not forsake her,' I said wearily. 'I will do all I can for her.'

'You will love her like you did before?'

(*Give my sister your wife a kiss from me. Love her as I did – oh yes I did. How can I promise that?*) I said nothing.

'It's she won't be satisfy. She is Creole girl, and she have the sun in her. Tell the truth now. She don't come to your house in this place England they tell me about, she don't come to your beautiful house to beg you to marry with her. No, it's you come all the long way to her house – it's you beg her to marry. And she love you and she give you all she have. Now you say you don't love her and you break her up. What you do with her money, eh?' Her voice was still quiet but with a hiss in it when she said 'money'. I thought, of course, that is what all the rigmarole is about. I no longer felt dazed, tired, half hypnotized, but alert and wary, ready to defend myself.

Why, she wanted to know, could I not return half of Antoinette's dowry and leave the island – 'leave the West Indies if you don't want her no more.'

I asked the exact sum she had in mind, but she was vague about that.

'You fix it up with lawyers and all those things.'

'And what will happen to her then?'

She, Christophine, would take good care of Antoinette (and the money of course).

'You will both stay here?' I hoped that my voice was as smooth as hers.

No, they would go to Martinique. Then to other places.

'I like to see the world before I die.'

Perhaps because I was so quiet and composed she added maliciously, 'She marry with someone else. She forget about you and live happy.'

A pang of rage and jealousy shot through me then. Oh no, she won't forget. I laughed.

'You laugh at me? Why you laugh at me?'

'Of course I laugh at you – you ridiculous old woman. I don't mean to discuss my affairs with you any longer. Or your mistress. I've listened to all you had to say and I don't believe you. Now, say good-bye to Antoinette, then go. You are to blame for all that has happened here, so don't come back.'

She drew herself up tall and straight and put her hands on her hips. 'Who you to tell me to go? This house belong to Miss Antoinette's mother, now it belong to her. Who you to tell me to go?'

'I assure you that it belongs to me now.[68] You'll go, or I'll get the men to put you out.'

'You think the men here touch me? They not damn fool like you to put their hand on me.'

'Then I will have the police up, I warn you. There must be some law and order even in this God-forsaken island.'

'No police here,' she said. 'No chain gang, no tread machine, no dark jail either. This is free country[69] and I am free woman.'

'Christophine,' I said, 'you lived in Jamaica for years, and you know Mr Fraser, the Spanish Town magistrate, well. I wrote to him about you. Would you like to hear what he answered?' She stared at me. I read the end of Fraser's letter aloud: '*I have written very discreetly to Hill, the white inspector of police in your town. If she lives near you and gets up to any of her nonsense let him know at once. He'll send a couple of policemen up to your place and she won't get off lightly this time . . .* You gave your mistress the poison that she put into my wine?'

'I tell you already – you talk foolishness.'

'We'll see about that – I kept some of that wine.'

'I tell her so,' she said. 'Always it don't work for *béké*. Always it bring trouble . . . So you send me away and you keep all her money. And what you do with her?'

'I don't see why I should tell you my plans. I mean to go back to Jamaica to consult the Spanish Town doctors and her brother. I'll follow their advice. That is all I mean to do. She is not well.'

'Her brother!' She spat on the floor. 'Richard Mason is no brother to her. You think you fool me? You want her money but you don't want her. It is in your mind to pretend she is mad. I know it. The doctors say what you tell them to say. That man Richard he say what you want him to say – glad and willing too, I know. She will be like her mother. You do that for money? But you wicked like Satan self!'

I said loudly and wildly, 'And do you think that I wanted all this? I would give my life to undo it. I would give my eyes never to have seen this abominable place.'

She laughed. 'And that's the first damn word of truth you speak. You choose what you give, eh? Then you choose. You meddle in something and perhaps you don't know what it is.' She began to mutter to herself. Not in patois. I knew the sound of patois now.

She's as mad as the other, I thought, and turned to the window.

The servants were standing in a group under the clove tree. Baptiste, the boy who helped with the horses and the little girl Hilda.

Christophine was right. They didn't intend to get mixed up in this business.

When I looked at her there was a mask on her face and her eyes were undaunted. She was a fighter, I had to admit. Against my will I repeated, 'Do you wish to say good-bye to Antoinette?'

'I give her something to sleep – nothing to hurt her. I don't wake her up to no misery. I leave that for you.'

'You can write to her,' I said stiffly.

'Read and write I don't know. Other things I know.'

She walked away without looking back.

All wish to sleep had left me. I walked up and down the room and felt the blood tingle in my finger-tips. It ran up my arms and reached my heart, which began to beat very fast. I spoke aloud as I walked. I spoke the letter I meant to write.

'I know now that you planned this because you wanted to be rid of me. You had no love at all for me. Nor had my brother. Your plan succeeded because I was young, conceited, foolish, trusting. Above all because I was young. You were able to do this to me . . .'

But I am not young now, I thought, stopped pacing and drank. Indeed this rum is mild as mother's milk or father's blessing.

I could imagine his expression if I sent that letter and he read it.

I wrote:

Dear Father,

We are leaving this island for Jamaica very shortly. Unforeseen circumstances, at least unforeseen by me, have forced me to make this decision.
I am certain that you know or can guess what has happened, and I am
certain you will believe that the less you talk to anyone about my affairs,
especially my marriage, the better. This is in your interest as well as
mine. You will hear from me again. Soon I hope.

Then I wrote to the firm of lawyers I had dealt with in Spanish
Town. I told them that I wished to rent a furnished house not too near
the town, commodious enough to allow for two separate suites of
rooms. I also told them to engage a staff of servants whom I was
prepared to pay very liberally – so long as they keep their mouths
shut, I thought – provided that they are discreet, I wrote. My wife
and myself would be in Jamaica in about a week and expected to find
everything ready.

All the time I was writing this letter a cock crowed persistently
outside. I took the first book I could lay hands on and threw it at him,
but he stalked a few yards away and started again.

Baptiste appeared, looking towards Antoinette's silent room.

'Have you got much more of this famous rum?'

'Plenty rum,' he said.

'Is it really a hundred years old?'

He nodded indifferently. A hundred years, a thousand all the same
to *le bon Dieu*[70] and Baptiste too.

'What's that damn cock crowing about?'

'Crowing for change of weather.'

Because his eyes were fixed on the bedroom I shouted at him,
'Asleep, *dormi, dormi*.'[71]

He shook his head and went away.

He scowled at me then, I thought. I scowled too as I re-read the
letter I had written to the lawyers. However much I paid Jamaican
servants I would never buy discretion. I'd be gossiped about, sung
about (but they make up songs about everything, everybody. You
should hear the one about the Governor's wife). Wherever I went I
would be talked about. I drank some more rum and, drinking, I drew
a house[72] surrounded by trees. A large house. I divided the third
floor into rooms and in one room I drew a standing woman – a

child's scribble, a dot for a head, a larger one for the body, a triangle for a skirt, slanting lines for arms and feet. But it was an English house.

English trees. I wondered if I ever should see England again.

*

Under the oleanders[73] . . . I watched the hidden mountains and the mists drawn over their faces. It's cool today; cool, calm and cloudy as an English summer. But a lovely place in any weather, however far I travel I'll never see a lovelier.

The hurricane months are not so far away, I thought, and saw that tree strike its roots deeper, making ready to fight the wind. Useless. If and when it comes they'll all go. Some of the royal palms stand (she told me). Stripped of their branches, like tall brown pillars, still they stand – defiant. Not for nothing are they called royal. The bamboos take an easier way, they bend to the earth and lie there, creaking, groaning, crying for mercy. The contemptuous wind passes, not caring for these abject things. (*Let them live.*) Howling, shrieking, laughing the wild blast passes.

But all that's some months away. It's an English summer now, so cool, so grey. Yet I think of my revenge and hurricanes. Words rush through my head (deeds too). Words. Pity is one of them. It gives me no rest.

Pity like a naked new-born babe striding the blast.[74]

I read that long ago when I was young – I hate poets now and poetry. As I hate music which I loved once. Sing your songs, Rupert the Rine, but I'll not listen, though they tell me you've a sweet voice . . .

Pity. Is there none for me? Tied to a lunatic for life – a drunken lying lunatic – gone her mother's way.

'*She love you so much, so much. She thirsty for you. Love her a little like she say. It's all that you can love – a little.*'

Sneer to the last, Devil. Do you think that I don't know? She thirsts for *anyone* – not for me . . .

She'll loosen her black hair, and laugh and coax and flatter (a mad girl. She'll not care who she's loving). She'll moan and cry and give herself as no sane woman would – or could. *Or could.* Then lie so still,

still as this cloudy day. A lunatic who always knows the time. But never does.

Till she's drunk so deep, played her games so often that the lowest shrug and jeer at her. And I'm to know it – I? No, I've a trick worth two of that.

'*She love you so much, so much. Try her once more.*'

I tell you she loves no one, anyone. I could not touch her. Excepting as the hurricane will touch that tree – and break it. You say I did? No. That was love's fierce play. Now I'll do it.

She'll not laugh in the sun again. She'll not dress up and smile at herself in that damnable looking-glass. So pleased, so satisfied.

Vain, silly creature. Made for loving? Yes, but she'll have no lover, for I don't want her and she'll see no other.

The tree shivers. Shivers and gathers all its strength. And waits.

(There is a cool wind blowing now – a cold wind. Does it carry the babe born to stride the blast of hurricanes?)

She said she loved this place. This is the last she'll see of it. I'll watch for one tear, one human tear. Not that blank hating moonstruck face. I'll listen . . . If she says good-bye perhaps adieu. *Adieu* – like those old-time songs she sang. Always *adieu* (and all songs say it). If she too says it, or weeps, I'll take her in my arms, my lunatic. She's mad but *mine, mine*. What will I care for gods or devils or for Fate itself. If she smiles or weeps or both. *For me.*

Antoinetta – I can be gentle too. Hide your face. Hide yourself but in my arms. You'll soon see how gentle. My lunatic. My mad girl.

Here's a cloudy day to help you. No brazen sun.

No sun . . . No sun. The weather's changed.

*

Baptiste was waiting and the horses saddled. That boy stood by the clove tree and near him the basket he was to carry. These baskets are light and waterproof. I'd decided to use one for a few necessary clothes – most of our belongings were to follow in a day or two. A carriage was to meet us at Massacre. I'd seen to everything, arranged everything.

She was there in the *ajoupa*; carefully dressed for the journey, I noticed, but her face blank, no expression at all. Tears? There's not a

tear in her. Well, we will see. Did she remember anything, I wondered, feel anything? (That blue cloud, that shadow, is Martinique. It's
clear now . . . Or the names of the mountains. No, not mountain.
Morne, she'd say. 'Mountain is an ugly word – for them.' Or the
stories about Jack Spaniards. Long ago. And when she said, 'Look!
The Emerald Drop! That brings good fortune.' Yes, for a moment the
sky was green – a bright green sunset. Strange. But not half so strange
as saying it brought good fortune.)

After all I was prepared for her blank indifference. I knew that my
dreams were dreams. But the sadness I felt looking at the shabby white
house – I wasn't prepared for that. More than ever before it strained
away from the black snake-like forest. Louder and more desperately it
called: Save me from destruction, ruin and desolation. Save me from
the long slow death by ants. But what are you doing here you folly?
So near the forest. Don't you know that this is a dangerous place? And
that the dark forest always wins? Always. If you don't, you soon will,
and I can do nothing to help you.

Baptiste looked very different. Not a trace of the polite domestic.
He wore a very wide-brimmed straw hat, like the fishermen's hats,
but the crown flat, not high and pointed. His wide leather belt was
polished, so was the handle of his sheathed cutlass, and his blue cotton
shirt and trousers were spotless. The hat, I knew, was waterproof. He
was ready for the rain and it was certainly on its way.

I said that I would like to say good-bye to the little girl who laughed
– Hilda. 'Hilda is not here,' he answered in his careful English. 'Hilda
has left – yesterday.'

He spoke politely enough, but I could feel his dislike and contempt.
The same contempt as that devil's when she said, 'Taste my bull's
blood.' Meaning that will make you a man. Perhaps. Much I cared for
what they thought of me! As for her, I'd forgotten her for the moment.
So I shall never understand why, suddenly, bewilderingly, I was certain
that everything I had imagined to be truth was false. False. Only the
magic and the dream are true – all the rest's a lie. Let it go. Here is
the secret. Here.

(*But it is lost, that secret, and those who know it cannot tell it.*)

Not lost. I had found it in a hidden place and I'd keep it, hold it
fast. As I'd hold her.

I looked at her. She was staring out to the distant sea. She was silence itself.

Sing, Antoinetta. I can hear you now.

> Here the wind says it has been, it has been
> And the sea says it must be, it must be
> And the sun says it can be, it will be
> And the rain . . . ?

'You must listen to that. Our rain knows all the songs.'
'And all the tears?'
'All, all, all.'

Yes, I will listen to the rain. I will listen to the mountain bird. Oh, a heartstopper is the solitaire's[75] one note – high, sweet, lonely, magic. You hold your breath to listen . . . No . . . Gone. What was I to say to her?

Do not be sad. Or think Adieu. Never Adieu. We will watch the sun set again – many times, and perhaps we'll see the Emerald Drop, the green flash that brings good fortune. And you must laugh and chatter as you used to do – telling me about the battle off the Saints or the picnic at Marie Galante[76] – that famous picnic that turned into a fight. Or the pirates[77] and what they did between voyages. For every voyage might be their last. Sun and sangoree's a heady mixture. Then – the earthquake.[78] Oh yes, people say that God was angry at the things they did, woke from his sleep, one breath and they were gone. He slept again. But they left their treasure, gold and more than gold. Some of it is found – but the finders never tell, because you see they'd only get one-third then: that's the law of treasure.[79] They want it all, so never speak of it. Sometimes precious things, or jewels. There's no end to what they find and sell in secret to some cautious man who weighs and measures, hesitates, asks questions which are not answered, then hands over money in exchange. Everybody knows that gold pieces, treasures, appear in Spanish Town – (here too). In all the islands, from nowhere, from no one knows where. For it is better not to speak of treasure. Better not to tell them.

Yes, better not to tell them. I won't tell you that I scarcely listened to your stories. I was longing for night and darkness and the time when the moonflowers open.

Blot out the moon,
Pull down the stars.
Love in the dark, for we're for the dark
    So soon, so soon.

Like the swaggering pirates, let's make the most and best and worst
of what we have. Give not one-third but everything. All – all – all.
Keep nothing back . . .

No, I would say – I knew what I would say. 'I have made a terrible
mistake. Forgive me.'

I said it, looking at her, seeing the hatred in her eyes – and feeling
my own hate spring up to meet it. Again the giddy change, the
remembering, the sickening swing back to hate. They bought me, *me*
with your paltry money. You helped them to do it. You deceived me,
betrayed me, and you'll do worse if you get the chance . . . (*That girl
she look you straight in the eye and talk sweet talk – and it's lies she tell you.
Lies. Her mother was so. They say she worse than her mother*.)

. . . If I was bound for hell let it be hell. No more false heavens.
No more damned magic. You hate me and I hate you. We'll see who
hates best. But first, first I will destroy your hatred. Now. My hate is
colder, stronger, and you'll have no hate to warm yourself. You will
have nothing.

I did it too. I saw the hate go out of her eyes. I forced it out. And
with the hate her beauty. She was only a ghost. A ghost in the grey
daylight. Nothing left but hopelessness. *Say die and I will die. Say die
and watch me die.*

She lifted her eyes. Blank lovely eyes. Mad eyes. A mad girl. I don't
know what I would have said or done. In the balance – everything.
But at this moment the nameless boy leaned his head against the clove
tree and sobbed. Loud heartbreaking sobs. I could have strangled him
with pleasure. But I managed to control myself, walk up to them and
say coldly, 'What is the matter with him? What is he crying about?'
Baptiste did not answer. His sullen face grew a shade more sullen and
that was all I got from Baptiste.

She had followed me and she answered. I scarcely recognized her
voice. No warmth, no sweetness. The doll had a doll's voice, a
breathless but curiously indifferent voice.

'He asked me when we first came if we – if you – would take him with you when we left. He doesn't want any money. Just to be with you. Because –' she stopped and ran her tongue over her lips, 'he loves you very much. So I said you would. Take him. Baptiste has told him that you will not. So he is crying.'

'I certainly will not,' I said angrily. (God! A half-savage boy as well as . . . as well as . . .)

'He knows English,' she said, still indifferently. 'He has tried very hard to learn English.'

'He hasn't learned any English that I can understand,' I said. And looking at her stiff white face my fury grew. 'What right have you to make promises in my name? Or to speak for me at all?'

'No, I had no right, I am sorry. I don't understand you. I know nothing about you, and I cannot speak for you . . .'

And that was all. I said good-bye to Baptiste. He bowed stiffly, unwillingly and muttered – wishes for a pleasant journey, I suppose. He hoped, I am sure, that he'd never set eyes on me again.

She had mounted and he went over to her. When she stretched her hand out he took it and still holding it spoke to her very earnestly. I did not hear what he said but I thought she would cry then. No, the doll's smile came back – nailed to her face. Even if she had wept like Magdalene[80] it would have made no difference. I was exhausted. All the mad conflicting emotions had gone and left me wearied and empty. Sane.

I was tired of these people. I disliked their laughter and their tears, their flattery and envy, conceit and deceit. And I hated the place.

I hated the mountains and the hills, the rivers and the rain. I hated the sunsets of whatever colour, I hated its beauty and its magic and the secret I would never know. I hated its indifference and the cruelty which was part of its loveliness. Above all I hated her. For she belonged to the magic and the loveliness. She had left me thirsty and all my life would be thirst and longing for what I had lost before I found it.

So we rode away and left it – the hidden place. Not for me and not for her. I'd look after that. She's far along the road now.

Very soon she'll join all the others who know the secret and will not tell it. Or cannot. Or try and fail because they do not know enough. They can be recognized. White faces, dazed eyes, aimless gestures, high-pitched laughter. The way they walk and talk and scream or try to kill (themselves or you) if you laugh back at them. Yes, they've got to be watched. For the time comes when they try to kill, then disappear. But others are waiting to take their places, it's a long, long line. She's one of them. I too can wait – for the day when she is only a memory to be avoided, locked away, and like all memories a legend. Or a lie . . .

I remember that as we turned the corner, I thought about Baptiste and wondered if he had another name – I'd never asked. And then that I'd sell the place for what it would fetch. I had meant to give it back to her. Now – what's the use?

That stupid boy followed us, the basket balanced on his head. He used the back of his hand to wipe away his tears. Who would have thought that any boy would cry like that. For nothing. Nothing . . .

PART THREE

'They knew that he was in Jamaica when his father and his brother died,' Grace Poole said.[1] 'He inherited everything, but he was a wealthy man before that. Some people are fortunate, they said, and there were hints about the woman he brought back to England with him. Next day Mrs Eff[2] wanted to see me and she complained about gossip. I don't allow gossip. I told you that when you came. Servants will talk and you can't stop them, I said. And I am not certain that the situation will suit me, madam. First when I answered your advertisement you said that the person I had to look after was not a young girl. I asked if she was an old woman and you said no. Now that I see her I don't know what to think. She sits shivering and she is so thin. If she dies on my hands who will get the blame? Wait, Grace, she said. She was holding a letter. Before you decide will you listen to what the master of the house has to say about this matter. "If Mrs Poole is satisfactory why not give her double, treble the money," she read, and folded the letter away but not before I had seen the words on the next page, "but for God's sake let me hear no more of it." There was a foreign stamp on the envelope. "I don't serve the devil for no money," I said. She said, "If you imagine that when you serve this gentleman you are serving the devil you never made a greater mistake in your life. I knew him as a boy. I knew him as a young man. He was gentle, generous, brave. His stay in the West Indies has changed him out of all knowledge. He has grey in his hair and misery in his eyes. Don't ask me to pity anyone who had a hand in that. I've said enough and too much. I am not prepared to treble your money, Grace, but I am prepared to double it. But there must be no more gossip. If there is I will dismiss you at once. I do not think it will be impossible to fill your place. I'm sure you understand." Yes, I understand, I said.

'Then all the servants were sent away and she engaged a cook, one maid and you, Leah. They were sent away but how could she stop them talking? If you ask me the whole county knows. The rumours I've heard — very far from the truth. But I don't contradict, I know better than to say a word. After all *the house is big and safe, a shelter from the world outside which, say what you like, can be a black and cruel world to a woman. Maybe that's why I stayed on.'*

The thick walls, she thought. Past the lodge gate a long avenue of trees and inside the house the blazing fires and the crimson and white rooms. But above all the thick walls, keeping away all the things that you have fought till you can fight no more. Yes, maybe that's why we all stay — Mrs Eff and Leah and me. All of us except that girl who lives in her own darkness. I'll say one thing for her, she hasn't lost her spirit. She's still fierce. I don't turn my back on her when her eyes have that look. I know it.

In this room I wake early and lie shivering for it is very cold. At last Grace Poole, the woman who looks after me, lights a fire with paper and sticks and lumps of coal. She kneels to blow it with bellows. The paper shrivels, the sticks crackle and spit, the coal smoulders and glowers. In the end flames shoot up and they are beautiful. I get out of bed and go close to watch them and to wonder why I have been brought here. For what reason? There must be a reason. What is it that I must do? When I first came I thought it would be for a day, two days, a week perhaps. I thought that when I saw him and spoke to him I would be wise as serpents, harmless as doves. 'I give you all I have freely,' I would say, 'and I will not trouble you again if you will let me go.' But he never came.

The woman Grace sleeps in my room. At night I sometimes see her sitting at the table counting money. She holds a gold piece in her hand and smiles. Then she puts it all into a little canvas bag with a drawstring and hangs the bag round her neck so that it is hidden in her dress. At first she used to look at me before she did this but I always pretended to be asleep, now she does not trouble about me. She drinks from a bottle on the table then she goes to bed, or puts her arms on the table, her head on her arms, and sleeps. But I lie watching the fire die out. When she is snoring I get up and I have tasted the drink without colour in the bottle.[3] The first time I did this I wanted to spit it out but managed to swallow it. When I got back into bed I could remember more and think again. I was not so cold.

There is one window high up — you cannot see out of it. My bed had doors but they have been taken away. There is not much else in the room. Her bed, a black press, the table in the middle and two black chairs carved with fruit and flowers. They have high backs and no arms. The dressing-room is very small, the room next to this one is hung with tapestry. Looking at the tapestry one day I recognized my mother dressed in an evening gown but with bare feet. She looked away from me, over my head just as she used to do. I wouldn't tell Grace this. Her name oughtn't to be Grace. Names matter, like when he wouldn't call me Antoinette, and I saw Antoinette drifting out of the window with her scents, her pretty clothes and her looking-glass.

There is no looking-glass here and I don't know what I am like now. I remember watching myself brush my hair and how my eyes looked back at me. The girl I saw was myself yet not quite myself. Long ago when I was a child and very lonely I tried to kiss her. But the glass was between us – hard, cold and misted over with my breath. Now they have taken everything away. What am I doing in this place and who am I?

The door of the tapestry room is kept locked. It leads, I know, into a passage. That is where Grace stands and talks to another woman whom I have never seen. Her name is Leah. I listen but I cannot understand what they say.

So there is still the sound of whispering that I have heard all my life, but these are different voices.

When night comes, and she has had several drinks and sleeps, it is easy to take the keys. I know now where she keeps them. Then I open the door and walk into their world. It is, as I always knew, made of cardboard. I have seen it before somewhere, this cardboard world where everything is coloured brown or dark red or yellow that has no light in it. As I walk along the passages I wish I could see what is behind the cardboard. They tell me I am in England but I don't believe them. We lost our way to England. When? Where? I don't remember, but we lost it. Was it that evening in the cabin when he found me talking to the young man who brought me my food? I put my arms round his neck and asked him to help me. He said, 'I didn't know what to do, sir.' I smashed the glasses and plates against the porthole. I hoped it would break and the sea come in. A woman came and then an older man who cleared up the broken things on the floor. He did not look at me while he was doing it.

The third man said drink this and you will sleep. I drank it and I said, 'It isn't like it seems to be.' — 'I know. It never is,' he said. And then I slept. When I woke it was a different sea. Colder. It was that night, I think, that we changed course and lost our way to England. This cardboard house where I walk at night is not England.

One morning when I woke I ached all over. Not the cold, another sort of ache. I saw that my wrists were red and swollen.[4] Grace said, 'I suppose you're going to tell me that you don't remember anything about last night.'

'When was last night?' I said.

'Yesterday.'

'I don't remember yesterday.'

'Last night a gentleman came to see you,' she said.

'Which of them was that?'

Because I knew that there were strange people in the house. When I took the keys and went into the passage I heard them laughing and talking in the distance, like birds, and there were lights on the floor beneath.

Turning a corner I saw a girl coming out of her bedroom.[5] She wore a white dress and she was humming to herself. I flattened myself against the wall for I did not wish her to see me, but she stopped and looked round. She saw nothing but shadows, I took care of that, but she didn't walk to the head of the stairs. She ran. She met another girl and the second girl said, 'Have you seen a ghost?' — 'I didn't see anything but I thought I felt something.' — 'That is the ghost,' the second one said and they went down the stairs together.

'Which of these people came to see me, Grace Poole?' I said.

He didn't come. Even if I was asleep I would have known. He hasn't come yet. She said, 'It's my belief that you remember much more than you pretend to remember. Why did you behave like that when I had promised you would be quiet and sensible? I'll never try and do you a good turn again. Your brother came to see you.'

'I have no brother.'

'He said he was your brother.'

A long long way my mind reached back.

'Was his name Richard?'

'He didn't tell me what his name was.'

'I know him,' I said, and jumped out of bed. 'It's all here, it's all here, but I hid it from your beastly eyes as I hide everything. But where is it? Where did I hide it? The sole of my shoes? Underneath the mattress? On top of the press? In the pocket of my red dress? Where, where is this letter? It was short because I remembered that Richard did not like long letters. Dear Richard please take me away from this place where I am dying because it is so cold and dark.'

Mrs Poole said, 'It's no use running around and looking now. He's gone and he won't come back — nor would I in his place.'

I said, 'I can't remember what happened. I can't remember.'

'When he came in,' said Grace Poole, 'he didn't recognize you.'

'Will you light the fire,' I said, 'because I'm so cold.'

'This gentleman arrived suddenly and insisted on seeing you and that was all the thanks he got. You rushed at him with a knife and when he got the knife away you bit his arm. You won't see him again. And where did you get that knife? I told them you stole it from me but I'm much too careful. I'm used to your sort. You got no knife from me. You must have bought it that day when I took you out. I told Mrs Eff you ought to be taken out.'

'When we went to England,' I said.

'You fool,' she said, 'this is England.'

'I don't believe it,' I said, 'and I never will believe it.'

(That afternoon we went to England. There was grass and olive-green water and tall trees looking into the water. This, I thought, is England. If I could be here I could be well again and the sound in my head would stop. Let me stay a little longer, I said, and she sat down under a tree and went to sleep. A little way off there was a cart and horse — a woman was driving it. It was she who sold me the knife, I gave her the locket round my neck for it.)

Grace Poole said, 'So you don't remember that you attacked this gentleman with a knife? I said that you would be quiet. "I must speak to her," he said. Oh he was warned but he wouldn't listen. I was in the room but I didn't hear all he said except "I cannot interfere legally between yourself and your husband." It was when he said "legally" that you flew at him and when he twisted the knife out of your hand you bit him. Do you mean to say that you don't remember any of this?'

I remember now that he did not recognize me. I saw him look at me and his eyes went first to one corner and then to another, not finding what they expected. He looked at me and spoke to me as though I were a stranger. What do you do when something happens to you like that? Why are you laughing at me? 'Have you hidden my red dress too? If I'd been wearing that he'd have known me.'

'Nobody's hidden your dress,' she said. 'It's hanging in the press.'

She looked at me and said, 'I don't believe you know how long you've been here, you poor creature.'

'On the contrary,' I said, 'only I know how long I have been here. Nights and days and days and nights, hundreds of them slipping through my fingers. But that does not matter. Time has no meaning. But something you can touch and hold like my red dress, that has a meaning. Where is it?'

She jerked her head towards the press and the corners of her mouth turned down. As soon as I turned the key I saw it hanging, the colour of fire and sunset. The colour of flamboyant flowers.[6] 'If you are buried under a flamboyant tree,' I said, 'your soul is lifted up when it flowers. Everyone wants that.'

She shook her head but she did not move or touch me.

The scent that came from the dress was very faint at first, then it grew stronger. The smell of vetivert and frangipani, of cinnamon and dust and lime trees when they are flowering. The smell of the sun and the smell of the rain.

. . . I was wearing a dress of that colour when Sandi came to see me for the last time.

'Will you come with me?' he said. 'No,' I said, 'I cannot.'

'So this is good-bye?'

'Yes, this is good-bye.'

'But I can't leave you like this,' he said, 'you are unhappy.'

'You are wasting time,' I said, 'and we have so little.'

Sandi often came to see me when that man was away and when I went out driving I would meet him. I could go out driving then. The servants knew, but none of them told.

Now there was no time left so we kissed each other in that stupid room. Spread fans decorated the walls. We had often kissed before but not like that. That was the life and death kiss and you only know a long time afterwards what it is, the life and death kiss. The white ship whistled three times, once gaily, once calling, once to say goodbye.

I took the red dress down and put it against myself. 'Does it make me look intemperate and unchaste?' I said. That man told me so. He had found out that Sandi had been to the house and that I went to see him. I never knew who told. 'Infamous daughter of an infamous mother,' he said to me.

'Oh put it away,' Grace Poole said, 'come and eat your food. Here's your grey wrapper. Why they can't give you anything better is more than I can understand. They're rich enough.'

But I held the dress in my hand wondering if they had done the last and worst thing. If they had *changed* it when I wasn't looking. If they had changed it and it wasn't my dress at all – but how could they get the scent?

'Well don't stand there shivering,' she said, quite kindly for her.

I let the dress fall on the floor, and looked from the fire to the dress and from the dress to the fire.

I put the grey wrapper round my shoulders, but I told her I wasn't hungry and she didn't try to force me to eat as she sometimes does.

'It's just as well that you don't remember last night,' she said. 'The gentleman fainted and a fine outcry there was up here. Blood all over the place and I was blamed for letting you attack him. And the master is expected in a few days. I'll never try to help you again. You are too far gone to be helped.'

I said, 'If I had been wearing my red dress Richard would have known me.'

'Your red dress,' she said, and laughed.

But I looked at the dress on the floor and it was as if the fire had spread across the room. It was beautiful and it reminded me of something I must do. I will remember I thought. I will remember quite soon now.

That was the third time I had my dream, and it ended. I know now that the flight of steps leads to this room where I lie watching the woman asleep with her head on her arms. In my dream I waited till she began to snore, then I got up, took the keys and let myself out with a candle in my hand. It was easier this time than ever before and I walked as though I were flying.

All the people who had been staying in the house had gone, for the bedroom doors were shut, but it seemed to me that someone was following me, someone was chasing me, laughing. Sometimes I looked to the right or to the left but I never looked behind me for I did not want to see that ghost of a woman who they say haunts this place. I went down the staircase. I went further than I had ever been before. There was someone talking in one of the rooms. I passed it without noise, slowly.

At last I was in the hall where a lamp was burning. I remember that when I came. A lamp and the dark staircase and the veil over my face. They think I don't remember but I do. There was a door to the right. I opened it and went in. It was a large room with a red carpet and red curtains. Everything else was white. I sat down on a couch to look at it and it seemed sad and cold and empty to me, like a church without an altar. I wished to see it clearly so I lit all the candles, and there were many. I lit them carefully from the one I was carrying but I couldn't reach up to the chandelier. Then I looked round for the altar for with so many candles and so much red, the room reminded me of a church. Then I heard a clock ticking and it was made of gold. Gold is the idol they worship.

Suddenly I felt very miserable in that room, though the couch I was sitting on was so soft that I sank into it. It seemed to me that I was going to sleep. Then I imagined that I heard a footstep and I thought what will they say, what will they do if they find me here? I held my right wrist with my left hand and waited. But it was nothing. I was very tired after this. Very tired. I wanted to get out of the room but my own candle had burned down and I took one of the others. Suddenly I was in Aunt Cora's room. I saw the sunlight coming through the window, the tree outside and the shadows of the leaves on the floor, but I saw the wax candles too and I hated them. So I knocked them all down. Most of them went out but one caught the thin curtains that were behind the red ones. I laughed when I saw the lovely colour spreading so fast, but I did not stay to watch it. I went into the hall again with the tall candle in my hand. It was then that I saw her – the ghost. The woman with streaming hair. She was surrounded by a gilt frame but I knew her. I dropped the candle I was carrying and it caught the end of a tablecloth and I saw flames shoot up. As I ran or perhaps floated or flew I called help me Christophine help me and looking behind me I saw that I had been helped. There was a wall of fire protecting me but it was too hot, it scorched me and I went away from it.

There were more candles on a table and I took one of them and ran up the first flight of stairs and the second. On the second floor I threw away the candle. But I did not stay to watch. I ran up the last flight of stairs and along the passage. I passed the room where they brought me yesterday or the day before yesterday, I don't remember. Perhaps it was quite long ago for I seemed to know the house quite well. I knew how to get away from the heat and the shouting, for there was shouting now. When I was out on the battlements it was cool and I could hardly hear them. I sat there quietly. I don't know how long I sat. Then I turned round and saw the sky. It was red and all my life was in it. I saw the grandfather clock and Aunt Cora's patchwork, all colours, I saw the orchids and the stephanotis[7] and the jasmine[8] and the tree of life in flames. I saw the chandelier and the red carpet downstairs and the bamboos and the tree ferns, the gold ferns and the silver, and the soft green velvet of the moss on the garden wall. I saw my doll's house and the books and the picture of the Miller's Daughter. I heard the parrot call as he did when he saw a stranger, *Qui est là? Qui est là?* and the man who hated me was calling too, Bertha! Bertha! The wind caught my hair and it streamed out like wings.[9] It might bear me up, I thought, if I jumped to those hard stones. But when I looked over the edge I saw the pool at Coulibri. Tia was there. She beckoned to me and when I hesitated, she laughed. I heard her say, You frightened? And I heard the man's voice, Bertha! Bertha! All this I saw and heard in a fraction of a second. And the sky so red. Someone screamed and I thought, *Why did I scream?* I called 'Tia!' and jumped and woke.

Grace Poole was sitting at the table but she had heard the scream too, for she said, 'What was that?' She got up, came over and looked at me. I lay still, breathing evenly with my eyes shut. 'I must have been dreaming,' she said. Then she went back, not to the table but to her bed. I waited a long time after I heard her snore, then I got up, took the keys and unlocked the door. I was outside holding my candle. Now at last I know why I was brought here and what I have to do. There must have been a draught for the flame flickered and I thought it was out. But I shielded it with my hand and it burned up again to light me along the dark passage.

APPENDIX

INTRODUCTION TO THE FIRST EDITION (1966)
by Francis Wyndham

Rhys was born at Roseau, Dominica, one of the Windward Islands, and spent her childhood there. Her father was a Welsh doctor and her mother a Creole – that is, a white West Indian. At the age of sixteen she came to England, where she spent the First World War. Then she married a Dutch poet and for ten years lived a rootless, wandering life on the Continent, mainly in Paris and Vienna. This was during the 1920s, and the essence of the artist's life in Europe at that time is contained in her first book, *The Left Bank* (Cape, 1927), which was described on the dust-jacket as 'sketches and studies of present-day Bohemian Paris'. In an enthusiastic preface, Ford Madox Ford comments on 'a terrifying instinct and a terrific – an almost lurid! – passion for stating the case of the underdog . . .' He goes on: 'When I, lately, edited a periodical, Miss Rhys sent in several communications with which I was immensely struck, and of which I published as many as I could. What struck me on the technical side . . . was the singular instinct for form possessed by this young lady, an instinct for form being possessed by singularly few writers of English and by almost no English women writers.' There is something patronizing about this preface (Ford was, in literal fact, her patron) but he must be credited with recognizing, so early in her career, the main elements which (increasing in intensity as her art developed) were to place her among the purest writers of our time. These are her 'passion for stating the case of the underdog' and her 'singular instinct for form' – a rare, but necessary combination. Without the instinct, the passion might so easily be either sentimental or sensational; without the passion, the instinct might lead to only formal beauty; together, they result in original art, at the same time exquisite and deeply disturbing.

It is likely that Ford Madox Ford was somewhat taken aback by his protégée's next book, a novel published in England as *Postures* (Chatto & Windus, 1928) and in the USA as *Quartet* (Simon & Schuster) — it is the American title that Miss Rhys prefers. The character of H. J. Heidler, a cold-eyed Anglicized German dilettante, may have been in part suggested by Ford himself. In *Quartet* we find the first embodiment of the Jean Rhys heroine: for essentially the first four novels deal with the same woman at different stages of her life, although her name and minor details of her circumstances alter from volume to volume. Marya Zelli has been a chorus girl in England and is now (the year is 1926) adrift in Montparnasse with a charming, feckless Pole whom she has married. This aimless, passive existence is suddenly disrupted when her husband is sent to prison. She is befriended by the Heidlers: a middle-aged picture-dealer and his very English, rather bossily 'emancipated' wife. It is taken for granted by this couple that Marya should become the husband's mistress. She is at first revolted by him, and then falls passionately in love with him: throughout she views him with a kind of hypnotized terror. The story describes the grisly *ménage à trois* that ensues (briskly broadminded wife, selfish petulant lover and their bewildered, uncomfortably candid victim) until the husband comes out of prison. Numbed by misery, Marya mismanages the situation and loses both men. The actual writing of *Quartet* betrays a few uncertainties that were later eliminated from Miss Rhys's style, but it is conceived with that mixture of quivering immediacy and glassy objectivity that is among her most extraordinary distinctions.

After Leaving Mr Mackenzie (Cape, 1930) also starts in Paris, about the year 1928. Julia Martin has been pensioned off by an ex-lover and is leading a lonely, dream-like life in a cheap hotel. One morning the weekly cheque from Mr Mackenzie's solicitor arrives with a letter explaining that it is to be the last. Julia has no money, and is losing confidence in her power to attract men. She decides to visit London, to look up former lovers and ask them for money. The visit (spent in boarding-houses at Bayswater and Notting Hill Gate) is not a success. She is met with patronizing incomprehension, with exasperation and moral disapproval. She has an affair with a young man called Mr

Horsfield which goes farcically wrong; she returns to Paris to face an empty, threatening future. The novel is written in the third person; it has a clear, bitter quality, but it does not reach so deep into the central character as the two that followed it, in which the heroines tell their own stories.

Jean Rhys returned to England after writing this book, and it is there that *Voyage in the Dark* (Constable, 1934) is set: the date, however, revealed casually half-way through, is 1914. Anna Morgan, who is nineteen, is touring the provinces in the chorus of a pantomime. Memories of her childhood on a West Indian island, of kind coloured servants and tropical beauty, form a poignant accompaniment to her adventures in an icy, suspicious land. At Southsea she is picked up by a man called Walter Jeffries; he seduces her and offers to keep her. She falls in love with him ('You shut the door and you pull the curtains and then it's as long as a thousand years and yet so soon ended'); she moves, a shivering dreaming creature, to rooms near Chalk Farm. But her lover's house in Green Street is 'dark and cold and not friendly to me. Sneering faintly, sneering discreetly, as a servant would. Who's this? Where on earth did he pick her up?' And Mr Jeffries is clearly made uneasy by her absent manner, and sometimes shocked by her sudden directness. When he is tired of her, his handsome cousin Victor tells her so in a letter. 'My dear Infant, I am writing this in the country, and I can assure you that when you get into a garden and smell the flowers and all that all this rather beastly sort of love simply doesn't matter. However, you will think I am preaching at you, so I will shut up . . . Have you kept any of the letters Walter wrote to you? If so you ought to send them back.' Stunned by this *coup de grâce* (although she has always expected it), Anna drifts into prostitution: in its treatment of a subject often falsified in fiction, this part of the book stands comparison with the novels of Charles Louis Philippe, and with Godard's film *Vivre sa Vie*. The story ends with Anna recovering from an abortion to hear the doctor say, 'She'll be all right. Ready to start all over again in no time, I've no doubt.'

In the next and most alarming instalment, *Good Morning, Midnight* (Constable, 1939), we see Sasha Jansen revisiting Paris in 1937, over forty, mistrustful of the men she tries to attract, expecting insults but unarmed against them, trying, as she says, to drink herself to death. Some restaurants may not be entered, because of the memories they inspire; the atmosphere of others is subtly hostile; the effort needed to buy a hat she cannot afford, to dye her hair, to follow up a promising encounter, is almost too much for her. Sasha meets a young man who turns out to be a gigolo, deceived by her fur coat into thinking her a rich woman. They embark on a complicated relationship, both at cross purposes. Sasha wants to work off on this boy her resentment at all men; she enjoys watching his desperate anxiety to please her, planning her revenge. 'This is where I might be able to get some of my own back. You talk to them, you pretend to sympathize; then, just at the moment when they are not expecting it, you say: "Go to Hell".' The gigolo is not so easy to shake off; he seems to be planning some sort of revenge of his own. What starts as mutual teasing becomes mutual torture. This involved episode is worked out with great subtlety; its climax, which brings the novel to an end, is brilliantly written and indescribably unnerving to read.

Sasha is the culmination of Jean Rhys's composite heroine. Although she is aggressively unhappy, she is always good company; her self-knowledge is exact, her observation of others comical and freezing. She is often unreasonable, and at moments one even pities the well-meaning men who found her so difficult to deal with. But she is not malicious: pity extends beyond herself to embrace all other sufferers. For her suffering transcends its cause. This is not only a study of a lonely, ageing woman, who has been deserted by husbands and lovers and has taken to drink; it is the tragedy of a distinguished mind and a generous nature that have gone unappreciated in a conventional, unimaginative world. A victim of men's incomprehension of women, a symptom of women's mistrust of men, Sasha belongs to a universal type that is seldom well written about; for the writer must treat her, as Miss Rhys does, with understanding and restraint.

After *Good Morning, Midnight*, Jean Rhys disappeared and her five books went out of print. Although these had enjoyed a critical success, their true quality had never been appreciated. The reason for this is simple: they were ahead of their age, both in spirit and in style. One has only to compare Miss Rhys's early books, written during the 1920s, with contemporary work by Katherine Mansfield, Aldous Huxley, Jean

Cocteau, and other celebrated writers of the period, to be struck by how little the actual text has 'dated': the style belongs to today. More important, the novels of the 1930s are much closer in *feeling* to life as it is lived and understood in the 1960s than to the accepted attitudes of their time. The elegant surface and the paranoid content, the brutal honesty of the feminine psychology and the muted nostalgia for lost beauty, all create an effect which is peculiarly modern.

The few people who remembered their admiration for these books, and those even fewer who (like myself) were introduced to them later and with great difficulty managed to obtain second-hand copies, for a while formed a small but passionate band. But nobody could find her; and nobody would reprint the novels. Then, as the result of a dramatized version of *Good Morning, Midnight* broadcast on the Third Programme in 1958, she was finally traced to an address in Cornwall. She had a collection of unpublished stories, written during and immediately after the Second World War, and she was at work on a novel.

Of these stories, *Till September Petronella, The Day They Burned the Books* and *Tigers are Better-Looking* have since been published in *The London Magazine* (which also printed a new, long story, *Let Them Call it Jazz*, written in 1961); *Outside the Machine* appeared in the sixth edition of *Winter's Tales* (Macmillan, 1960) and *A Solid House* in an anthology entitled *Voices* (Michael Joseph, 1963). *I Spy a Stranger, The Sound of the River, The Lotus* and *Temps Perdi* were published in the eighth, ninth, eleventh and twelfth editions of *Art and Literature*.

For many years, Jean Rhys has been haunted by the figure of the first Mrs Rochester — the mad wife in *Jane Eyre*. The present novel — completed at last after much revision and agonized rejection of earlier versions — is her story. Not, of course, literally so: it is in no sense a pastiche of Charlotte Brontë and exists in its own right, quite independent of *Jane Eyre*. But the Brontë book provided the initial inspiration for an imaginative feat almost uncanny in its vivid intensity. From her personal knowledge of the West Indies, and her reading of their history, Miss Rhys knew about the mad Creole heiresses in the early nineteenth century, whose dowries were only an additional burden to them: products of an inbred, decadent, expatriate society, resented by the recently freed slaves whose superstitions they shared, they languished uneasily in the oppressive beauty of their tropical surroundings, ripe for exploitation. It is one of these that she has chosen for her latest heroine: and Antoinette Cosway seems a logical development of Marya, Julia, Anna and Sasha, who were also alienated, menaced, at odds with life.

The novel is divided into three parts. The first is told in the heroine's own words. In the second the young Mr Rochester describes his arrival in the West Indies, his marriage and its disastrous sequel. The last part is once more narrated by his wife: but the scene is now England, and she writes from the attic room in Thornfield Hall . . .

All Jean Rhys's books to date have shared a modern, urban background: Montparnasse cafés, cheap Left Bank hotels, Bloomsbury boarding-houses, furnished rooms near Notting Hill Gate are evoked with a bitter poetry that is entirely her own. Only the West Indian flashbacks in *Voyage in the Dark* and some episodes in *The Left Bank* strike a different note – one of regret for innocent sensuality in a lush, beguiling land. In *Wide Sargasso Sea*, which is set in Jamaica and Dominica during the 1830s, she returns to that spiritual country as to a distant dream: and discovers it, for all its beauty (and she conjures up this beauty with haunting perfection) to have been a nightmare.

F.W.

(Francis Wyndham's introduction and the first part of this novel were first published in *Art and Literature,* No. 1.)

GENERAL NOTES

SARGASSO SEA

The identification and naming of the Sargasso Sea are inextricably linked with the history of colonialism. The sea is a tract of the North Atlantic Ocean lying roughly between the West Indies and the Azores, in the Horse Latitudes. It is a relatively still sea but is the centre of a great swirl of ocean currents. Columbus was becalmed in it on his first voyage; its name derives from the tracts of floating weed on its surface. An Englishman who encountered the weed in the Sargasso Sea in 1598 describes it as being like samphire, but yellow, and says that the Portuguese named the sea after the weed that grew in their wells at home, sargassum. One of the myths about it was that ships could become entangled in the weed and be unable to escape. The term Horse Latitudes is thought to originate from the period when Spanish sailing ships transported horses to the West Indies. The ships were often becalmed in this latitude, and horses had to be thrown overboard because of water shortages on board. The poem called 'Obeah Night', which Jean Rhys wrote when she was finishing *Wide Sargasso Sea* using the persona of Rochester, Antoinette's husband, touches on the novel's title, though the novel itself does not do so:

> Perhaps Love would have smiled then
> Shown us the way
> Across that sea. They say it's strewn with wrecks
> And weed-infested
> Few dare it, fewer still escape[1]

ISLANDS

Grouping the islands of the archipelago under such comprehensive terms as the West Indies or the Caribbean annihilates the particularity of their individual characteristics. The islands differ because of their original indigenous inhabitants, their land and seascape, their languages, and their encounters with European and North American colonialism. Rochester, in *Jane Eyre*, includes all the ingredients that a Victorian reader would expect to find in what he calls 'a fiery West Indian night'[2]: hurricanes, claustrophobic heat, mosquitoes, the sound of the sea, pineapples and pomegranates. Though detailed scholarship exists to show that Jean Rhys sometimes conflates Jamaica and Dominica, Jamaica and the honeymoon island, which is unnamed but physically resembles Dominica, are distinct, suggesting particular histories with different weather and geographical features. The servants at Coulibri, in Jamaica, are Protestants and disapprove of Annette's foreign ways; she and Christophine are from Martinique which was a French colony. Christophine's Catholicism and French patois are alien to Godfrey and Myra, and her clothes are different from theirs; in the novel St Pierre, in Martinique, is described as '"the Paris of the West Indies"'. (p. 49) As Daniel Cosway says, 'French and English like cat and dog in these islands since long time.' (p. 60) Richard Mason is described as having been to school in Barbados, which used to be known as 'Little England' because it was the only Caribbean island that was colonized exclusively by the British; Baptiste comes from St Kitts which was colonized by both British and French, and he seems alien to Rochester when he comes in search of him wearing 'blue cotton trousers pulled up above his knees and a broad ornamented belt round his slim waist' (p. 66) and carrying a razor-sharp machete.

The text hints at secret histories, with the suggestion that the descendants of both the exploiter and the exploited want to hide what happened from Antoinette's husband. The significance of the name of the village on the honeymoon island, Massacre, has oblique links with the plot of the novel, in that the massacre it records was the probable murder of the illegitimate mixed race Indian Warner by his half-brother, Colonel Philip Warner, in 1675; Indian Warner was the supposed son of Sir Thomas Warner, Governor of St Kitts, and a Carib woman.[3] The Caribs were the indigenous inhabitants of Dominica and St Vincent. Preoccupation with race, exemplified in this story in that Philip Warner denied that Indian Warner was his half-brother, is part of the texture of *Jane Eyre* and *Wide Sargasso Sea*. Rochester tells Jane that his wife's family ' "wished to secure me, because I was of a good race" ',[4] and anxiety about race permeates Antoinette's consciousness. When her aunt reassures her that her hair will grow back after the fire, she remarks tersely, ' "But darker." ' (p. 24) The language of colour gradations in the period at which the novel is set suggests a neurotic obsession with defining racial mixture: sambo, mulatto, quadroon, mustee, mustiphini, quintroon and octoroon were all gradations current in the nineteenth century, but it was possible to refine them further, to 128 gradations.[5] Being in between black and white is often seen as dispossession; in an anonymous novel called *Marly*, published in 1828, a black slave tells a coloured one: 'You brown man hab no country – Only de neger and de buckra [whites] hab country.'[6] Rochester reflects this anxiety about race when he comments, about his wife: 'Creole of pure English descent she may be, but they are not English or European either.'(p. 40)

The cultural baggage that European colonizers brought with them affected each of the colonized islands differently, in terms of religion, language, dress and gender relations. This is exemplified in the text, though it is blurred, as the only island that Rhys knew well was Dominica; she had not been to Jamaica. Coulibri, though it is in Jamaica in the novel, was an estate she remembered from childhood; Granbois resembles what she remembers about her father's estate:

the place I have called Coulibri *existed*, and still does . . . 'Coulibri' was, for Dominica, an 'old' estate – about 178-something (I rather think before that too) on sea level very fertile and so on. It had that feeling too of that time. The place my father bought was way up – mountains, forest – oh incredibly beautiful but *wild*.[7]

SLAVERY

The Emancipation Act was passed in 1833; a transitional phase of seven years' apprenticeship for the slaves before they attained liberty was originally intended, but this was amended and August 1838 became the date for full emancipation. The British government awarded owners a compensation rate of £19 per slave; the market value of slaves was £35. In addition to the loss of free labour on the plantations, the price of sugar fell by half with the introduction of free trade; the planters were no longer in a privileged trading position and compensation for the loss of the slaves often went to the planters' creditors, not to them. Sugar estates were frequently heavily mortgaged already and the planters felt betrayed by the British government. The racial balance in the islands at the time of the Emancipation Act is suggested by the number of claims that were made; in Jamaica there were 255,290 slaves and 16,435 claims for compensation were lodged, and in Dominica the equivalent figures were 11,664 and 1,041.[8] This demonstrates that the British West Indian plantation economy was a small-scale one, in that the figures average out at 15 slaves per claim in Jamaica and 11 in Dominica. The Creole planters were at a disadvantage in relation to incoming businessmen, like Mason in the novel, who could buy up estates in their depressed state. In Jamaica in 1830 the coloured population, like Sandi Cosway in the novel, was about 60,000, of whom about 15,000 were slaves and 45,000 free.[9] The indigenous population of Arawak Amerindians had been exterminated or expelled in the early colonial period, but in Dominica the Caribs had survived as part of the population.

CREOLE

Creole was the title that Jean Rhys gave to her writings about the West Indies. Creole can be used as a noun of both language and people, and as an adjective. The word is thought to be a colonial corruption of the past participle of the Spanish *criar*, meaning 'to breed'. It is used in the West Indies of people of European or African descent who are born and naturalized in the Caribbean: Rhys and her mother were Creoles but her father was not; the descendants of slaves were Creoles but the remaining indigenous people, Arawaks and Caribs, were not. There is sometimes an assumption that the word applies only to people of European descent but Edward Brathwaite, for instance, uses it more widely in the title of his book *The Development of Creole Society in Jamaica*. It is also used of animals and plants that were imported to the West Indies and naturalized there, modifying in response to the climate and conditions for their growth.

A separate but related usage of the word is for language in the West

Indies. When the slaves were taken from Africa on the Middle Passage they were separated from people of their own area who spoke their language, to inhibit insurrection. When they arrived in the plantations they could not understand the language their masters spoke, nor that of their fellow workers. In these circumstances, what happens first in a situation where the masters are English-speaking is that a pidgin English develops, that is a marginal language for restricted communication between people with no common language. Pidgin discards the inessentials of the original language. A Creole language develops when pidgin becomes the mother tongue of a community: children born to the slaves on board ship or in the plantations acquired pidgin first but it was inadequate to express the whole range of human experience. In this way a more complex language evolved, retaining some of the characteristics of pidgin; for example Godfrey leaves out the verb when he says, ' "I too old now." ' (p. 6) The omission of the inessentials creates an impression of vitality to speakers of the language that was the source of the Creole, for instance when Christophine leaves out the verb and the preposition, and turns an adjective into a noun in ' "she pretty like pretty self" '. (p. 5) Similarly Christophine's omission of inessentials makes her sound much more direct and emphatic than English speakers: ' "Read and write I don't know" ' (p. 104) has a totally different impact from 'I do not know how to read and write.'

OBEAH

There are various accounts of the derivation of *obeah*; one persuasive version is that it is a corruption of the Twi *obayi* or sorcery; the practitioner of *obayi* was called an *obayifo*. Twi is the language of the Akan people of Ghana, many of whom were sold into slavery in the Caribbean. The influence of obeah practitioners is clear from the Jamaican Slave Laws of 1760, passed soon after the Tacky slave rebellion:

And in order to prevent the many Mischiefs that may hereafter arise from the wicked Art of Negroes, going under the Appellation of Obeah Men and Women, pretending to have Communication with the Devil and other evil spirits, whereby the weak and superstitious are deluded into a Belief of their having full Power to exempt them, whilst under their Protection, from any Evils that might otherwise happen: Be it therefore enacted [. . .] That from and after the First Day of June [1760], any Negro or other Slave, who shall pretend to any supernatural Power, and be detected in making use of any Blood, Feathers, Parrots Beaks, Dogs Teeth, Alligators Teeth, broken Bottles, Grave Dirt, Rum, Egg-shells or any other Materials relative to the Practice of Obeah or Witchcraft, in order to delude and impose on the Minds of others, shall upon Conviction thereof, before two Magistrates and three Freeholders, suffer Death or Transportation.[10]

Present-day obeah laws are not very different apart from the penalties; the eighteenth-century laws were well researched, suggesting that the authorities were aware of the subversive power of obeah in the society.

Originally obeah practitioners cast spells and used witchcraft against their victims, harming them through psychic powers and the use of the kinds of magical objects listed in the law. Practitioners were believed to be able to turn people into zombis through spirit theft, leaving them as the living dead. Myal practitioners were those who countered the malign power of the obeah men and women, and cured the bewitched. However, during slavery myal priests and obeah practitioners functioned together sometimes, as a secret society, to counter the power of the slave-owners, who were themselves thought guilty of spirit theft in their treatment of slaves. The Barbadian poet and scholar Edward Brathwaite describes it:

In African and Caribbean folk practice, where religion had not been externalized and institutionalized as in Europe, the obeah-man was doctor, philosopher, and priest. Healing was, in a sense, an act of faith, as it was in the early Christian church, and the fetish (*suman*) had come to mediate (in many instances to replace and obscure the connection) between man and god . . . Each man was also, in a way not understood by Europeans, a priest, and through possession (induced by communal dancing to drums) could not only communicate with the gods, but become and assume the god. In Jamaica, Black Baptist worshippers were often possessed.[11]

Christophine in *Wide Sargasso Sea* has the status of both healer and witch, partly because she speaks a strange language and her food and clothes are Martinican rather than Jamaican. The fear of being poisoned that pervades the novel reflects relationships in what had been until very recently a slave society. The casual cruelties inflicted on house slaves, as opposed to the systematic cruelty of the way the plantations were run, suggests that slaves employed in kitchens had a rare opportunity for wreaking revenge on their masters. A witness in a House of Commons Inquiry in 1790/1 describes how a 'house wench' of a doctor in Jamaica 'had either broken a plate, or spilt a cup of tea, which raised his passion so much, that he took a hammer and a tenpenny nail, and nailed one of her ears to a bullet-tree post.'[12] Antoinette's husband's power over her is seen by her as a form of obeah; when he calls her Bertha instead of Antoinette she says: '"You are trying to make me into someone else, calling me by another name. I know, that's obeah too."' (p. 94) Christophine regards his sexual control over Antoinette as a form of enchantment which turns her into a zombi; he describes Antoinette just before they leave the honeymoon island as 'a ghost in the grey daylight'. (p. 110)

Notes

1. *Letters*, p. 264.
2. Charlotte Brontë, *Jane Eyre*, chapter 27.
3. See Peter Hulme and Neil L. Whitehead (eds), *Wild Majesty: Encounters with Caribs from Columbus to the Present Day* (Oxford: Oxford University Press, 1992), pp. 89 ff.
4. Brontë, loc. cit.
5. Edward Brathwaite, *The Development of Creole Society in Jamaica 1770–1820* (Oxford: Clarendon Press, 1971), p. 167.
6. Brathwaite, p. 156.
7. *Letters*, pp. 276–7.
8. Eric Williams, *From Columbus to Castro: The History of the Caribbean 1492–1969* (London: André Deutsch, 1970), p. 283.
9. Brathwaite, p. 168.
10. Brathwaite, p. 162.
11. Brathwaite, p. 219.
12. Brathwaite, p. 156.

NOTES TO THE TEXT

The notes below are amplified in the General Notes above. The relevant passages are indicated as follows:

SS Sargasso Sea   *I* Islands   *S* Slavery   *C* Creole   *O* Obeah

PART ONE

1. *we were not in their ranks*: Antoinette, the narrator, sees the situation as a quasi-military one; as Creoles, she and her family feel themselves to be excluded by white European incomers and by the more respectable plantation owners. *C*

2. *'she pretty like pretty self'*: she is as pretty as prettiness itself is. *C*

3. *Martinique*: an island of the Windward Islands colonized by the French, between Dominica and St Lucia, officially British colonies at the time when the novel is set. Most of the people in Martinique speak a Creole patois. *C*

4. *Jamaican ladies* [. . .] *Martinique girl*: see *I* for the tensions between the islands' populations. Jamaica was a British colony.

5. *Spanish Town*: the town was founded in 1523 and was the capital of Jamaica from 1692 until 1872. Its name reflects the fact that Columbus visited it in 1494 and it was claimed for Spain in 1509. It became a British colony in the seventeenth century; from 1672 it had one of the world's major slave markets.

6. *Coulibri*: the name of an estate on Dominica (*I*); its name means 'humming bird'.

7. *this compensation the English promised when the Emancipation Act was passed*: this provides an approximate date for the opening of the novel as the Emancipation Act was passed in 1833 (*S*); when Antoinette is at school she embroiders '1839' on her sampler (p. 29). Jean Rhys has shifted the approximate date of *Jane Eyre* which is earlier than this. Though the novel is not precisely dated, Jane says that she has been married ten years at the time she writes her story. If we assume that to be the year in which it was published, 1847, it means that Jane and Rochester were reunited in 1837. He tells Jane that he roved round Europe in a frantic state for ten years after he had incarcerated his wife in the attic at Thornfield, which means that Antoinette could not have been born after about 1805. These details probably do not bother the reader of either novel but it is significant that Jean Rhys shifts the date of *Wide Sargasso Sea* to the period when the Creole planters were most disorientated and, from her perspective, to be pitied.

8. *Nelson's Rest*: the French threatened to invade Jamaica at the end of the eighteenth century and in 1806; the name of the property identifies it with one of the British heroes of the wars against Napoleon. Nelson married a West Indian heiress in Nevis and opposed the abolition of the slave trade.

9. *frangipani tree*: shrub or small tree with fragrant white, yellow or pink flowers.

10. *marooned*: a significant choice of word as 'maroon' is the name in Jamaica for the descendants of the slaves of the Spaniards who fled to the interior when the island was captured by the British. Annette uses the word again on p. 11.

11. '*The devil prince of this world*': Godfrey quotes, like a Presbyterian elder of the church, from St John 12.31.

12. *that garden in the Bible – the tree of life grew there*: the Garden of Eden where Adam and Eve ate from the tree of knowledge but were driven out by God's command before they could eat from the tree of life, which would have given them immortality (Genesis 3.22).

13. *tree ferns*: ferns with a trunk-like stem reaching up to 25 metres.

14. *Adieu* [. . .] *à dieu*: 'adieu' is a farewell before a long, or final, parting: '*à dieu*' means 'we're in God's hands'.

15. *She was your father's wedding present to me*: Christophine had been owned as a slave by Cosway but is now (some time after 1833) free. S

16. *These new ones*: people like Mason who were not born and brought up in the West Indies but came either as part of the colonial government or as entrepreneurs. S

17. *white cockroaches*: cockroaches are nocturnal scavengers and household pests; they are usually black or brown and are associated with dirt and decay.

18. *calabash*: gourd, used in Africa and the West Indies as a bowl or container.

19. *We ate salt fish*: slaves on the plantations were issued with salt fish rations, and fresh fish was reserved for the owners.

20. *chain gang*: convicts who are chained together and forced to do hard labour.

21. *They got tread machine to mash up people's feet*: the treadmill was invented in Britain early in the nineteenth century as a form of hard labour for convicts. 'Mash' is Creole for 'crush'.

22. *the old sugar works and the water wheel*: Coulibri was a sugar estate, but political and economic changes mean that it has become derelict. S

23. *bastards*: many of the plantation-owners, like Cosway and like Indian Warner's father, had children by African slaves and, in some islands, by Carib women.

24. *Trinidad*: a British colony from 1802.

25. *Some of the big estates are going cheap*: entrepreneurs with capital could take advantage of the slump in the sugar market and the emancipation of the slaves. *S*

26. *obeah woman*: obeah is a religious folk practice originating in Africa; obeah was seen by Europeans as superstition, witchcraft and poison but by the slaves and their descendants as a source of healing and religious belief. Originally obeah was a practice used to harm an enemy, but it changed and took on different characteristics in different islands. *O*

27. *the pictures of the Holy Family and the prayer for a happy death*: this indicates that Christophine is a Roman Catholic, whereas most black Jamaicans belonged to nonconformist churches. Christianity is not thought to be incompatible with traditional practices such as obeah in many parts of Africa and the Caribbean. *O*

28. *the old black press*: wardrobe or cupboard. There are echoes of *Wuthering Heights* as well as *Jane Eyre* in *Wide Sargasso Sea*; this is a reminder of the black press that Catherine imagines in the twelfth chapter of *Wuthering Heights*. Godfrey plays a role similar to Joseph's in *Wuthering Heights*. Jean Rhys read the novel at the time when she was writing *Wide Sargasso Sea*.

29. *a dead man's dried hand* [. . .] *hear it*: ritual sacrifice of creatures such as a cock is common in traditional religious practice, but Antoinette fuses what she has picked up about it with European stories of witchcraft. *O*

30. *your estate in Trinidad? And the Antigua property?*: as a non-Creole incomer, Mason has bought up properties in various parts of the West Indies. Antigua was named by Columbus but became a British colony in the late seventeenth century. Sir Thomas Bertram, in Jane Austen's *Mansfield Park*, visits his estates in Antigua in the course of that novel.

31. *A wedding perhaps?*: Mason's assumptions about the social mores of the newly liberated slaves are eurocentric; Antoinette implies that they do not marry.

32. *a plan* [. . .] *East Indies*: indentured labourers from India were brought to the West Indies immediately after the Emancipation Act, on fixed time contracts. The term 'coolies' derives from a word that exists in all Indian vernaculars meaning hired labourer or burden carrier.

33. *the people here won't work*: Mason is committed to the Protestant work ethic. Indian labourers were thought to work harder than the ex-slaves were willing to do.

34. *Unhappily children do hurt flies*: an echo of *King Lear* IV.i.36: 'As flies to wanton boys, are we to the gods, They kill us for their sport.'

35. *you had to belong to her sect to be saved*: Myra belongs to a nonconformist sect. *I*

36. *yellow roses*: probably imported, like 'The Miller's Daughter', to suggest English aesthetic values.

37. *tamarinds*: pulp from the pod of the tamarind tree is mixed with sugar and water to make a drink.

38. *they set fire to the back of the house*: Jean Rhys claims in her autobiography *Smile Please* that her grandfather's house was burnt down immediately after the Emancipation Act by freed slaves. Peter Hulme in 'The locked heart: the creole family romance of *Wide Sargasso Sea*' (in Barker, Hulme and Iversen (eds), *Colonial discourse/postcolonial theory*) shows how the incidents and attitudes of the novel have been accepted as being based on actual events, for instance in the standard biography of Rhys by Carole Angier, whereas there is no evidence that the house was destroyed. Angier corrects the mistake in an afterword.

39. *Qui est là?*: here the parrot speaks French and asks, 'Who is there?'

40. *Ché Coco*: he replies to himself in patois, 'Dear Coco.' C

41. *flambeaux*: flaming torches.

42. *it was very unlucky to kill a parrot*: superstitions accrued round parrots; their beaks were used in obeah ceremonies. O

43. *machete*: a broad, heavy knife or cutlass, used as a tool and a weapon.

44. *You mash centipede* [. . .] *it grow again*: If you leave one little bit of a centipede when you crush it, it will grow whole again.

45. *jumby*: ghost.

46. *sangoree*: a drink made from wine, diluted and spiced; from the Spanish, meaning 'bleeding'.

47. *hammock*: used as a means of conveyance in the tropics.

48. *a white skin*: the boy is an albino.

49. *sans culottes*: without pants; the term was a derogatory one used during the French Revolution of extreme republicans. Then it meant that they wore long trousers instead of the fashionable knee-breeches worn by aristocrats; there as here it comments on class.

50. *zombi*: either a dead person brought back from the grave by obeah, or a living person whose spirit has been stolen from them by witchcraft. Zombis were known as the living dead. O.

51. *The Relics*: Antoinette's Roman Catholic education cuts her off from local children, and from the family into which she marries.

52. *the garden of my Spouse*: the nun is wedded to Christ, and the garden is heaven.

53. *vetiver*: a grass plant that can be used to produce aromatic oil.

54. *chemise*[s]: smock or shift, used as an undergarment.

55. *now and at the hour of our death*: quotation from the Roman Catholic prayer, the Hail Mary.

56. *Let perpetual light shine on them*: from the Prayer for the Dead.

PART TWO

1. *for better or for worse*: a quotation from the Anglican marriage service. The narrator is now Antoinette's husband, the Rochester of *Jane Eyre*, though he is never named in *Wide Sargasso Sea*.

2. *mango*: an evergreen tree with dark green leaves and sweet-tasting fruit.

3. *Massacre*: a village north of Roseau on Dominica; the honeymoon island is not named. *I*

4. *Windward Islands*: southern group of the Lesser Antilles, including Martinique, Grenada, Dominica, St Lucia and St Vincent.

5. *tricorne hat*: three-cornered hats with cocked brims had been worn by men and women throughout the eighteenth century but were no longer fashionable in Europe by the mid-nineteenth century.

6. *Creole* [. . .] *or European either*: Rochester is obsessed by anxiety that Antoinette's ancestry may not be entirely white. *I, C*

7. *debased French patois*: Creole French, which Rochester regards as inferior. *C*

8. *not civilized*: this reflects the cultural competitiveness between the islands. *I*

9. *blue rag* [. . .] *head*: the speaker is protecting his head to carry a head-load, in the African manner.

10. *A cock crowed loudly*: an indication of impending betrayal from the episode in the New Testament when Peter denies knowledge of Christ before the crucifixion: 'And Peter said, Man, I know not what thou sayest. And immediately, while he yet spake, the cock crew. And the Lord turned, and looked upon Peter. And Peter remembered the word of the Lord, how he had said unto him, Before the cock crow, thou shalt deny me thrice.' Luke 22.60–61.

11. *Bon sirop*: 'Good syrup'; a street vendor is selling a refreshing drink.

12. *thirty thousand pounds*: in *Jane Eyre* Rochester's father is a grasping man who does not want to split up his estate. He settles it on his elder son, Rowland, leaving nothing for Edward, the younger son, but negotiates a marriage for Edward with the daughter of a planter in the West Indies, Mason. Edward is sent to the West Indies without knowing that Mason is prepared to settle a dowry of thirty thousand pounds (a huge sum of money at that time) on his daughter in exchange for Rochester, because, as he says, he is of a good race. Ironically, once he is married, Rochester's father and brother die and he inherits the estate anyway.

13. *No provision made for her*: in English law at this period, a woman's property passed to her husband at her marriage unless special safeguards had been legally negotiated for her before the wedding.

14. *I have sold my soul*: the Faust legend; Faust sold his soul to the devil in exchange for pleasure, knowledge and power in his mortal life.

15. *screw pine*: evergreen tree resembling a palm with sword-shaped leaves and pineapple-shaped fruits.

16. *my da*: Creole meaning 'my nurse'.

17. *Doudou, ché cocotte*: 'dear little chicken' in Creole. In French, *cocotte* is used as a term of affection to a loved one or a child, but also to mean prostitute, tart.

18. *shingles*: a piece of wood used as a tile.

19. *Confessions of an [English] Opium Eater*: by Thomas de Quincey, published in 1821.

20. *Richard Mason*: In *Jane Eyre*, Richard Mason visits Thornfield and is bitten by his mad sister, not step-sister, as in *Wide Sargasso Sea*. Later he intervenes to prevent Rochester's bigamous marriage to Jane Eyre.

21. *à la Joséphine*: in the style of the Empress Josephine, who was divorced by Napoleon in 1809. As with the tricorne hat, fashions on this island seem rather behind the times in comparison with Europe. One of Christophine's names is Josephine (p. 91).

22. *Coralita*: coral-coloured flowers.

23. *Crac-crac[s]*: an insect like a cricket.

24. *La belle*: the beauty.

25. *very bad* [. . .] *the moon is full*: a superstition that associates the full moon with madness.

26. *cassava*: a food plant whose fleshy roots can be made into flour, bread, tapioca etc.

27. *guava*: the fruit of an evergreen tropical tree, usually used for stewing or for jams and jellies.

28. *'Rose elle a vécu'*: from a poem written in 1599 by François de Malherbe entitled *'Consolation à M du Périer'*. The lines read: *'Et rose elle a vécu ce que vivent les roses /L'espace d'un matin'*: 'Rose has lived as roses live, for one morning.' The poem is an elegy for M du Périer's daughter.

29. *fer de lance*: a venomous snake.

30. *ajoupa*: a small shelter.

31. *Adieu foulard, adieu madras*: the singer says good-bye to two fine materials. Foulard can be silk and madras can be cotton, and both can be a mixture of silk and cotton.

32. *Ma belle ka di maman li*: there is a translation of this in the next line. A recording of Jean Rhys singing this song exists in the archive at the University of Tulsa; its theme is that the beautiful girl asks her mother why pretty flowers die in a day or an instant, and the mother replies that a day and a thousand years are the same to God.

33. *If I could die. Now, when I am happy*: an echo of *Othello* II.i.189, 'If it were now to die /'Twere now to be most happy.'

34. *I watched her die many times*: the 'little death', orgasm.

35. *nancy stories*, from Ananse, the Akan spider-hero, a trickster who uses his intelligence to outwit powerful opponents.

36. *spunks*: guts.

37. *plantain*: a large tough species of banana that must be cooked before being eaten.

38. pp. 67–75: the narration reverts to Antoinette for this section.

39. *beating them against the stones*: a traditional method of washing clothes in Africa.

40. *hibiscus*: a spectacular flowering plant with pink, red and white blossoms.

41. *wolds*: the usual meaning is rolling uplands.

42. *tim-tim*: fairy story.

43. *béké*: a white person.

44. *doudou*: little darling.

45. *doudou ché*: dear little darling.

46. *soucriant*: a wailing ghost.

47. *why Judas did what he did*: the reference to the crowing of the cock, the palm leaf from Palm Sunday and to Judas are all reminders of the ways in which Christ was betrayed by the disciples who were with him on Palm Sunday when he rode in triumph into Jerusalem on a donkey. Judas sold him for thirty pieces of silver; Rochester's family sold him for thirty thousand pounds.

48. p. 75: Rochester resumes the narration.

49. *Esau*: a biblical name (Genesis 25). Esau sold his birthright, as the elder of twin sons, to his brother Jacob for a bowl of food; his name is often used to signify a failure to sort out priorities. His story can also be interpreted as an intimate betrayal of one brother by another. Both Daniel Cosway's names are from the Old Testament: Daniel braved the lions' den and emerged unscathed because of the strength of his faith.

50. *It have [. . .] big black letters*: Jean Rhys's great-grandfather, James Potter Lockhart, was commemorated in this way in the Anglican church in Dominica. He was the cousin of Sir Walter Scott's biographer; Scott's novels are among the books in Rochester's dressing room.

51. *Perhaps they are related*: Rochester's neurosis about race and incest becomes stronger. *1*

52. *Bertha*: in *Jane Eyre* the madwoman's name was Bertha Antoinetta Mason, and her marriage certificate describes her parents as ' "Jonas Mason, merchant, and Antoinetta Mason, his wife, a Creole" ' (*Jane Eyre*, chapter 26).

53. *the frown between her thick eyebrows*: an almost exact repetition of Antoinette's description of her mother on p. 7.

54. *Demerara*: an area of what was then British Guiana, the only British possession in South America.

55. *Rio*: at that time the capital of Brazil.

56. *I had his reply in a few days*: Rhys's local knowledge slips here; it would take more time for a message and a reply to it to get from one of the Windward Islands to Spanish Town and back.

57. *she won't get off lightly this time*: the laws against the practice of obeah were strict. *O*

58. *Martinique*: the main exports of the French colony of Martinique, where slavery was not abolished until 1848, were sugar and rum.

59. *Que komesse!*: Creole meaning 'What's wrong?'

60. *Grandpappy passing his glass over the water decanter*: James II went into exile in 1688; his Stuart descendants remained in exile but laid claim to the British Crown. Their supporters, mainly Roman Catholic and many of them Scots, shared secret signs of their support for the Jacobite cause. Until the accession of Edward VII in 1901, finger-bowls were not placed on royal dinner tables because in former times Jacobite sympathizers were in the habit of drinking to the king over the water.

61. *A Benky [. . .] Charlie*: 'benky' means crooked; 'Charlie' refers to Bonnie Prince Charlie, the Young Pretender to the British Crown who led the 1745 rebellion. Sir Walter Scott's *Waverley* rekindled interest in the nineteenth century in the romantic appeal of the Jacobite cause.

62. *Ma belle ka di*: this refers back to the poem quoted on p. 56, about the mother telling her daughter that to God one day and a thousand years are the same.

63. *Ti moun*: little one.

64. *Doudou ché*: dear darling.

65. *Do do l'enfant do*: sleep, sleep, child, sleep.

66. *Rupert [. . .] I think it's from old time they get it*: Prince Rupert of the Rhine supported the Stuarts and arrived in England in 1642 to fight for Charles I and the Royalist cause in the English Civil War. He was made general of the king's army in 1644; after the Restoration he settled permanently in England.

67. *swear like half past midnight*: like a drunkard swears after an evening's drinking.

68. *it belongs to me now*: all Antoinette's property, in accordance with English law, passed to her husband when they married because no safeguards had been written into the marriage settlement.

69. *This is free country*: Christophine asserts her status as a member of post-Emancipation society; Rochester reminds her that she has a police record.

70. *le bon Dieu*: the good God, another reference to the Creole song.

71. *dormi, dormi*: asleep, asleep.

72. *I drew a house*: Rochester anticipates what Thornfield will be like, with the madwoman in the attic.

73. *oleanders*: ornamental evergreen shrubs, all parts of which are poisonous.

74. *Pity* [. . .] *blast*: from *Macbeth* I. vii. 21. The speech goes on to say that pity 'Shall blow the horrid deed in every eye / That tears shall drown the wind.' This suggests that Rochester feels guilt as well as self-pity.

75. *solitaire[s]*: a species of thrush.

76. *Marie Galante*: an island named from the ship in which Columbus was sailing when he first saw it; a French island which was attacked by the Dutch and the British.

77. *the pirates*: one of the most notorious was Sir Henry Morgan who became lieutenant-governor of Jamaica in 1674, but matched his daring exploits against the Spaniards with flamboyant cruelty and depravity. His drunkenness sometimes cost him the booty he had acquired, though he did capture Spanish galleons carrying treasure.

78. *the earthquake*: possibly the cataclysmic earthquake in which Port Royal, the capital of Jamaica, sank into the sea in 1692, and Spanish Town became the capital.

79. *the law of treasure*: the law of treasure trove that operates in most countries is that the finder has the responsibility of reporting the discovery of treasure to the state authorities; the state keeps the larger part of the treasure but returns a proportion of it or of its value to the finder.

80. *Magdalene*: Mary Magdalene, traditionally thought to have been a prostitute, had 'seven devils' cast out of her by Christ (Luke 8.2) and was present at the Crucifixion; Christ appeared to her after his resurrection.

PART THREE

1. pp. 115–16: Grace Poole, who is mad Mrs Rochester's keeper in *Jane Eyre*, takes up the narration while it is in italics; while it is also in quotation marks she is talking to Leah, the maid. On p. 116 Antoinette resumes.

2. *Mrs Eff*: Mrs Fairfax, Rochester's housekeeper in *Jane Eyre*.

3. *the drink without colour in the bottle*: gin.

4. *my wrists were red and swollen*: the narrative intersects here with *Jane Eyre* (chapter

20). Richard Mason has visited Thornfield and has secretly seen the madwoman, who attacks him and is restrained by being tied up.

5. *a girl coming out of her bedroom*: One of Rochester's guests.

6. *flamboyant flowers*: bright scarlet flowers of the flamboyant or flame tree.

7. *stephanotis*: twining evergreen perennial with fragrant white flowers.

8. *jasmine*: shrub with fragrant white flowers.

9. *the man* [. . .] *streamed out like wings*: ' "She was a big woman, and had long black hair: we could see it streaming against the flames as she stood . . . we heard him call 'Bertha!' We saw him approach her." ' (*Jane Eyre*, chapter 36.)

FURTHER READING

WORKS BY JEAN RHYS

Novels

Postures, London: Chatto & Windus, 1928; published as *Quartet*, New York: Simon & Schuster, 1929; republished London: André Deutsch, 1969; Harmondsworth: Penguin, 1973

After Leaving Mr Mackenzie, London: Cape, 1931; republished by André Deutsch, 1969; Penguin, 1971

Voyage in the Dark, London: Constable, 1934; republished by André Deutsch, 1967; Penguin, 1969

Good Morning, Midnight, Constable, 1939; republished by André Deutsch, 1967; Penguin, 1969

Wide Sargasso Sea, André Deutsch, 1966; Penguin, 1968

The Early Novels, André Deutsch, 1984

The Complete Novels, New York: W. W. Norton, 1985

Short Stories

Tigers Are Better-Looking, André Deutsch, 1968; Penguin, 1973

My Day: Three Pieces by Jean Rhys, New York: Frank Hallman, 1975

Sleep It Off Lady, André Deutsch, 1976; Penguin, 1981

The Collected Short Stories, W. W. Norton, 1987

Tales of the Wide Caribbean, ed. Kenneth Ramchand, London: Heinemann, 1985

Letters and Autobiography

Smile Please: An Unfinished Autobiography, André Deutsch, 1979; Penguin, 1981

Jean Rhys: Letters, 1931–1966, ed. Francis Wyndham & Diana Melly, André Deutsch, 1984; Penguin, 1985

WORKS ABOUT JEAN RHYS

Biography and Bibliography

Carole Angier, *Jean Rhys, Life and Work*, André Deutsch, 1990; Penguin, 1992

Elgin W. Mellown, *Jean Rhys, A Descriptive and Annotated Bibliography of Works and Criticism*, New York & London: Garland Publishing, 1984

David Plante, *Difficult Women*, London: Gollancz, 1983

Ruth Webb, 'Swimming the Wide Sargasso Sea: The Manuscripts of Jean Rhys's Novel', *The British Library Journal*, Autumn 1988

Critical Studies

Helen Carr, *Jean Rhys*, Plymouth: Northcote House in association with the British Council, 1996

Arnold E. Davidson, *Jean Rhys*, New York: Frederick Ungar, 1985

Mary-Lou Emery, *Jean Rhys at 'World's End': Novels of Colonial and Sexual Exile*, Austin: University of Texas Press, 1990

Pierette Frickey (ed.), *Critical Perspectives on Jean Rhys*, Washington DC: Three Continents, 1990

Veronica-Marie Gregg, *Jean Rhys's Historical Imagination: Reading and Writing the Creole*, Chapel Hill: University of Carolina Press, 1995

Nancy C. Harrison, *Jean Rhys and the Novel as Women's Text*, Chapel Hill & London: University of North Carolina Press, 1988

Kristien Hemmerechts, *A Plausible Story and a Plausible Way of Telling It, A Structuralist Analysis of Jean Rhys's Novels*, Berne: Peter Lang, 1986

Coral Ann Howells, *Jean Rhys*, London: Harvester Wheatsheaf, 1991

Louis James, *Jean Rhys*, Harlow: Longman, 1978

Selma James, *The Ladies and the Mammies: Jane Austen and Jean Rhys*, Bristol: Falling Wall Press, 1983

Deborah Kelly Kloepfer, *The Unspeakable Mother: Forbidden Discourse in Jean Rhys and H D,* Ithaca: Cornell University Press, 1989

Paula Le Gallez, *The Rhys Woman*, London: Macmillan, 1990

Helen Nebeker, *Jean Rhys, Woman in Passage*, Montreal: Eden Press, 1981

Teresa O'Connor, *Jean Rhys: The West Indian Novels*, New York & London: New York University Press, 1986

Thomas Staley, *Jean Rhys: A Critical Study*, Macmillan, 1979

Loreto Todd, *York Notes on Wide Sargasso Sea*, Harlow: Addison Wesley Longman, 1995 (study guide)

Peter Wolfe, *Jean Rhys*, Boston: Twayne Publishers, 1980

Chapters in Books

Peter Hulme, 'The locked heart: the creole family romance of *Wide Sargasso Sea*' in Francis Barker, Peter Hulme & Margaret Iversen (eds), *Colonial discourse/postcolonial theory*, Manchester: Manchester University Press, 1994

Judie Newman, 'I walked with a zombie' in *The Ballistic Bard: Postcolonial Fictions*, London: Arnold, 1995

Caroline Rody, 'The Revisionary Paradigm of Jean Rhys's *Wide Sargasso Sea*' in Alison Booth (ed.), *Famous Last Words: Changes in Gender and Narrative Closure*, Charlottesville: University of Virginia Press, 1993

Gayatri Chakravorty Spivak, 'Three Women's Texts and a Critique of Imperialism', in Fred Botting (ed.), *Frankenstein, Mary Shelley*, New Casebook, Macmillan, 1995

West Indian History and Culture

Leonard Barrett, *The Sun and the Drum: African Roots in Jamaican Folk Tradition*, Heinemann, 1976

Edward Brathwaite, *The Development of Creole Society in Jamaica 1770–1820*, Oxford: Clarendon Press, 1971

FURTHER READING

Philip D. Curtin, *The Rise and Fall of the Plantation Complex: Essays in Atlantic History*, Cambridge: Cambridge University Press, 1990

Peter Hulme & Neil L. Whitehead (eds), *Wild Majesty: Encounters with Caribs from Columbus to the Present Day*, Clarendon Press, 1992

Loreto Todd, *Pidgins and Creoles*, London: Routledge, 1990

Eric Williams, *From Columbus to Castro: The History of the Caribbean 1492–1969*, André Deutsch, 1970

Visit Penguin on the Internet
and browse at your leisure

- preview sample extracts of our forthcoming books
- read about your favourite authors
- investigate over 10,000 titles
- enter one of our literary quizzes
- win some fantastic prizes in our competitions
- e-mail us with your comments and book reviews
- instantly order any Penguin book

and masses more!

'To be recommended without reservation ... a rich and rewarding on-line experience' – Internet Magazine

www.penguin.co.uk

READ MORE IN PENGUIN

In every corner of the world, on every subject under the sun, Penguin represents quality and variety – the very best in publishing today.

For complete information about books available from Penguin – including Puffins, Penguin Classics and Arkana – and how to order them, write to us at the appropriate address below. Please note that for copyright reasons the selection of books varies from country to country.

In the United Kingdom: Please write to *Dept. EP, Penguin Books Ltd, Bath Road, Harmondsworth, West Drayton, Middlesex UB7 0DA*

In the United States: Please write to *Consumer Sales, Penguin USA, P.O. Box 999, Dept. 17109, Bergenfield, New Jersey 07621-0120.* VISA and MasterCard holders call 1-800-253-6476 to order Penguin titles

In Canada: Please write to *Penguin Books Canada Ltd, 10 Alcorn Avenue, Suite 300, Toronto, Ontario M4V 3B2*

In Australia: Please write to *Penguin Books Australia Ltd, P.O. Box 257, Ringwood, Victoria 3134*

In New Zealand: Please write to *Penguin Books (NZ) Ltd, Private Bag 102902, North Shore Mail Centre, Auckland 10*

In India: Please write to *Penguin Books India Pvt Ltd, 706 Eros Apartments, 56 Nehru Place, New Delhi 110 019*

In the Netherlands: Please write to *Penguin Books Netherlands bv, Postbus 3507, NL-1001 AH Amsterdam*

In Germany: Please write to *Penguin Books Deutschland GmbH, Metzlerstrasse 26, 60594 Frankfurt am Main*

In Spain: Please write to *Penguin Books S. A., Bravo Murillo 19, 1° B, 28015 Madrid*

In Italy: Please write to *Penguin Italia s.r.l., Via Felice Casati 20, I–20124 Milano*

In France: Please write to *Penguin France S. A., 17 rue Lejeune, F–31000 Toulouse*

In Japan: Please write to *Penguin Books Japan, Ishikiribashi Building, 2–5–4, Suido, Bunkyo-ku, Tokyo 112*

In South Africa: Please write to *Longman Penguin Southern Africa (Pty) Ltd, Private Bag X08, Bertsham 2013*

READ MORE IN PENGUIN

Penguin Twentieth-Century Classics offer a selection of the finest works of literature published this century. Spanning the globe from Argentina to America, from France to India, the masters of prose and poetry are represented by the Penguin.

If you would like a catalogue of the Twentieth-Century Classics library, please write to:

Penguin Marketing, 27 Wrights Lane, London W8 5TZ

(Available while stocks last)

READ MORE IN PENGUIN

A CHOICE OF TWENTIETH-CENTURY CLASSICS

Flight to Arras Antoine de Saint-Exupéry

On 22 May 1940 Antoine de Saint-Exupéry set off on a reconnaissance operation from Orly over Nazi-occupied France to Arras. It was such a dangerous mission that he was not expected to survive it. *Flight to Arras* is his profound and passionate meditation on mortality and war, on his wretched, defeated country and the seeds of its regeneration.

Mrs Dalloway Virginia Woolf

Into *Mrs Dalloway* Virginia Woolf poured all her passionate sense of how other people live, remember and love as well as hate, and in prose of astonishing beauty she struggled to catch, impression by impression and minute by minute, the feel of life itself.

The Counterfeiters André Gide

'It's only after our death that we shall really be able to hear.' From puberty through adolescence to death, *The Counterfeiters* is a rare encyclopedia of human disorder, weakness and despair.

A House for Mr Biswas V. S. Naipaul

'*A House for Mr Biswas* can be seen as the struggle of a man not naturally rebellious, but in whom rebellion is inspired by the forces of ritual, myth and custom ... It has the Dickensian largeness and luxuriance without any of the Dickensian sentimentality, apostrophizing or preaching' – Paul Theroux

Talkative Man R. K. Narayan

Bizarre happenings at Malgudi are heralded by the arrival of a stranger on the Delhi train who takes up residence in the station waiting-room and, to the dismay of the station master, will not leave. 'His lean, matter-of-fact prose has lost none of its chuckling sparkle mixed with melancholy' – *Spectator*

READ MORE IN PENGUIN

A CHOICE OF TWENTIETH-CENTURY CLASSICS

Details of a Sunset and Other Stories   Vladimir Nabokov

More than mere footnotes to the masterly novels of his maturity, these early Russian stories are rich in the glittering surfaces and deep undercurrents of Nabokov's genius. '*Details of a Sunset* is much concerned with different kinds of loss ... and yet the effects of these stories are mainly exhilarating, even affirmative' – *The New York Times Book Review*

Jean Santeuil   Marcel Proust

Drawing on the intense emotional experiences of his youth, Proust tells the story of boyhood summers of strawberries and cream cheese, of garlands of pink blossom under branches of white may, of love and its lies, of political scandal and of his deep feeling for his parents.

Under Western Eyes   Joseph Conrad

Razumov aims to overcome the denial of his noble birth by a brilliant career in the tsarist bureaucracy created by Peter the Great. But in pre-revolutionary Russia Peter's legacy is autocracy tempered by assassination; and Razumov is soon caught in a tragic web with fellow-student Victor Haldin's sister Natalia in spy-haunted Geneva ...

The Reef   Edith Wharton

Anna Leath, an American widow living in France, has renewed her relationship with her first love, diplomat George Darrow. But on his way to her beautiful French château, where he hopes to consolidate his marriage plans, Darrow encounters Sophy Viner, who is as vibrant and spontaneous as Anna is reserved and restrained.

The Claudine Novels   Colette

Seldom have the experiences of a young girl growing to maturity been evoked with such lyricism and candour, and in Colette's hands Claudine emerges as a true original, first and most beguiling of this century's emancipated women.

READ MORE IN PENGUIN

A CHOICE OF TWENTIETH-CENTURY CLASSICS

The Prodigy   Hermann Hesse

Hesse's early novel *The Prodigy* is based on his own experiences of a narrow and uncaring education. Hans Giebenrath is a gifted child and the victim of provincial ambitions. Sent to theological school, the intelligent and imaginative boy is gradually driven to nervous collapse in a situation from which there seems to be no escape.

Something Childish and Other Stories   Katherine Mansfield

'The singular beauty of her language consists, partly, in its hardly seeming to be language at all, so glass-transparent is it to her meaning. Words had but one appeal for her, that of speakingness' – Elizabeth Bowen

Collected Poems 1947–1985   Allen Ginsberg

Leading poet of the Beat generation, spokesman for the anti-war generation, an icon of the counter-culture, Allen Ginsberg remains an authentically American voice. This volume brings together four decades of bold experiment and provocative verse from *Howl*, one of the most widely read poems of the century, to his later, highly acclaimed collection, *White Shroud*.

Incest   Anaïs Nin

Spanning the years 1932–4, the material in *Incest* was considered too explosive to include when the journals were originally published. In it, Nin reveals her incestuous affair with her pianist father, and recounts other relationships, loves and desires.

The Last Summer   Boris Pasternak

Pasternak's autobiographical novella is a series of beautifully interwoven reminiscences, half-dreamed, half-recalled by Serezha, an intensely romantic young man and former tutor to a wealthy Moscow family. Here he broods over the last summer before the First World War, 'when life appeared to pay heed to individuals, and when it was easier and more natural to love than to hate'.

READ MORE IN PENGUIN

A CHOICE OF TWENTIETH-CENTURY CLASSICS

Tender is the Night F. Scott Fitzgerald

In *Tender is the Night*, the author distilled much of his and Zelda's life, and the knowledge of the wrecked, fabulous Fitzgeralds adds poignancy and regret to his supple, tender and poetically tantalizing portrait of destructive affluence and spoiled idealism.

Extinction Thomas Bernhard

'A merciless denunciation of Austrian hypocrisy and mediocrity ... although Bernhard's critique of his own nation gives no quarter, it is both funny and humane ... a magnificent elegy for an Austria destroyed by Hitler and for Bernhard's own blighted childhood' – *Observer*

Vile Bodies Evelyn Waugh

In the years following the First World War a new generation emerges, wistful and vulnerable beneath the glitter. The Bright Young Things of twenties' Mayfair, with their paradoxical mix of innocence and sophistication, exercise their inventive minds and vile bodies in every kind of capricious escapade.

The Little Prince Antoine de Saint-Exupéry

Moral fable and spiritual autobiography, this is the story of a little boy who lives alone on a planet not much bigger than himself. One day he leaves behind the safety of his childlike world to travel around the universe where he is introduced to the vagaries of adult behaviour through a series of extraordinary encounters. His personal odyssey culminates in a trip to Earth and further adventures.

The Amen Corner James Baldwin

Sister Margaret presides over a thriving gospel-singing community in New York's Harlem. Proud and silent, for the last ten years she has successfully turned her heart to the Lord and her back on the past. But then her husband Luke unexpectedly reappears. He is a burnt-out jazz musician, a scandal of a man who none the less is seeking love and redemption.

READ MORE IN PENGUIN

A CHOICE OF TWENTIETH-CENTURY CLASSICS

Ulysses James Joyce

Ulysses is unquestionably one of the supreme masterpieces, in any artistic form, of the twentieth century. 'It is the book to which we are all indebted and from which none of us can escape' – T. S. Eliot

The Heart of the Matter Graham Greene

Scobie is a highly principled police officer in a war-torn West African state. When he is passed over for promotion he is forced to borrow money to send his despairing wife on holiday. With a duty to repay his debts and an inability to distinguish between love, pity and responsibility to others and to God, Scobie moves inexorably towards his final damnation.

The Age of Innocence Edith Wharton

To the rigid world of propriety, of which Old New York is composed, returns the Countess Olenska. Separated from her European husband and displaying an independence and impulsive awareness of life, she stirs the educated sensitivity of Newland Archer, who is engaged to be married to young May Welland.

Mr Noon D. H. Lawrence

This Penguin edition is the first annotated paperback publication of Lawrence's autobiographical and strikingly innovative unfinished novel. Abandoning a promising academic career, Gilbert Noon becomes embroiled in an affair which causes him to flee to Germany, there to find true passion with the unhappily married wife of an English doctor.

Black List, Section H Francis Stuart

This astonishingly powerful novel follows H on a spiritual quest for revelation and redemption, from his disastrous marriage to Iseult Gonne, the Irish Civil War and internment, to his life as a writer, poultry farmer, racehorse owner and Bohemian in 1930s London, and his arrival in Hitler's Germany in 1940.

READ MORE IN PENGUIN

A CHOICE OF TWENTIETH-CENTURY CLASSICS

Orlando Virginia Woolf

Sliding in and out of three centuries, and slipping between genders, Orlando is the sparkling incarnation of the personality of Vita Sackville-West as Virginia Woolf saw it.

Selected Poems Patrick Kavanagh

One of the major figures in the modern Irish poetic canon, Patrick Kavanagh (1904–67) was a post-colonial poet who released Anglo-Irish verse from its prolonged obsession with history, ethnicity and national politics. His poetry, written in an uninhibited vernacular style, focused on the 'common and banal' aspects of contemporary life.

More Die of Heartbreak Saul Bellow

'One turns the last pages of *More Die of Heartbreak* feeling that no image has been left unexplored by a mind not only at constant work but standing outside itself, mercilessly examining the workings, tracking the leading issues of our times and the composite man in an age of hybrids' – *New York Book Review*

Tell Me How Long the Train's Been Gone James Baldwin

Leo Proudhammer, a successful Broadway actor, is recovering from a near-fatal heart attack. Talent, luck and ambition have brought him a long way from the Harlem ghetto of his childhood. With Barbara, a white woman who has the courage to love the wrong man, and Christopher, a charismatic black revolutionary, Leo faces a turning-point in his life.

Memories of a Catholic Girlhood Mary McCarthy

Blending memories and family myths, Mary McCarthy takes us back to the twenties, when she was orphaned in a world of relations as colourful, potent and mysterious as the Catholic religion. 'Superb . . . so heartbreaking that in comparison Jane Eyre seems to have got off lightly' – Anita Brookner

BY THE SAME AUTHOR

Quartet

The winter-wet streets of Montparnasse, *pernods* in smoke-filled cafés, cheap hotel rooms and Marya Zelli, trying to make something substantial of her life – to resist the unreality that surrounds her. Alone, her Polish husband in prison, she has been taken up by an English couple who slowly overwhelm her with their passions. The husband demands, the wife fosters. Marya is left – as always – to comfort herself.

Voyage in the Dark

A brief liaison with a kindly but unimaginative man leads Anna to abandon the theatre and drift into the demi-monde of 1914 London: red-plush dinners in private rooms 'up West'; ragtime, champagne and whisky back at the flat; these, and a discreet tinkle of sovereigns in the small hours pave the way to disaster . . .

Good Morning, Midnight

Back in Paris for a 'quiet, sane fortnight', Sasha Jensen has just been rescued by a friend from drinking herself to death in a Bloomsbury bedsitter. Despite a transformation act, new clothes and blonde cendré hair dye, Sasha still feels 'not quite as good as new'. Streets, shops and bars vividly evoke her Paris past: feckless husband Enno, baby born dead, sundry humiliations in abject jobs . . .

One night, a gigolo mistakes Sasha for a rich woman – she still has her fur coat – and their subsequent liaison somehow distils the essence of all that has gone before.

BY THE SAME AUTHOR

Sleep It Off Lady

Sixteen tales, uncannily and vividly drawn together like the fragments of a single life – childhood innocence destroyed under a louring Caribbean sky; youthful disenchantment with the London stage life of the 1910s; brief encounters in the brittle gaiety of a Parisian nightclub and in London during the Blitz; followed by the slow, inevitable descent into old age and loneliness; and after death, the return.

After Leaving Mr Mackenzie

Julia felt too old and tired to worry about men, but she knew she could not survive without them.

For six months, she had lived alone in a drab Parisian hotel on an allowance from her ex-lover, Mr Mackenzie. When his cheques stopped, she supposed there was no alternative but to rally her spirits, return to London and try again. But London was not an easy city to survive in without money.

The story of Julia's ten-day visit includes some of Jean Rhys's most sensitive and poignant writing. Once lovely, now exhausted by broken love-affairs and too much drink, Julia knows that the odds are against her. Lovers old, lovers new – none can offer what she really wants. Nor can her bitter, martyred sister or her paralysed mother, now on the threshold of death. For what Julia wants is expensive: she wants love.

BY THE SAME AUTHOR

Tigers are Better-Looking

A collection of short stories, first published in 1939, which includes a selection from Jean Rhys's 1927 volumn of Paris stories, *The Left Bank*, of which Ford Madox Ford wrote in the Preface: 'One likes, in short to be connected with something good, and Miss Rhys's work seems to me to be very good, so vivid, so extraordinarily distinguished by the rendering of passion, and so true, that I wish to be connected with it.'

Letters 1931–1966

The publication of *Wide Sargasso Sea* finally brought Jean Rhys to fame at the age of seventy-six. These letters span the period of the completion of her masterpiece and make exhilarating as well as painful reading, providing a frank self-portrait of a fascinating, complex, tormented personality striving to know herself.

Smile Please

Begun when she was eighty-six and left unfinished only by her death three years later, *Smile Please* is a collection of autobiographical vignettes, which reveal the influences that shaped Jean Rhys's life, the tensions of her childhood in Dominica, and the rebellious uncertainties of her later life in London and Paris.

Wide Sargasso Sea is also available as a Penguin Audiobook, read by Jane Lapotaire and Michael Kitchen.